Time of Death

The Story of Jared

by

Mitch Bensel

Time of Death

The Story of Jared

by Mitch Bensel

First Printing August 2018

For all those brave souls that work in the

medical field…

\

Warning…

This book contains graphic material…

not for the faint of heart

Jared Walker

Within all of us there are levels of becoming a human being or a real person. Some grow quickly in life with confidence and skill while others flounder in the realm of their minds and wished for something of importance to happen in their lives. Jared Walker was a different kind of human. He thought of himself as a divorced loser, but in reality his whole existence had helped everyone and anyone that crossed his path. He had compassion and was always there for anyone that needed. He chose to forget about love and just existed in his work. He worked with death on a daily basis as an emergency room tech. He drew the blood, did the redundant EKG's and bagged the fresh dead, he was stuck in a loop of death. He had no interest in being a nurse, he worked to make a steady bit of money and that was that. His only relief was his gloriously dangerous life as a pool hustler. And even that was a weak attempt at living. He was born with a gift, one of those spiritual gifts the type that people mocked and made fun of. He was a spiritual healer and he could also see the dark spirits that roamed the emergency room. They would attempt to follow him home at times but he was able to make them leave him alone. His day consisted of battling energy and his own lack of self worth. Jared Walker stumbled into a new existence, one of love. This was his story. A story of life from the side of different, a story of darkness being destroyed and payments being fulfilled. Debt is something cumulative in life, it is also a deep cavern within the soul and consequences of actions. Delivered into the hands of hope the tests began would he do the right thing?

Acknowledgments

Thank you God for your guidance through the many battles in my life. My co-workers, who truly were my core family through horrific trauma's. My daughter's for putting up with me and my stories over dinner. God bless all, as a nurse I worked with would always say, "peace, love and happiness, get the blood, get the pee!"

Time Of Death

The Story Of Jared

by

Mitch Bensel

Chapter 1

Jared walked toward the beach and looked down at his feet while they moved across the pavement. His black EMS boots were a little beaten from time but they seemed to be his only friend. They had seen everything he had, been through the blood as he had, never judged him, just sturdy under him. He was preparing himself for another day in the ER, the usual of fresh dead with tears and screams from the ones left behind. He took a deep breath and pulled in the ocean air. "Memories and moments," he observed every moment of the oceans movement to use when that time would come, for him to pull away from reality, when that parking place became too strange. His mind flew to a moment in the ER. He watched as they dropped the mans right leg to the floor. Blood spurted in an interesting way when an artery was opened. Nice rhythm, he thought, as the mans left leg was dropped to the floor torn from his body when his motorcycle slid down the highway. He stopped the thought and inhaled again deeper than before. The ocean seemed to be able to remove any visuals, at least temporarily, of death and family members as they screamed at the dead body to wake up. But it returned as quickly as it slowed. Her voice shook through him, "please get her some more blankets her skin is just too cold, wake up grandma." Yes, she was cold and dead but the grandchild just didn't understand how she could be gone, when she was right there. The oceans current became the artery of his very existence. With each waves push the ebb of tide

filled with images and voices, feelings, tears and pain. "Oh my baby please don't let her be dead." Screams and sobs were an interesting combination, they subsided then gained pitch with the next exhale. The beach released for a moment the voices and the memories of that mixed of death and the clash of life. But only for a moment. He finally reached the stairs that would take him down to the sand and the ocean. He felt a familiar presence, a jagged kind of spiritual presence. That same feel at times after someone died, someone of not good energy and a little upset they were dead. With a quick thought he tossed the dark away from him, not in the mood to be messed with at his ocean. He examined the oceans flow it was in control, its currents were strong and could pull anyone from their feet if caught. It held life, thousands of types of life surrounded by the liquid of salt water. Even in the colors of a wave there was the amazement of magic, a lure or was it a wonder. What would it be like to be part of that oceans flow? He tried to be part of the flow in his youth by body surfing. The idiocy of a human trying to be a surf board. His body fresh against the wave he leaned then swam fast and was lifted by the wave. There was a cool silence inside the turbulence of a wave as it crashed literally around you while your body protruded from it. The end was not graceful as he slammed into the beach, like a piece of sand tossed.

The prison guard, his watch, announced the need to get to work. He waved to the ocean and bowed to its beauty, "I bid thee farewell but shall return." He had always thought that the ocean had to be a woman, the way it could so easily captivate, engulf and roll him up onto the sand, aching and hot, waiting for her moisture once more to satisfy his reach. When he was tired he got poetic, he laughed at that thought and knew he was tired already and he had twelve hours of dead's to go before he could play some pool.

He watched his boots carry him back to his van. Just at the start of the stairs he found a fascinating rock, he held it up to the sun, the fascination to him was that he could see through the rock. He lowered the rock and thought of how he could see through people. He could see the souls, the lights and the darks with the swirls of both. Which made it difficult not to wrap someone up immediately in a judgement. For all give in to the dark at times and all can change. He walked toward his van thinking of all the souls he had seen, within those alive and the ones that left the fresh dead. Was it a gift, he paused and looked back at the ocean before heading to work. "Or is it a curse." He got into the van and moaned at his constant thoughts.

He drove slowly with his mind still crashing against memories and vomiting them out into his reality. He had seen the demons that slithered around the ER waiting for those that chose the dark to take away to their world. He had seen the light so bright of those souls that happened to choose right in life, on a path of love.

He had seen so many souls, sometimes he could handle the ones of blind and idiocy, but other times he wanted to crack them on the head to knock some sense into them. Or more like knock the sense out of them. The brainwashed sheep mode kind of sense. Confuse the wise with wisdom, annoy the calm with silence, hit the pod heads with the real world. Pod heads were programmed people that slipped into the blind of life. A pod heads spirituality was the redundant putridity of herd mentality of normal. Get the money, get the power, step on anyone to acquire such normal goals. He turned on the radio to block his constant thoughts, he wasn't in the mood to think on all the depth of life and mankind. But it didn't matter his thoughts were still arranging their furniture in his brain. The visuals of brain matter splattered across his scrub top, blood falling to his shoes from that exposed artery. The sounds of screams from a family member looking upon their mother's cold dead body. Escape was a tree moving just right with the wind or the ocean and its constant washing with its waves or a daisy pushing through darkest of asphalt.

He turned up the radio, the music was loud and the rhythm was good but he knew it was but for a short time. The spirits were everywhere, he exhaled slowly as he turned into the parking lot of the hospital. It was full so he must be late. He pulled in and swiped his badge for the parking lot and drove slowly to find a spot. He watched as a nurse got out of her blue Mercedes. "Well, how nice." He slowed and parked a few cars away from hers. "Would you like to go out?" He laughed at himself, turned off the van and got out quickly. Jared had an issue with his life and doubted himself on a constant.

He walked behind her and thought of his life and the small bubble in which he lived. It was a bubble of time not released with laughter or pleasure. Work the ER, hustle at the pool hall and go to bed. Wake and work, the circle had him and it was his own fault.

He had given up his martial arts school to change for a woman but she left him anyway. He had an occasional blip of a date, that would always turn into the normal games women played of control and sex. The sex part wasn't bad, he smiled as he thought of all the women he had been with. But then he frowned as the memory that he was only good for sex, they would get someone else to travel with. He wanted to find a woman that had some depth, how twisted and messed up was that? To not want to just have sex with a woman, but to want to have romance and depth and someone to walk through the rest of his existence with him.

He put his badge against the door and it unlocked. The click of the lock removed his ramble of thoughts and the smell of the ER wrapped him back into the world of blood and dead. "Here I go.."

Chapter 2

Cool Factor

There were factors in his life, the cool factor in his was the important one. May not have much but damn I'm cool. The cool factor of working EMS faded quickly when he injured his back. The injury wasn't even a cool moment of injury. Someone slipped in their own pee and the traditional standing take down was about to happen. So the backboard was put against her back as she stood and was slowly lowered. Then the four hundred pound person was lifted and carried through their home to the ambulance. The only problem was that Jared twisted just a little as they moved with the patient through the door. Jared's back did a scream from inside, it twisted and did the 'cha cha cha' to his L4 and L5 vertebrae.

The cool factor of working in an emergency room was fading. His day by choice was of screams, blood, death and stench. The familiar rot of flesh or toss of blood dried against the skin. His wonderful moments of wiping feces off the wall and off the patient's hands after they literally pulled it from their own bottom while standing on the stretcher. "Just tired…" again his voice found the air. Even his talking to himself had increased. and if the saying fit the answer, He was crazy in the land of normal folk. Although he felt the normal folk should walk the way he did, life was beautiful if you learned to lean your head and toss a smile at the flowers, the sun and the air that reaches for us to feel it. Most did not, some would inhale it others would wish it would cease. Normal folk were boring.

As he walked through the ER to his locker he saw the eyes of red and swollen from a young lady as the chaplain walked with her toward the made up viewing area for the fresh dead. It is one of the ER bays with the lighting dimmed so that the immediate viewing of a loved one freshly dead, was not so harsh. Her body began to slump as she got closer to the closed doors. Behind door number three is her husband or child or daughter, cold with expression and always with a tube sticking out of their mouth from being intubated. When the body doesn't work well the airway is always protected. Being intubated allows the medical types to breathe for the patient.

As he turned the corner to walk down the long hall to his locker he heard the scream of her sorrow. What do you say to someone that is looking at their dead loved one? Can you say, don't worry we are all going to die, or they are gone but will always be with you? That makes no sense to someone that is looking at their dead person they knew and loved for their whole life. If they are gone then why are they still here? Why can I touch them? so the answer to the sob is to allow it to happen.

Jared lost his grandmother when he was a young one. The air changed around him with a vacuum of silence that took years and years to leave him. He did not like death, even with the understanding of forever being where all will go, he did not like death. It's like an echo without an echo that echoed.

The first time he experienced death in his life was the dog he had when he was a kid. Skitch, named after the conductor of Mayvilles Orchestra, was a french terrier of fast and happy that didn't belong in a cage when they left the house. At least in his mind it didn't, so just before the door was locked and his family of six were in the car he ran over and let the dog out of the cage. Yay! but no yay, when they returned home the dog had torn up several rolls of toilet paper and gleefully ran through the house literally covering just about every inch of living space with toilet paper.

His father took out the belt and the lean over so the leather strap could hit your bottom began. He gritted his teeth and refused to cry, if one did cry when getting a spanking with belt or hand, who knew what would happen. The words don't cry or I will give you something to cry about had an ominous ring. So the tears never occurred just a grit of teeth and searing pain.

As punishment to the dog, he was put in the backyard. But someone decided to cut through the yard and left the gate open and he got out.

Jared frantically ran through the dark night and called the dogs name. He found him, first he saw the blood on the street then he saw Skitch. Blood pooled around his mouth and his body was smashed. The thought of a pancake slapped him in his wee mind. The air shifted inside him and he ran back home. He sat outside alone and wept, he knew it was his fault Skitch was dead, "my fault," he whispered into his tear soaked hands. The practice of push and shove emotions away began then and it had never left.

He fell back into the present as his thought zoomed away from Skitch lying in blood and the feel of that smack of silence and death. In the middle of the pull back to reality was the flash of all the people he had seen smashed and blown open, ripped apart by concrete or bullets. The locker room door was a pleasant pause that softened and finally removed the images in his mind. He removed his coat and lifted the trauma sheers from his locker. He felt the rhythm of the ocean, he was doing the Jared thing, walls inside slammed down to protect his heart. Tears dried on his face, "sadness sucks.." He tossed it away and smiled to create the false of happy and began once more his attempt to find something good in every moment. "I am healthy," he paused as a hint of back pain filtered across him, "not wealthy," visions of the past when money was not a worry, marriage and a house of large gone with divorce. He finished his thought and whispered, "and maybe wise?"

His hand found the agate in his pocket he held it up to the light fascinated with its translucence. How can someone see through a rock, he smiled and put it back in his cargo pants pocket.

Chapter 3

Night shift was done and wanted away, It was time to give report to the oncoming tech and nurse, the passing of the torch. He lowered his head and listened to what he had in store for the next twelve hours. A chorus of vomiting with curse words that flew from behind one of the curtained rooms gave him a clear moment of what the day would hold. He wanted to turn and walk out of there but he had to stay. A scream from the back of the ER caused all to turn, another family member was looking at their freshly dead loved one. He turned back and began his duties, distraction was a good thing, even if it was distraction right in the middle of the battlefield.

It was time to draw some blood from a patient, he walked toward the room and a vision filtered through the moment into his mind. The lights were bright, the ceiling tiles of the familiar surrounded by the usual hospital lights. He was lying on a stretcher and felt a pressure on his chest, voices around him spoke of blood pressures, familiar voices and suddenly a face. One of the nurses he knew asked him questions, a sudden stab of pain from the vision caused him to wince, "what the hell?" He said as he walked into the patients room. "No my name is not what the hell," came the response from the lady on the stretcher. "Oh I'm sorry," He said quickly, "Are you Ms. Lights?" She shifted in the stretcher and looked him in the eyes, "yes," she said dryly. He opened the butterfly needle and got the blood tubes ready. A butterfly needle aptly named because of the two flaps that the blood taker holds as they shove the needle into the patients vein, or gently slide, depending on the vein and the mood of the blood taker. Veins could be interesting animals and become more interesting when one draws blood daily. With a gasp and an "ooo nice veins," followed by a reach to touch the vein, was a common occurrence with blood takers. Vampires had to do the same, check out the veins on that one! But when in the hospital most people are sick and dehydrated or drug users or very old. All of the above offers not the best veins to get blood. When the needle goes in the vein says no thanks and collapses. skin can also be rough from using them at work or rough from time but there are some people with very, very tough skin. So tough that when the needle was pushed into the vein and it literally bent the needle. "Are you an alien?" His famous retort to the patient with the skin of iron. Some veins were huge and created a sense of over confidence. Something about huge thick and fat veins was they had huge thick fat walls. The needle would move in and no blood returned. Nothing, nada, embarrassment 101 was when the tech had to ask someone else to get the blood from that guy in bay three that had huge tree trunk veins, but Jared couldn't get a drop. The other wonderful type of veins are the ones that as soon as the needle goes in they blow, which causes the blood to flow around the needle and puff up like a huge balloon. Pushing ever upward causing the patient's eyes to get very wide followed with a, "what have you done to me!"

The worst time of blood drawing, the needle near the skin, the patient is calm with head turned and right as the needle begins to pierce their skin they scream and yank their arm away. Well, the moment that all phlebotomist's fear had just occurred. The needle is hot, meaning there is blood on it and can infect you. The needle in the air above Jared, how fast can an old martial artist move? Fast, evading once more a sharp from finding him, he grabbed the patients arm and yelled, "Don't move!" Before the patient could recover, he pushed a new needle into capture the much needed, always wanted, usually unnecessary blood.

The patient had tattoos of death and skulls of the grim reaper that flew across skin muscular and taught. But as soon as the small needle went into his arm he began to cry like a baby. Jared looked at the tattoos and wondered why he wore such macho if inside there was such weakness. People do like to hide their true self, for in life does anyone know who they really are?

Back to the way of blood drawing, he looked at Ms. Lights, she was a young woman of distress, life had not been kind to her. Lines of worry showed on her face, she could be considered beautiful but the edges of her choices showed. Alcohol and smoking and drugs. So death was what she wished for but some how it didn't happen. Her wrists were covered with bandages with dried blood still on her forearm. The ones that truly want to die, usually succeed. The percentage of those that tried made up a large percentage of the visitors to the emergency room. Some overdosed on various drugs, or they fell in front of a train. The ER received parts of their bodies with a slight pulse still popping the blood through the opened cavities where legs used to be.

One came in with half of her head blown away. She put the gun to her head and made it so. Brain matter was on the backboard and the blood had pooled throughout her hair. To help handle the constant avalanche of death, medical people find humor somewhere in everything. One of the nurses pointed to a piece of her brain matter on the board, "look there's kindergarten right there." Jared shifted his thoughts quickly away from her life of play and school and children. He put her in the body bag, she watched him with those dead eyes. Just like all the dead, glassed like and fake. Factoid number one on fresh dead types, their eyelids never seem to want to stay closed. Even if you are lucky to get the eyelashes to stick momentarily and hold the lid, as you zip up the body bag, one of the eyes inevitably opens and peeks at you. "Peek a boo" words that come out of ones mouth in place of just not normal are usually ones of humor. Like icing on a cake, have to smooth the horror of the reality of death. Jared always wished the fresh dead to find peace and to tell his mother hello.

The flash of some of the suicide moments fell away and he was back to drawing blood. "Where shall I get blood from you today?" People knew their bodies better than anybody, they definitely knew the best veins were located for getting blood. He walked back with the tubes to ship them off to lab. He held his head for a moment, Sarah the phlebotomist and a friend of his, noticed something a little off with him. "Are you ok Jared?" "Just not feeling right today Sarah." Behind them the sound of a head slamming onto the floor is heard. There is no other sound in the world than someones skull crashing to the ground. "We have a seizure!..." his head was bleeding from the hit which caused the visitor with another patient to scream, thats what loved ones do, they scream a lot and often. Jared turned the patient on his side and put a towel under his head to stop the repetitive hit against the hard surface. Not much else can be done, he waited for the nurses with the meds to show up. He looked at how the body tightened every muscle during this seizure, it was a good seizure. He wondered what it would be like to have one, would be a good work out. The only problem with that work out was that the muscles can only do it for so long. After a time the kidneys begin to fail due to the sludge from your muscles that clog the way to filter. The name for the breakdown is a cool one, RABDO.

Chapter 4

The trauma buzzer made its horrible buzz sound and Jared had to get to the trauma room. The nurses had the seizure dude so he walked quickly to the room of death or crippled or bloody.

The patient was a lady with blonde hair that was covered in blood. An interesting way to become a red head, as thoughts of re-arrange occur once more, now in the world of reality any red head he would see, a flash of blood dripping through, would visit his thoughts in one quick flash. The doc wiped the blood with a towel and began to staple the lacerated scalp back together. Her skin fell away from the bone that protected her precious brain matter. Interesting the way the skin falls way from our bones, the skull sometimes intact, sometimes cracked with the ebb and flow of the arterial bleed almost hypnotizing the watcher. We are fascinated with the body's interior, showing itself to us while we medical types practice medicine.

Her brains were inside that protective place where they be-longed. Her skull was intact. While the doc stapled her skin together Jared had to get a rectal temperature. Vitals have to be done and this time it would be a rectal, like most of the temperatures taken at that hospital. Traumas usually are too torn up to get oral. She began to fight him as the thermometer probe entered, "John don't touch me there I told you only Jimmie can touch me there!"

The room continued with their duties but smiled when one of the docs mimicked the patient, he looked at Jared, "Yea John stop it." All are used to patients with head wounds or repetitive speak or just plain out of the normal way of flow because they were on drugs or too much of some substance.

The click and trigger of eight thousand more moments flew through his mind. The time when brain matter was on the sheet next to a freshly opened skull due to a bullet. Or the nice touch of a hatchet slammed perfectly into the skull. A butcher knife had an interesting slant when it was left inside the skull. Or the EMS backboard splattered with brain matter. In a moment the mind showed the many images when triggered, every opened skull that his eyes had ever seen. Then the images shifted to every head that didn't quite hang right off of the body. Hanging oneself puts a twist in the get-a-long. The head off to the side with a stair step look as the spine angled outwardly pushing to escape the hold of skin. The click click of the staple gun brought Jared back to the present. Her head would soon have the Frankenstein look with shiny metal.

Ah, my trauma room always the trauma tech never a trauma be? The trauma room was trashed from the last body that rolled through. Gloves thrown to the floor, blood on the floor, anything the docs and nurses used was on the floor. Even with garbage cans wonderfully supplied in easily accessible places, everything was always thrown to the floor. He called environmental services to help him put the room back to await yet another sad soul that had driven under the influence or hit by a car while walking or just medically unsound and the heart ceased it's rhythm.

He watched the environmental lady walk into the trauma room. She was limping a bit. She was a good soul that had worked hard her whole life and he wanted to help. "Alexandria you ok?" He hoped he could help, he was a spiritual healer after all. He kept it secret so that no one would put him in the place of crazy. "My back hurts horribly today Jared." He tried to think of a way to touch her lower back without it looking inappropriate. He hoped he could see if he could help her. Sometimes the push would come to shove and the nudge to just touch someone would hit him. He had no choice but to watch as his hand would reach to rest on a patients head or their side. The rest was up to the Big Guy whether or not they were helped by his touch. Energies of light and dark surround all of us and wait for us to call on them to do our duties of help or hurt. Some people though deserve a little smack in the souls face. That is also up to the the Big Guy. The Big Guy was God to him and sometimes he would call Him the Biggest Guy. Not many people believed anymore in God, they especially didn't believe there were healers out in the world with the gift of the spirit to heal. Which was really just a prayer said with faith, when God hears you because you ask from your heart, miracles happen. He could heal by sending light from a distance but sometimes he had to put his hand on the area that needed help. "Show me where it hurts." He moved his hand to where she pointed. He lightly touched and pressed against her lower back. But he had to continue the touch without her thinking it was strange. He had to find a way to keep his hand on her back. He had to wait for the exchange of the pull of light and the heat of healing to move into her back. "Jared? What are you doing it feels hot?" He just continued with his touch and sent healing light. His hand became too hot to keep on her back and he had to pull it away. "I don't know whats wrong but if you let me touch you there once in awhile I may be able to fix you." He knew that didn't sound right especially when one of the nurses walked into the trauma room and heard him. "Touch where Jared?" She smiled and winked at him. She was a new nurse and admired and respected him. "What are you two up to in here?" Alexandria grabbed her dust mop and just shook her head. "Jared you are truly wearing me out." The nurse got the meds she needed out of the trauma room med pyxis. "I'm just messing with you Jared." She winked at him and walked out. The trauma room was cleaned and stocked and ready for the new arrival of almost dead person.

The doors open to a new trauma as soon as the thought left his brain. EMS was doing compressions so obviously some kind of heart failure. Either traumatic or medical either way the person they brought into the room was dead. A traumatic one was caused by an impact of some sort, either the patient slammed into the steering wheel or the seatbelt smashed them. Or they were thrown from the car and tossed like a limp doll across the pavement.

Jared waved them toward a clean bay, he rolled his shoulders and readied himself to take over the compressions. They are a work out with attitude and he is about to get very tired pushing on the chest of a dead person. The patient was tied neatly to the backboard and presented in the normal way by EMS. Fully immobilized and fully dead. She was t'boned, a wonderful expression of being hit on the side of the car. He would never think of a t'bone steak the same. Her head bled profusely down the back board onto the floor. Her brain matter began to ooze with the blood out of her cracked skull. The compressions stopped after only a few minutes of compressions. He saw them look at the clock, hey TOD they are looking at you. He named the clock they used to call time, TOD. The time of death called and all left him alone with the fresh dead lady. The silence after the storm, his muscles tired and flexed his heart pounded in his chest and just in front of him was a fresh dead. No movement, stillness with attitude followed his workout with attitude. He lowered his head and wished her to find peace and to tell his mother hello. He laughed suddenly at the site of all of the fresh dead types showing up where his mother was on the other side of reality and saying, "Jared says hello."

He prepared her for the family to visit and lifted her head gently to place a towel underneath. The sound and feel of two of his fingers slipping into her brain caused him to grimace as he pulled his fingers out of her brains as quickly as he could. "I am so sorry Ma'am." The back of her head was gone, the skull was gone, and now he had the wonderful memory of pushing against her brains with his fingers. "Just great…" He walked to the side of the trauma room and apologized again to her, he could feel she was in the room. Her spirit lingered then left with a speed that only spirits have. He slammed the walls down inside himself so he wouldn't see the flash of her life but it was too late. It did its dance through his mind. Her children, her love, her life in one second of a blip across his mind. He hated death. "I do not like death!" God should have put post it notes somewhere so we could communicate with our loved ones of fresh dead.

He thought of his mother and began to cry unexpectedly. Tears were a waste of time in his book. Nothing to be done nothing can be done, nothing ..can..be..done! "I hate death and I hate tears!" The body is moved to one of the bays in the trauma room, to allow family to look at their loved one for the first time as a dead loved one. There are patterns in an ER, some days it's knees other days it's strokes, this may be the day to die.

Pause::::::::::

The air is hot

..water   cool

..jumping high through the sprinkler,

I fly.. becoming the water .. soft yet

strong

reaching to find the magic of it's release

from the metal sprinkler

I am lost inside it's hold..

the air is hot.......

======

I walked in rain ..

of drops so small ...

they filtered easily into my soul...

feet were wet but

no matter as yet ...

for the day only holds so much of this gold

He heard them call another trauma on the way he stood to the side and watched as EMS brought in yet another dead. The patients stocking was ripped down the side. The stocking she put on to ready herself for work. She was dead on my stretcher, her shoe was off to the side as was her foot. Open fractures of the ankle show the stub of bone for all to see and the fragile nature of our flesh. Her skirt carried dark red blood that was coming from her abdomen. He got caught up in the flow of compressions and the watch as her leg moved with the rhythm of each push.

The flash began as it did with Jared. He saw her morning as she got out of bed slowly because she was tired. He saw her applying her make up and slipping her foot into her shoe, the one he saw off to the side. She pulled up her skirt and adjusted it just right, now the slip of into death. Her body rocked with each compression her arms off to the side of the stretcher limp and white cloudy way that dead skin gets her feet had that dead look.

Sunrise, the start of a beautiful moment a vision of light falling across green fields onto our back porch, then finding its way to our coffee pot. Sunrise, the start of a day that someone would die. He walked to the other bay to make sure it was fully stocked. He heard them call the time of death. He didn't look at TOD, he didn't want to look at TOD. Numbers on a clock marked a moment of yet another one of us that slowed into not breathing, no breath, no rhythm of anything, just dead.

He was in automatic mode and pulled the body bag off of the shelf. The push began as he rearranged the furniture of his reality. He waited for the images of the wonderful flash of dead ones he had bagged in his years. Kind of like watching an old movie, one of those movies you didn't want to watch because it is so poorly done, yet your eyes won't let you turn away. The film dumped and voila, the cavities of glassed eyes or bloodied faces. Heads blown open wide with metal bullets, swoosh slam, flip. The nudge of lift and the toss of thoughts occurred as he pushed with subtlety death away from his mind.

He always tied the toe tag on the right toe. No reason for it but it was the way of choice. The body fresh in the plastic shower curtain smell and his job was done. He will take her to the morgue and shut the door to the cold room but he would still see her stockings and a shoe that just didn't quite fit well on the foot as it dangled with blood flowing. Sunrise, what would it bring....

Chapter 5

His redundant walk of getting the trauma rooms ready, kerlix here tubing there, syringes and fluids all ready for the docs to find and the nurses to use. The room was ready to rock for the next contestant to come on down. A voice over the paging system once more shrills, "Trauma in five minutes!" He exhaled and flexed then pulled down his scrub top with a pop. "Lets do this."

She was intubated so we could push air into her lungs and very pregnant. She lost control of her car and slammed into a telephone pole. Her abdomen was crushed momentarily and her babies were ripped away from their life feeding source.

Slow motion with speed... contrast of noise with silence. Blood splattered to the floor as they cut her abdomen open to remove the babies. Baby girl A, baby girl B, the docs were covered in blood, they stepped and walked and moved through it, but did not stop their work. Compressions had begun the mother's heart had ceased when they cut her open and she lost pressure and blood. It was time for him to help with compressions.

His journey began again. His hands placed on her sternum, compressions. His only job was to move the blood and medicines through her body by becoming her heart. He glanced at the babies being pulled from her abdomen, he looked at his hands as they pushed, he looked at the face of the mother with the intubation tube rocking with each compression. He was suddenly relieved of compressions.

He was too tired to profuse well for her anymore. He stepped back and watched unable to move. The skills of the docs, the techs and the nurses. All worked with one purpose and one need and one hope. To keep all alive. Baby Girl A, they looked at TOD, Baby Girl B, little gentle compressions with two fingers pushed lightly on her heart, stopped their movement. TOD, time of death was called. He looked back at the mother, she had a rhythm, we had brought her back to life. They sewed her abdomen from where they cut the babies out and away to the operating room she went. All leave quickly, silence fell quickly, Jared looked at his trauma bay. Every inch of the floor was covered in blood. Several environmental workers came in, it took many to get it cleaned. The baby warmer that held the two fresh baby deads, was pushed slowly out of the room. "I wish you two to find peace and tell my mother … hello." Tears were silent and moved down his face. He walked quickly out of the trauma room into the daylight. He cried and was frozen for a moment in the sun. The sun had to remove the visual, it had to take it away. He had seen a lot in his days in the medical trauma world, but this hit him very hard. Everywhere he looked he saw the mother's head rocking and the dead babies being lifted out of her. It was a film in front of his vision. One of the nurses came running out to him. "Jared are you ok?" She actually looked worried. She was one of the newer nurses to the ER and she was very beautiful. Her eyes showed such concern he had to straighten up so she wouldn't worry. He didn't like to cause anyone trouble or worry. "I will be ok thanks for asking." He turned away from her and walked back to the trauma room. She watched him walk away, she saw a man with more heart in that one moment than she had met her whole life.

Chapter 6

This Man

She was new to this emergency room and was used to the many men hitting on her from the patients to the doctors and the techs and other nurses. This man didn't even notice her. She felt her heart pound a little bit as she thought of him. His eyes permeated her mind, his energy was of strong with gentleness. She had to get to know this man. Her walk back to the ER through the ambulance doors was slow as she imagined that she walked beside him. That she walked with him through time, "I know him.." Her whisper slammed through the ER and fell across Jared. He felt a touch, he would feel spirits often try to tempt him to go against God, or give up on love but this was a different feel. "Hello?" Maybe it was one of his guardian angels or maybe his mind was flipped some with the sorrow of the dead babies, "maybe." He didn't have much time to think of anything. His trauma bays were stocked and his timing was good as usual. For one moment though he looked at TOD and shook his finger at the clock, "look ashamed TOD, they should be alive." The clock with its digital movement was of course not fazed by the comment.

Another trauma rolled in and a stench followed it. She was old and frail and bent and smelled of rot. Something had died on this woman and it was her own skin. She was emaciated and contracted and stuck in the fetal position. The skin on her back was black and red and very dead. Her eyes held such a deep sorrow and pain. She was found stuck to the floor with straw under her. She lay in her own feces and urine. They had to pull her from the floor and ripped her skin away from where it was stuck. She was dying, her heart slowed its beat, compressions are called for and he grimaced at the thought of pushing on the frail bent soul. He lightly began the push on her sternum. Her ribs broke immediately and with every push he felt and heard the bones crunch

The medical types put in the central lines that would carry meds to her body quickly and hopefully bring her heart back to the normal of alive. He got angrier with each push on the literal skeleton at the lack of compassion and atrocity of this abuse. The fear, the pain from hunger, the pain of lack of love. Other med students came in to practice their works. Have to learn somehow so might as well practice. He pushed until the meds began to work and her heart began to beat on it's own.

She was moved to the main ER but the room smelled of her rotted skin. The room cleaned and a new stretcher pushed to the receiving spot of the next, most likely would be dead soon person. He sat on the edge of one of the stretchers to rest and push once more visuals of pain and the horrendous nature of daily abuse and trauma's. He felt a peace cover him for a moment, "you ok Jared?" He turned quickly to see that nurse with the beautiful blue eyes that was concerned about him earlier. She sat on the stretcher with him. His shoulders were rolled over some as he sat with such exhaustion and pain. She touched his shoulder and then patted it. "You need to take a break…" He stood suddenly a bit out of sorts, he wasn't used to a beautiful nurse or anyone for that matter worrying about him. "I am good, just a rough day." He forced a smile and pushed his hair out of his face. "You know, one of those days." She watched his strength as he moved through the room tossing stock on the shelves. He was aware she watched him but he didn't care at the moment. He was still very angry about the last patient. "If you need to talk to anyone you know where I am." She pointed to the main ER right outside the trauma room. He waved at her but did not look her way, "sure, thanks..um.." "I am Jen." He walked to her and reached to shake her hand. She saw him move but with a way of light and energy. She smiled but was shaking inside and had no idea why. " Nice to meet you also." He walked back to finish stocking the room. She started to walk out of the room but didn't want to leave him just yet. "Meet me in the break room, lets get a soda or water you need a break and I would like to talk to you some." He didn't have time to answer, the doors opened and a new trauma was being rolled in by EMS. He put his hands up with a shrug, "see ya round nursely." She smiled and walked out, "soon then."

Another full arrest complete with the triage tech Carrie, riding the stretcher and doing compressions on the man. He was dropped at the door and left. She was first there and called all to action. Whenever she worked triage something out of TV land would happen. She was a youngen heading to be a nurse which made him worry a bit, because she truly was a black cloud. Everything and anything would happen when she worked. They worked on intubating the man, the long silver blade went in to open the mouth so they could visualize the vocal chords then slipped a tube through and into the lungs. Sometimes a dead person was too dead and had already stiffened up or had rigor set in. TOD was involved as they called time of death and away another body went to the bags of glory and the cold room of storage. There was a different feel this time though, his thoughts were on Jen and those beautiful eyes and that contrasting beautiful jet black hair she had swept up some magical way.

He stocked the room and quickly and took a break. Maybe she would be in the break room, maybe he would see her working, maybe.. His stride felt different as he walked through the ER. The spirits were calm it seemed and gave him some peace. He got a drink out of the soda machine in the break room. The television was blaring so he shut it off. The chair felt good against his back, his old EMT back was a tad sore and he was just plain worn out. The overhead page was loud and startled him. "Jared to the trauma room please!" Short lived and she didn't show up. He tossed his cup in the garbage and pulled open the door quickly. She fell into his arms, she had just pushed on the door and the timing was perfect. He felt every bit of her against him and he held her for a moment. She felt his strength and also every bit of him. She smiled and did not try to get out of his arms. "Well hello Jared, we meet again." He stepped back to release her and laughed nervously. "Well, yes here we are but I have to go." He moved past her and down the hall quickly to the trauma room. She watched him and liked what she saw but she saw more than a man, she saw his light, his energy that surrounded him was of purity and strength.

He smiled as he walked into the trauma room. Whatever was going on he enjoyed every moment of it. He tilted his head and tried to make out what the next patient was, what was the trauma. He saw blood that covered every inch of the person. Bright red slippery blood complete with a french fry between her legs. She was a young girl maybe in her twenties and she was very much a dead bloodied mess. No compressions just a bloody dead girl. He prepared the body for the bag, blood was still her companion and that french fry was still nestled between her legs in a pool of blood. He added that to his visuals to his already overloaded brain. Ketchup will never look the same. "Yes, I will have a t-bone with fries to complete the loss of my sanity."

Removing jewelry from a fresh dead is a vision of contrast. Taking from them what they cannot take with them. Rings slipped easily from blood soaked fingers. He pulled harder than if they were alive. He tried to remove a most stubborn ring, it didn't want to leave her. He heard the finger crack and realized he pulled too hard. The ring slowly came off and with it came the feel of jagged energy. Her soul was confused or shattered or something because he felt it all around him. If you have ever felt jittery on too much caffeine and the air was not comfy that is what it felt like. "Go to the light or something but leave here." He plopped the rings in the bio bag to lock into the safe. He wanted the energy or ghost or whatever it was to leave.

There was something that happened with a fresh dead, there was always a presence. Sometimes the liquid peaceful kind of presence, sometimes a jagged hard angry kind.

He wrapped her up in a sheet and rolled her into the body bag and zipped it shut. A flash of her last moments hit him. He saw her put on those jeans that were soaked

in her blood. Silence finally came to the trauma room and the young one. She must have found the light and left because he felt her energy leave.

Chapter 7

The morgue had its own history of scary and sad. Security had to always open the locked morgue door for everyone, but they couldn't help with the body transfers. No one could help transfer the bodies but ER personnel too much liability. Once a guard dropped a dead, so they weren't allowed to help any longer. That left him to transfer the literal dead weight alone. The morgue had it's own stretchers, stainless steel and very cold. He transferred the white body bag to the stainless steel one and positioned it in the cooler. He would always quickly get out of dodge because that place was full of spirit types that were confused or angry or stuck there for some reason. He wanted no part of their after existence. He discovered if you showed them you were aware of their existence they turned into real pests.

Once the morgue showed what must have been a grumpy spirit trapped and not happy in the cooler. He opened the door and the stretchers were turned over and some of the body bags were tossed onto each other. This messed with his head and he wanted no part of the angry spirits. Security left after they opened the door. He pushed the body into the cooler but left them on the ER stretcher. He stood there a moment, almost a moment too long. The door began to close and there was no inside handle or way to open it from the inside. If someone was stuck in there they were stuck until somebody came to collect a dead or drop one off, or if you were missed in the ER, but that would be one too many minutes in a dark cooler with a bunch of tossed body bags.

Speed was interesting when fear of being trapped in a small very cold room with old dead things in bags was a possible reality. Just before it clamped itself shut he slammed into it and ran out. He walked quickly past the offices that were next to the morgue. How could anyone have an office next to fresh deads? He walked into his trauma room and did a quick once over of the stock. The room hadn't been cleaned but the stock was ready to rock for the next trauma. The trauma doors opened suddenly and startled him. Alexandria stood there with her cleaning cart and smiled at him. "What are you doing standing there like that Jared?" She pushed her cleaning cart into the room, "you wear me out," she said as she began to mop up the blood left from Ms. French fry. He asked her quickly, "see any EMS heading this way Alexandria?" "No, we are done with trauma's today." A hopeful thought but he knew differently. But maybe he could have a break and go visit that pretty nurse that had caused him to ponder. He walked into the main ER but she was nowhere to be seen. He walked to the break room to get another quick drink before another trauma would arrive. He pushed into the room quickly and ran into her. They fell back against one of the tables but he caught her and kept her from getting hurt. "Well hello again Jared, I didn't expect to see you this soon." He enjoyed the moment of her against him, her eyes sparkled in a way that took his breath. One of the nurses walked into the room and he stepped away from her suddenly. "I'm sorry I ran into you Jen, hope I didn't hurt you." She just smiled at him and sat down with her soft drink. "Thank you for catching me Jared." The nurse that walked in laughed at them, "you two look good together you should do something about that." She made herself some coffee and before Jared could say anything the trauma buzzer went off and he had to go. "See you soon.." he turned and ran back down the hall to the room. He was happy, "who knows?" His mind flew with thoughts and wishes and desires but that left quickly as he walked into his reality. The trauma room was clean just in time for more blood. A young girl, packaged and wrapped from another hospital. She had a perforated colon, how did this happen? The docs ask the EMS as report found the ears of all in the room. X-ray was there ready to do the quick look inside as were the residents two nurses and registration. A whole lot of nurses, docs and techs are present when one arrived at the trauma room. The patient had been brutally raped and sodomized with some kind of metal object. She was torn way up into her colon. They moved her quickly to the OR, this one was safe now, if she survived. Memories found him of all the abused women that had been to the ER. One was raped by her husband beaten and sent off to the hospital with a story of falling down the stairs. While in the ER she was visited by her abuser. He closed the curtains and beat her while she lay in the bed. Casually slipped into the hospital bed with her then raped her once more. A quick few thrusts and he was complete in his terror into her world. She will feel she can never escape him for even in the hospital she wasn't safe. Yes abusers know their job and they do it well. If she doesn't want to press charges he would walk free to do whatever he wished. He lowered his head and saw the look on the ladies face as she rolled into the trauma room. She had been shot in the vagina but the angle was perfect it somehow didn't kill her. He slammed the wall down on those memories and finished stocking the room. It wasn't too dirty so he cleaned it himself and didn't bother environmental. As the trauma room stilled for a moment his job became one to float in the main ER and help with whatever was needed. The ER was a usual mess, with people scattered about moaning, vomiting and cursing. He looked out across his wonderful emergency room at the disarray.

A naked older gentleman was walking past every bay, looking into each one, then walking to the next. He walked up to him with a hospital gown in hand, the ones that never quite cover any part of the patient. It's a simple way to tease them with the feel of almost decency, but their parts still hang out the back of the gown. The old man was talking of someone that most likely had been gone many years or doesn't even exist. The man had Alzheimer's, that nasty thing older types get that removes proper thought processes and memory. Reducing an adult to that of a child, lost in their minds, in another world, they have to be controlled medicated and watched. He walked him back to his room, "You have to stay on this stretcher ok?" The old man just smiled and began to stand again to walk past him. He gently

46

pulled him back to the stretcher, "You have to stay here, or I have to tie you to the bed." He sat down for a moment, settled into the stretcher, but for a moment. In rushes Uma, one of the techs, a German lady of interesting qualities.

"You must stay in zee bed Mr. Johnson." She pushed him back into the stretcher. He watched as she moved around him. He will be restrained soon, but for now Uma has him under control. She was slight of build, blondish red hair and had an uncanny ability to almost kill every patient she came in contact with. He chuckled at her, he liked her, enjoyed her, she was not very skilled but she always meant well in her attempts to give patient comfort.

He walked past a man on a stretcher covered in maggots. They were in his eyes, his nose, they moved with their slippery way all over his skin. Is this maggot day? He was found down in an alley covered with maggots. He smelled of alcohol and looked like something out of a movie of living dead types. The eye docs were called in to pull the maggots from his eyes. With a warm wash cloth he begin his tech duty to wipe away the maggots. This wasn't working for they started to fall onto the floor and near his shoes. He wheeled him into a shower room and lowered the nozzle to wash him on the stretcher. The maggots fell away into the drain. "I love my job." He repeated a few times. "Thank you for doing this I'm sorry I'm like this." The man said as he looked down at the things crawling and falling away from his groin. "It is my job dude no worries." He finished the task of

47

maggot duty, the patient was put back into his room. Fresh gown and sheets waited for the eye docs to pull them from his eyes, he fell back away into dream land. He washed his hands with the alcohol jell. He slid it quickly across and up onto his arms. "No maggots allowed." He turned to the doors of the ER and he saw EMS bringing in a patient that had a familiar ailment, little white rice things crawling to the top of the patients pants. "Great, it is maggot day." "Jared?" The charge nurse looked at him and smiled. "Please?" EMS put the patient into the shower room. He was a frail young homeless man, hair was thinned black with specks of dirt and pieces of grass mixed with the premature grey. He sat the frail one on a chair in the room and pulled down the shower head that would once more wipe away maggots to the drain. The maggots were crawling under his balls and into and out of his bottom. "Help me here dude." He asked, as the frail man lifted parts of his anatomy so he could hose the maggots from his red skin. His skin was broken down for some reason, an infection had taken the healthy skin away and left dead skin for the maggots to feed on. The patient looked down at himself. "What are those things?" His eyes were wide. "Maggots, they are eating your dead skin, you need to learn to wash yourself out there in the world." The man sat once more on the stretcher, silence was the companion between time and water washing. The man was in tears. A sudden feel across the moment was a sorrow of wishes that didn't occur, wants that weren't followed through with in this frail patient's life. "Choices." He said to the man then finished washing away the maggots. He needed a break and headed back to the break room. Diet coke, "I need sustenance." He pushed open the lounge door and grabbed a cup. The lounge had free fountain drinks for the employee's, although truly it was for the patients.

As soon as he sat down the page for a trauma came in over the intercom. He walked quickly back to the trauma room through the main ER, he saw Uma as she reached to take a blood pressure cuff off of a patients arm. But this cuff wasn't being used to take blood pressure; it was being used to keep an arterial bleed contained until the docs could fix it. He yelled at her to stop, but it was too late, she removed the cuff, the blood began to spurt from the mans artery that was now exposed. The patient just laughed as Uma ran out of the room screaming, "help! It's going poof, poof!" She tossed her hands up with every poof and ran past him. Another tech had already gone into the room, with a gloved hand grabbed the arm and asked in anger, "What did she do to you?" The patient just laughed, he wanted to kill himself, he tried by doing the slice of arm thing, so he laughed, Uma almost finished him off.

The trauma room buzzer went off again with an added bonus, because he was late getting to the room. "We need a tech in the trauma room," there was a pause, then added "Jared!" He walked quickly back to his trauma room, he placed the trauma tag on the pt's ankle but he didn't see any trauma on the man. His shirt was opened, and there in a small place in the center of his chest was a dimple. It seemed he was working with a nail gun and shot himself in the chest. He was moving a ladder he was holding the nail gun and, boom, dead center shot. His vitals suddenly began to drop, blood pressure, oxygen saturation; his skin began to get mottled. His skin just didn't look right, and he started to pass out. Before he could even get his temperature, he was rolled immediately out of the room to the operating room. The nail had been piercing the heart with each beat. He survived, so we were told later.

Another minute another trauma. "Great one of those stuck in the trauma room, days." He hated those back to back trauma's, especially when they come in with a leg on the side. No not fries with that, a leg with that. Drugs and motorcycles don't mix, especially this time, a leg missing and a dude high on cocaine. His right leg was detached from the knee down and EMS was carrying it in. He handed it to Jared and states flatly "find a home for this." Yea a leg on the side." The bony ripped open side near his blue gloved hand. He had to get a patient valuables bag to put his leg in.. "This just isn't natural," his thought as he shoved and turned and maneuvered the limb to find a temporary resting place inside the bag. But it wasn't working.

He watched his blue gloved hands turn the mans leg, then he grabbed the foot. He should have chosen a different job what the hell was he thinking? The hairy limb wasn't going to allow itself to be shoved into the not tall enough clothing bag. He had to improvise and put another bag on top, then taped it together. He had to find a place to put the partial leg with the patient. They were about to be rushed up to the OR. It wasn't going to be re-attached or he would have had it on ice already. But you have to keep the parts with the body, maybe there was a warranty? The patient was ready to go, the warming blanket on him, a monitor to keep an eye on his vitals, left no room to place the leg on top of the stretcher. He put the leg underneath the stretcher with the visual of all of the lost clothing under stretchers daily. He wrote clearly on wide silk tape, LEG IS UNDER THE STRETCHER, taped to the patient's chest. He hoped it would keep the leg from separating further from it's owner. He watched as they wheeled the patient to the operating room. The patient was still high on cocaine and felt no pain and laughed all the way down the hall.

Without time to stock or even pee, EMS rolled another one in. He was at work and a fork lift truck driven by one of his co-workers crushed him against the wall. He seemed ok at first. Pulled off his jeans a surprise was found, he was crushed alright. Crushed a fresh bowel movement right out of him, there lodged in the pants legs are clumps of turds. "What is this." He stopped his words in mid-sentence, the patient was awake and aware and could hear and see him. Not wanting to embarrass him he just folded the jeans up after dumping the surprise into the garbage.

Somehow this man was ok and away he went to the CT scan. His loss of bowels kept decently respected. Although some med students chuckled a little as one of the turds did a floor dance. Much better than a gun spinning away from falling out of a motorcyclists pocket. That was a fun moment, while he waited for his foot to be shot. He also had a moment of holy crap, when he thought he was trying to remove a knife from a pocket. Instead he pulled out a gun. Well, he immediately pointed it away from himself which then pointed it to all in the room.

Jen leaned into the room to check on Jared. She missed him and had just become aware of him. She watched him move with skill as he worked on the patients and then quickly stocked the room. She had to leave him there and go back to her patients. She would get to know him, "oh yes…" She whispered as she walked away from the trauma room.

The double doors in the ambulance bay open like clouds dumping their held moisture, another trauma literally flew into the room. EMS was doing compressions and he was intubated. He immediately took over CPR. He pushed hard and quick on the chest, but felt this man had left the building long ago. His head was crushed, not much of any resemblance of a head was left. The docs flew into action throwing in the central lines that would send lifesaving meds immediately into the system, but to no avail. He was long gone, been long gone. The time of death was called as once more, TOD was called into duty and CPR was stopped.

The body bag brought out to prepare the fresh dead for family to view. They would be arriving soon and he would feel their loss, hear their screams and watch them fall to the floor begging just to hear them one last time. To tell them goodbye, to say something they wished they would have said. It was always the same it was always difficult and they were always full of regret.

Putting the fresh dead over to bay four in the trauma room he got ready to feel the possible side effect of pain, it hits when least expected. Sorrow, sadness ripping kind of what the hell feeling, he does not like death. He moved the body to the morgue quickly removed the body and the bag from his stretcher. As he tossed it onto the cold cart into the cooler, he looked at the room full this day of deads, he felt the temporariness of life here, he felt his mortality.

"I think I want a blue body bag, or maybe one with decorations and such?" His voice trailed off as he walked down the long hall in the basement that headed back to the main ER. Visuals of decorated body bags for sale fell into his mind of play. "Maybe I am insane?" One of those flesh people heard him talking to himself. The ones that do the studies on the deads to find out why they died, pathologists they are called. "Insanity is over rated." She said then smiled at him as he walked past. Nodding in agreement, he just wanted to go play pool or fall into a place of writing, where a story could take him away relieving him of pain. Flight was an interesting thing all want it, they climb high with wings to carry them over and off the mountain cliff.

We fly in planes, we fly on skies, we fly from reality when someone pushed that vile of their anger into us. Yea, flight was something that he wanted, away from their pain and his own pain from his past, his life, his walk.

He did the marriage thing, did it for twenty two years. The one great reward from the place of, let me spit in your face, was three daughters and a knowing of what true abuse is. It is an insidious creature that spills over the words of love and touch into hatred and anger. Something like mixing shit with ice cream, yea that's what abuse is like. And he had ice cream on a daily basis.

Words were interesting and they meant things and words of anger and control was something he left at the doorstep. He liked his little things, writing poetry and stories of short for kids and no anger anywhere near. Yes, flight from the way of pain is an ever constant want into his world. But the grown up thing he had to do was work in the world of normal. Unless and until, something broke into his life that had that continued flow and feel of love and comfy, he would have to work in the world of pod heads and reality playing the games to walk this place.

-- there is the calm that

comes with love

that love doesn't have to be of earth

it can come from an angels ..sigh

or a light touch of eternity that just happened to slip

from Gods fingers....

The hospital high five is a finger in your bottom is necessary but most of the patients yell while it's being done. It is to check for tone, or to see if they may have blood in their bottom. Tone is to see if they could possibly be paralyzed. So a finger up the bottom is a medical necessity. If a bottom goes into a trauma room a virgin, it leaves experienced. When patients are awake and aware but are breathing through their mouth or have on a non re-breather oxygen mask and cold air is blowing over their mouth. The most horrible rectal temperature time occurs. They are going to watch you do it, feel you do it. He told the lady as she eyeballed him of a rectal temperature moment. She waited he pushed, she said calmly and flatly, "you are in the wrong hole." Red is an interesting color on paper and in art but there was no brighter red than on his face that rectal temperature day.

Women have the other place, and at times it is accidentally used. It is still a viable place to get a temperature as is placing the thermometer underneath the balls or ball, if you will. But when awake and looking at said tech inserting said thermometer with finger pursuing the issue first, can be a rough moment. The trauma room silent for a moment, cleaned and stocked. He opened the doors to the back hall that lead to the trauma elevator. There in the hall was a stretcher. He leaned to look underneath to see and yes, lo and behold the leg from the patient before. He picked up the bag with the forgotten leg, he hummed a tune while in the elevator and looked down to see the toes in the bag, they looked like they wiggled. He averted his eyes quickly and pushed the button once more to the surgery floor. Let them dispose of it.

Chapter 8

"Nurse!" She screamed from her stretcher in one of the rooms. "I want something to eat and I want pain meds now! I have been in here for an hour at least and I am starving to death!" He listened to the redundant wish for food and water from yet one more angry patient. He asked slowly, "what are you in here for ma'am?" "My stomach hurts real bad, and I can't stop puking. What is wrong with this hospital, it's horrible, people treat you like shit, and I am tired!" "Slow down with the yelling ma'am there are other patients here that are sick." He turned away from her and walked away as she continued to scream for food and pain meds."

No matter what is wrong with people they come into the ER and want to be fed. Maybe it's a hospital hotel confusion in their brains. As soon as he left the room there was a yell for help at the circle, in the back of the ER. A man was lying on the ground in the parking lot near an ambulance, he had been badly beaten. Jared grabbed a wheel chair and lifted the man into it. He was so badly beaten he had to be held in the chair while he pushed him into the trauma room. The man mumbled something. Was it about who hit him? Was it about what hurt? No, "I want something to drink I'm so thirsty." Even in the heat of pain, people want to be watered or fed. Jared smiled and pushed the button that called the necessary ones to the trauma room to help this badly beaten man to a drink of water. Maybe it was a medical condition that occurred when one was beaten or their legs were hanging off their body? No sense to be made of the hunger and thirst in an emergency room.

As he walked back into the hall of the ER one of the prisoner patients blasts past him, knocked him against the counter. The prisoner was running full out for the magnetically locked double doors. Everyone leaned over the counter and stepped into the hall to watch. If the ER was a boat at that moment, it would have turned over from the weight shift. The vision to behold, would be the prisoner slamming into the double doors and falling with the same slam to the floor in front of the doors. He was flat on his back, timing was everything in life, this guy didn't have good timing. The doors opened slowly and security lifted him up and walked him back to his bay for treatment. "Fascinating," was all he could say. The ER recovered from its lean position and continued with duties of drugs and patient care.

He heard one of the patients crying, he had no traumas he was floating to help in the ER wherever needed. He walked into the room, "what can I get for you?'" She was a middle aged lady, simple in way but with such fear. He could feel her fear, it was a liquid that filled the room and flew into his every thought, he felt it. She looked at him, her eyes wide, "I know I am about to have a seizure and I do not want to have it, they scare me." He walked slowly over to her calmly and stood next to her. "Well I am here to keep you from getting hurt, and your body knows what to do, so just relax and I will be here when you are finished." She smiled, "you are right," she relaxed. Sometimes there were moments that hit him at work. He would be compelled to reach out and touch a patient, maybe their head or shoulder or to give one of those side hugs. This was one of those times. He touched her head, he watched as his hand touched her head, it always happened quickly and without any control on his part. "You will be ok." He didn't know why it happened but when it did he had no control. He could feel and see a line of energy that flowed into the person. He never told anyone for he knew they would lock him up in a psych department. He could see her brain and the energy malfunction, he could see people, inside them and send light of healing to them. It was always from God and he did it with faith and he would never not do it. Didn't matter anyway, his hand would go where needed and his want to help others would always send a prayer of pure faith to God. He was a spiritual healer and would be until time slowed against his heart and soul.

The room filled with that liquid air, the kind that was thick but felt calm and comfortable. The patient calmed immediately. He removed his hand and she smiled. He said calmly, "no seizing today little one, not on my watch." He walked out of the room. He watched the doctors walk in and the nurse started the meds. She looked at him with a silent thank you. He walked back into his ER and felt refreshed and alive with energy and a feel of forever. Yes, forever covered him as he felt peace. He did not question what just happened for it was natural for him to reach for all that needed and God wished to be helped. He was there for whoever needed for that is what life was about. At least to Jared, it was about helping others.

Jen walked past him and ignored him for a moment. He watched her walk past and up to the place where the nurses mixed the meds ordered by the docs. She was one striking figure and a beautiful woman that would surely have nothing to do with him. A scream shattered the ER and Jared moved quickly to the room where it originated. Jen watched him and hoped he would be ok. She smiled, "he will be fine." She finished the meds ordered for her patent and walked away from the drama. She saw his strength and knew he had a healing gift. "We will need to talk soon," she paused, "of life and such."

Jared walked into the room where the yell came from, he saw what looked like Tarzan on steroids. The man was huge and his muscles bulged against the pull of the restraints that EMS had him tied down with. Somehow magically the only thing holding biceps of three feet wide are those triangle scarves used usually in EMS land as slings, but most the time they are used as restraints. "Will you help us with this one?" The EMS medic asked Jared. "I spose," he walked to the counter and put on some gloves he wasn't looking forward to messing with this maniac. The patient's eyes dashed back and forth and randomly flew up into his head, which showed only the whites for just a moment, then his eyes would dart back and forth. As if he was watching a fast and furious tennis match. Security was called to also assist, and the journey began.

The nurse for this one was Keri, she handled every patient easily. She always had a calm and patient way about her but mixed that with a strength from her core. Jared nicknamed her Keri Lee, after the martial artist of long ago. She walked into the room and rolled her shoulders to ready herself for the battle. The patients family thought he was possessed after he tore up their home. The truth of it is he was high on steroids. A dangerous mix with a body builder with eight feet wide biceps.

Security walked into the room to help move the patient from EMS stretcher to ER stretcher. Leather restraints, compliments of the hospital and our wonderful security staff, who had bondage 101 down pat, ready to wrap around wrists that will be attached to the ever growing biceps. Jared's image of this mans muscles was getting distorted. EMS released his hands and away he flew, literally. The patient jumped up onto the television set that hung on the wall in the room. The televisions hadn't been updated, so there was one of the old fat back TV's with Tarzan hanging on for life. Security grabbed at him while Jared and Keri stepped back out of the room. "These are the best seats Keri stay by me I have your back." Keri stood there with a syringe ready to sedate the young man. "Sounds like a plan to me." Jared was handed a blood order, "get this guys blood as soon as they restrain him." Oh great! was his first thought, he would get to somehow stick a needle in Tarzan and hope he remained still.

The patient was pulled down hard onto the stretcher. It took seven of them to hold him down, while the leather restraints were applied to his wrists and ankles. The patient yelled and cursed and started using words no one had ever heard. Finally done with their job, they filed out of the room. Jared and Keri sighed at the same time, "Ready?" he asked her as they stepped into the room. Jared waited until Keri gave the man his shot but there was trouble in paradise. No IV started, so no meds to be put in. The resident doc walked into the room. He was one of the young ones that many of the nurses liked. It was his boyish quality and muscular body mixed with that soon to be doctor mode that created the drool moments with those women. Jared had enjoyed many a wild party with him when he was invited to go along and act like a med student. He enjoyed the free meal and free drinks supplied by the drug rep's that were always bribing the docs with such pleasures. "Johnny, are you going to get some info from this patient?" Jared asked as he pushed the doc into the room while he and Keri stepped back out. "How am I going to get an IV in that guy?" "How am I going to get his blood?" The patient yelled in a language of not known to mankind.

The doc walked back out of the room. He looked at Jared with that hidden holy shit look, and walked away from the patient. A visitor went into the room, a family member so they were told. She went into the room and closed the door and the curtains. "Yea, let her talk to him maybe calm him down." A small group had now formed near the secretaries desk right outside the bay. His yells were getting louder, and the opinion was formed that obviously the visitor was upsetting him. Jared opened the door and pulled open the curtains. His mind was thrown into disbelief. The lady had candles lit on the floor and was rocking back and forth mumbling and tossing water onto her brother. Her brother was livid, he thrashed in the stretcher, moved his head around wildly and pulled at those leather restraints with those eight foot wide biceps. "Security, call security!" everyone closed on the room while he lifted the lady up and blew out the candles quickly.

"You could blow us up, there is oxygen everywhere in here what the hell are you doing?" The patient began to laugh maniacally then called his sister every animal name known to mankind. "He is possessed, he is possessed save me, save me!" Security walked her out to the waiting room, Jared picked up the instruments of exorcism and could not help but to laugh. Suddenly the patient calmed and just was just lying there without movement.

Dr. Johnny walked back and was ready to talk with the patient. Molly, one of the nurses, a cute little woman, small petite frame with short bright golden hair, walked up to Johnny and sprinkled normal saline solution on him in the shape of a cross. Keri got some silk tape and put a few tape crosses on his scrubs across his chest. "You are ready to go in doc." Molly smiled and stepped back, everyone stepped

64

back as he approached the patients room. He was in there all of three minutes, closed the door behind him and was a bit ashen in color. "I think that man may truly be possessed." He ordered meds and IV and walked away in a trance like state. "Yikes!" Jared looked at Keri, "you go in first," Keri picked up the pager phone, "security we need you at bed four." She got her IV supplies and states with strength, "I'm going in!" The seven guards stood around him, Keri explained to the patient the facts of IV and that it would happen no matter what. He looked around at all in the room, and settled his stare on Jared. Eye contact was a very personal thing, and to Jared on this day that eye contact shot through him like lightning. "I am going to kill everyone in this room, every last one of you." Keri didn't miss a beat, "well can you wait until I get this IV in first and give you some medicine?" He smiled and relaxed, "deal," but then immediately lifted his head once more, his eighteen foot wide biceps flexed. His finger tried to point to Jared, but being kind of stuck to the bed it pointed to the patients foot. "You I will kill first!'" Jared just smiled, "thank you for the honor," again the patient relaxed, then yelled just as Keri settled to push the needle into his vein, "get it the first time, or I will kill you first instead of macho over there." Jared thought of the small amount of money he was paid to work in this ER, then looked back at Tarzan who was calm for the moment. She got the IV and the blood, Jared would not have to stick him after all. She handed the blood to him and said, "here.." she stopped, then finished "Paul, take this blood." Jared stood there and looked behind him to see who the heck

Paul was then Keri winked. "Oh yea, thanks Mary Jane." He walked quickly out of the room, he said with a smile. "The names have been changed to protect the innocent."

Chapter 9

And there she is…

Time to take a lounge break again, Tarzan had worn Jared out and the trauma room tech must pace themselves, for one never knew when the multiple trauma's would come in. That was his excuse for the day to pace himself. Jared walked to the break room and the nurse Jen, she was on his mind and that wasn't anything new. He was used to admiring beauty from afar. But nurses don't mix with the lowly paid techs. Most of the time anyway at least that was what he put in his head to believe. She was a new nurse to the ER, came from the med surge floor in the hospital and was a cute thing, according to Jared anyway. She wore her hair wrapped around in swirls, jet black hair that seemed to tease anyone near it to untie it from it's hold and watch the cascade of shine fall down past her shoulders. Her eyes of light blue contrasted her beauty and her skin, oh her skin. His thoughts found his mouth against her skin. He sighed and walked past her and felt a little less than good enough for anybody. Divorced and old at the age of 52, hustler of pool an old martial artist that wrote goofy sentimental poetry, top that off with, just a tech, and you have the perfect non interesting type person all wrapped up in Jared.

"Hello Jared, we still need to talk some." Jared stopped and smiled. "We do? About what pray tell." He so enjoyed being near her. She was mixing meds for a patient and turned away from him for a moment. He straightened his black scrub top, she looked him up and down, "you look good today Jared, you are a strong one aren't you?" He slowly pushed his hand through his hair. He seemed unable to speak he just smiled and tugged on his scrub top to pull it down more. "I have been known to mess with some weights in my day." "I saw you helping that patient that had a seizure, you know just what to do." Jared leaned against the wall near the assignment board tried to act cool. He missed the wall and slipped some catching himself. She laughed, he laughed, "I have worked here many years in the medical world, have seen a lot." She finished filling her syringe with the meds, grabbed the patients chart and walked away. "Talk to you later?" He nodded and watched her walk, a walk of tease, that walk of I know you are watching. She seemed nice and she had a very nice walk, and most beautiful smile. He walked to the lounge to finish his interrupted diet coke. With fresh nice thoughts he could fantasize a bit, but knew she was just being nice.

Uma walked into the lounge cursing in German. She grabbed a cup and filled it with a soda, gulped it down then walked out as quickly as she came in. "The German is in an uproar." Jen walked into the room. "Hi again," she reached for a cup to get a drink then bent over to get some peanut butter out of the cabinet. He was enjoying the view quite nicely. She sat across from him, opened the small bit of peanut butter specially packed for hospitals, her finger slipped into and pulled out a taste. "Want some?" Her finger extended toward Jared, "No thank you, but I surely like your spoon." She slipped it into her mouth and smiled. "You are cute, I think I will enjoy working down here in the ER." Jared stood and tossed his cup into the garbage can. "Well thank you, you are very damned cute yourself." He couldn't believe that came out of his mouth, he left quickly. The trauma buzzer made its horrendous sound and he was off once more. "Saved by the bell." He ran down the hall, as he turned to walk into the ER he heard a whistle. He looked down the hall and there she was, she smiled and whistled again. "Nice rhythm there Jared," flustered, he walked to the trauma room. Blood was released from a fresh bullet through the head, a self inflicted act of waste. The med types worked to keep the patient alive for CODA, not for real life, just for organ life. The hole in the back of his head was large. A large caliber bullet, left large exit wound. Everyone watched the blood splatter onto the floor from the back of his head. Everyone put on their proper gowns to keep blood off and sometimes they were used to keep warm in a cold ER.

Jared just stared at the amount of blood that accumulated onto the floor around the stretcher. IV fluids moved into the guy to hydrate his organs, but the fluids had to go somewhere and they were literally spraying his blood out onto the floor. He grabbed a sheet and some towels and tossed them onto the never ending red sea, but to no avail. "Look guys, you are making a mess here, stop the bleeding." He looked at the docs, he pointed to the obvious blood covered floor, the response? "We are waiting on the OR, have to keep fluids moving through him to save the other organs." They walked out and left him there with a mess. He pushed the patient into another bay, the bay they usually kept the fresh dead ones for the family to see.

He wrapped the guys head with towels and put blankets and towels on the floor to catch the ever leaking movement of blood out of the bullet wound at the back of his head. Family would be arriving soon to view the body as the perpetual leak of blood formed to the right side of the stretcher. He called in the chaplain to stand on that side of the stretcher so the family wouldn't have to see the blood from their loved one, drip blood onto the floor or onto them. They walked in to view the body and the only sound he could hear was the dripping of blood onto the towels on the floor. Like a leaky faucet, drip, drip, drip. It was very loud in his mind, but luckily they didn't hear it. They were too busy crying and yelling at him for doing such a thing. "Whew." Alexandria walked in behind Jared, "do you need me in here yet?" He had closed the curtains around the original bay, he pointed to the curtains, which remained closed so the family wouldn't see. "Clean up in aisle bay one." She walked over to the curtain and slowly pulled it back, "oh my god!" She exclaimed before she could stop the words. The family turned to see her and unfortunately saw past her. As the daughter began to cry, "Look that's his blood, look!" She closed the curtains quickly and left to get her cleaning supplies. The chaplain walked the family away from the trauma room and hit Jared on the way out, with a look of cover the blood up next time! He smiled at her and nudged her out of the room. As they walked out of the back of the trauma room, Alexandria walked through the other door and began the mopping of the massive blood splat on the floor.

The doors flew open once more. The nurse Mike, a big strong dude, carried the guy in and put him on the stretcher in another bay. Jared began CPR and away the docs flew. The nurses moved around the patient getting the drugs out that were ordered quickly as Jared continued to push on the guys chest. Yea the man was blue from the shoulders up, dropped dead while being triaged into the ER. They hit him with all the heart failure drugs.

The doc ordered all to get back, ready to shock. "I'm clear, you're clear, we're all clear, clear!" Wham!, 200 joules of electricity slammed into the body. He almost sat up with the shock, his body lifted higher than any of them had ever seen. "Wow," was all Jared could get out. His arms were pumped from doing compressions, he waited for the order to continue. A few more pushes, and the docs ordered once more for a shock. Wham, they hit him again, he rose even higher than the first time. One of the docs said in a whisper to Jared, "wow just like on tv." The patient suddenly began to speak, "I just haven't felt right.." He stopped in mid sentence and looked around the trauma room, "Where the hell am I?" The doc proceeded to tell him that he was dead and we brought him back. The room calmed, the meds were in, the patient was alive. Jared had never in all of his years working the ER, ever see someone come back like that from a full arrest. They had come back to have a heart beat but they had brain damage or just long enough for their family to prepare for their death.

The doc that handled this one was a little strange, but brilliant, "well that's why we come to work isn't it my, my, look at that." He walked out of the room, the patient was wheeled over to x-ray and Jared had a mess to clean up. "Alexandria look!" He flexed his freshly pumped biceps, "Jared you wear me out." She had bay one ready to go, Jared pushed a stretcher in there and all was ready for the next trauma. He stocked the room quickly as she cleaned up the mess of stuff that the medical staff tossed so quickly to the floor. Although being clean isn't important when a life is at stake.

The doors flew open once more, a lady was sitting up in the stretcher, but the right side of her neck was wide open and it flapped in a weird way as she looked around the room. Jared directed them to go to the freshly cleaned bay. She had gotten some numbing meds somehow and numbed her neck and used a razor to hack away at her throat and her wrists. Why is she alive? Jared wondered, he couldn't believe the way her neck looked. It hung open with jagged edges and flapped as she talked. The docs looked into her neck and were a bit lost in what to do. Jared asked one of the docs why she wasn't dead, why was her neck wide open like that. "It's a miracle, for she clotted some how, now how to repair the damage to that artery." "I should be dead, I did it right, I watched my blood spurt and now I wake up here!" Jared just watches in amazement, she had money, she was beautiful, she was married, why was she hacking away at her neck? He felt a wave of complete sadness cover him. It was overwhelming and mixed with a feeling of total loss and alone. She was miserable and needed to escape. Too bad some people don't reach for the Big Guy. She was moved quickly to the OR but Jared won't know if she survived. He felt her sadness her wish to cease was strong, and if she didn't succeed this time he knew she would the next. There were people on this place of time and wishes that Jared felt were a test for others. Spirits or lights of good, whatever name they were real, they sacrificed a small amount of time living in flesh on earth to test the pod heads of life. One was Roger and he was homeless. He was also an alcoholic. His redundant visits to the emergency room created and attitude of disgust with most. EMS tossed his limp drunk body around on the stretcher as they waited to triage him into the ER. "Hey Roger ole buddy wake up."

Jared met him for the first time on a morning that was crazy as usual and he had to be cleaned off from messing on himself. He took him to one of the shower rooms and washed off all the dirt and feces. Roger was a gentle soul to Jared, he had a light inside him that was more than bright it was in the brilliant category. Once he made eye contact with him and it about knocked him back on the floor it was so bright. Jared felt he was an angel of some sort, or a test for those that walk life and see how they would treat a soul of no money and dirty clothes.

Chapter 10

Miracles happen

He finished cleaning Roger and went back to the main ER but as soon as he walked in a trauma came in. It was a multiple gunshot victim. He counted the wounds, nine to be exact. The docs looked at TOD and called the time of death, they all walked out and left him for dead, the nurse was there to finish her charting. He began to open the body bag and get the fresh dead into a fresh shower curtain, swimming pool smell place of rest. As he rolled the body to one side so he could tuck the body bag under him he saw something a wee bit off for a dead man, movement?

Nine minutes after the man stopped breathing and called dead he decided to breathe again. His chest rose. The nurse saw it the same time he did, "I see him breathing?" Jared stepped back and felt a flush of heat move through him while he looked at the dead guy. He felt and saw life move back into the fresh dead body. The doc had walked back in, "this man is not dead.." He shook his head. The staff was called back into the room to do what they do with people that are not dead. Push the right meds, stimulate the right organs and look with their mouths open at a miracle. The patient remembered nothing, he was sent to the OR, his vitals were great, he was awake he was alive. A miracle most say, Jared felt he was a miracle person or a jumper. They come to hospitals and groups, get killed, come back to life and voila all is good. Some would find a level of growth within and faith, others would just continue to walk blindly with the old voices of programming. Jared's mind continued to repeat the word programming until it was humming through his body. "Enough!" He yelled into the empty trauma room. Jared later heard the man was released and was fine, no brain problems nothing. He didn't remember anything about the shooting or being dead and he was as if nothing happened, a fine healthy young man. Jared's thoughts go back to the jumper theory, "yea he is a miracle man."

The doors flew open once more with another miracle man. His car broke down on the interstate and he tried to cross the interstate to the shoulder on the road. But instead of an easy walk he was hit by a car that was traveling 70 miles per hour, rode the top of the car for a time then was tossed to the pavement. EMS presented him to our trauma room. He was talking he was collared and on a back board but he showed no sign of trauma. The MD came into the room to begin his evaluation. Nothing was found, the man was laughing and talking, he told of his flight in time. We didn't keep him in the trauma room he would be rolled out to triage then sent to the main ER just to make sure they hadn't missed anything. The MD asked before he left the room. "What happened again son?" He told of seeing the car coming toward him and he jumped up as high as he could. The car instead of smacking him with full impact hit him with a glancing blow? "You need to buy a lottery ticket young man you are one lucky person." The boy was released a few hours later with absolutely no injuries. Miracle man or just not his time one or the other for sure.

The memory of Jared's own moment of not supposed to get hurt slipped across his mind. He was at his father's house at Christmas. His nephew Eric was in front of him as he ran up the back stairs to the house. Eric held the back door open to allow Jared to go into the house first. Somehow in his elegance of run up the stairs, Jared tripped. He could still see his right hand pushing to catch himself on the stairs. But his hand, open and spread waited to take part of the blunt of the trip never touched the stairs. He was held in the air for just a moment then let down with an easy klunk. His nephew yelled, "man you just did a matrix thing you were in the air!" Jared knew of those days of not supposed to get hurt. Blame it on luck or thick air but sometimes teeny miracle things happen.

He looked around the room and fell into thought, which was what he did a lot. He was different from all of them or at least most of them. He could help heal people and felt them leave their bodies or felt their energy of good and bad. He saw things that no one saw and could never tell anyone or he would be put away in a closet somewhere. He first noticed he was different in school. School was a place of torture for him, with uncomfortable uniforms and teachers that would rather be yelling than teaching. Lunch and recess were the favorite times of the day. He stood with his lunch money ready for milk and delicious potato sticks. On the lucky days when his mom was there to help serve the lunch he hoped to get extra. But no, she gave him the regular scoop as all the other kids got. He would fly out into the playground and was free from the walls of torture. Imagination is flight and he knew how to fly. Thoughts of the words of religion taught that day also found his recess moments. He attended a Catholic grade school and that in itself was a different kind of torture with mass daily. He did try to listen to all that was read from the bible, he would try to discern the reality or the common sense of what was said in the holy word thing. He didn't understand how he shouldn't steal money for his candy habit or not live forever in heaven. He had to think long and hard on that one. He had a talk with the Big Guy, he decided that yes he did not want to burn forever in hell, but a compromise would have to be found because he needed his candy and would continue to steal to get it if necessary. He asked with his eyes closed and all his heart for a ticket to go to heaven. He just knew he would never make it without help. After he asked for that ticket he felt he was good to go. So yay! He ran and played his best play day.

He watched the other kids playing they all had friends and companions to run with. Jared was a different type of person. He was crooked or not built right or his brain didn't fall into the same dots theirs did. If you ever felt out of place at a party or the first day at work then you knew what he felt all of the time.

He pushed a stretcher back to its parking place and stopped the thought of different and times of past. It had become second nature to block the bad spirits that were constantly attacking him. Witches in life were real and they spun their evil against anyone they could try to capture with their ways. Other evil things roamed beside the angels of light. If people only knew the battle going on right beside their every moment and thought. "Would they act differently?" He walked out the the ER and sighed, he was tired. It was filling up and never slowed its pace of patients and blood. He walked past bay one and heard a man with obvious tourettes syndrome yelling out. Tourettes syndrome was an interesting illness caused people to curse or have peculiar tics, uncontrollable tics. Next to the man cursing suddenly in bursts was a kind old man from a nursing home. Jared could see he was very upset with the language being presented, "Are you ok sir?" He walked in to comfort him. The Tourettes patient continued with his rant of inappropriate words, "cock sucker, shit face, face, face." he twitched as well. Jared touched the guy on the arm to comfort for a moment then turned back to the nursing home patient. "You will be ok, just push the button if you need someone." He handed him the nurse light, and smiled in hopes that would calm him. He walked out of the room and heard the cursing continue, he looked back at the nursing home man and saw him cringe.

To add to this wonderful sound of my people, a drunk was still on a backboard and yelled, "I have to poop!" along with this chorus of yells came a reply from another patient, "well go ahead!" his reply, "Sarah?" "No she left your sorry ass." Jared stood for a moment as the three voices created a song of a very odd nature. "Cock sucker, shit face, face, face," "I have to poop," "go ahead poop," "Sarah?" "No she left your sorry ass," "cock sucker shit face, face." The cycle didn't slow until Jared went to the guy on the backboard to speak to him. "Sir I can put you on a bedpan, but you can't get off the backboard." The smell of alcohol was strong, Jared stood back a little from the spit of response from the patient. "No! I will just wait!" He walked out and away but the voices continued their song. He looked at the clock it is almost time to go and he was ready. Jen saw him and walked up to him near the, I have to poop patient. "Interesting day isn't it Jared." She smiled then walked back to the nurses station to mix yet another drug. Jared just smiled at her, his history with women was not very good. He usually fell for them, gave them some amazing love making, opened them up to their core, and they took it to someone else to enjoy.

He leaned against the counter to watch her skill with the syringe and the push into the med bottle. "What are you doing after work Jared?" "Nothing," it came out before he could think of a lie, for he didn't feel like being hurt just yet, or go anywhere. The last lady he was with ripped him pretty quickly, and out of the blue. She just called one night and said goodbye, told him of his lack of's and poof she was gone. She did drop a thank you for the amazing sex, and how he taught her how to love, but just not love him. He had a gift of giving, and it seemed most women don't understand why they feel him so deeply and run away. They would find someone else pretty quickly, giving them love and comfort and trust. Everything he wanted, but just didn't seem to get. He was doomed in life to just show women how to love, and then let them fly to another. One of Jared's favorite poems, for it seemed to suit his life, he kept framed on his locker at work and on his desk at home.

...there is a spot the size of forever..

it sits upon my shoulder trying to find a life...

the fuel of her fire has been removed

now he will have what I showed her he will feel

what I gave her...there is a spot that I will place

into another.. then I will have.... forever

M.B.

"Let's go to dinner? We can talk of the trauma's you had today, I can talk of my horrible patients I had today," she shifted her weight and leaned toward him. "therapy?" Jared nodded, "sure, lets go for a little bite to eat." They settled on a place, Jared watched as the night shift walked in looking like a long line of zombies, awake barely and stiff in stride. He was tired from the day and tomorrow he would return,12 more hours of? His thoughts went to where he should be what should he be doing with his life. A tech is nothing in the way of work, barely pays and is very hard work. If it wasn't for his pool hustling, he would be in trouble financially. He plants thoughts in his mind, allowing them to have flight and cook. He had to let his thoughts play and find and examine all possible routes. Then out of the blue he would get an answer to the best possible action. Which in his reality is a prayer to the Big Guy.

A lady interrupts his thought as she walks out of the room her mother is in and called for people to come to the room. "Whats wrong? How can I help you?" The mother was very close to dying, "Look at her she needs some meds or something." The daughter walked over and picked at her mother's skin, then put whatever she picked off of her into her mouth. He couldn't believe what he just saw, "I will get your nurse." She nodded slowly but continued her taste of what was on her mothers skin. She pulled off scabs and popped them into her mouth. He felt a wave of nausea over this.. "Ma'am maybe you should wait out in the waiting room for a bit until we get your mother settled." Jen was the nurse for this room, she walked up, "what's wrong Ms. Johnson?" Jared stepped back away from the lady, she wasn't natural in his eyes. The daughter told of her concern, but all the while she picked at her mothers skin. The mother's pressure was dropping, all of her vitals were not good, she would not be alive long. Jen told the daughter she could be with her just a little longer then she would have to leave. She closed the curtain for her to be with her for some alone time. "Did you see her?" Jared whispered to Jen. She pushed lightly against him and whispered back, pressing purposefully her lips against his ear. "She is a nut case." She walked away to finish mixing the med's she was working on and glanced back at Jared. He was immobilized, still felt her against him. Balance that's what that was, gross of eating moms skin to the pressure of a beautiful woman's lips against his ear. Jared walked over to tell the lady she needed to wait in the waiting room. He pulled back the curtains and he could not believe what he saw. "No!" He pulled the catheter away from the daughter. The catheter that was just inside her mother's bladder. She ripped it out and was sucking the urine out of the tube. Jared just about lost his stomach contents, security was called and she was escorted away. Her mother was dead, the words from the daughter as she was being taken away, "Can I go to the morgue with you?" Jared was done with this day, done, done, done.

--

Silence of beauty

…is that one moment

when the air mixes with

your inhale..

flowers know the secret to rise

trees know the way to survive

..but the air has the power

to involve…..me in the life

of ..beauty

John, a night tech was assigned the trauma room, he and Jared head toward it while Jared gives him report on the room and any possible items missing. John was an interesting fellow, Jared had watched him grow in the medical world. John was one of the good guys he genuinely cared for the patients and would treat them with respect, no matter what they spit at him, he was always polite and calm on the return. And if you came in with a full arrest and John was on duty, your heart would have no choice but to beat. Jared had never seen such hard compressions done by anyone, John made it look easy.

Jen smacked Jared on the rear as he walked past her with John. "See you at the time clock." John looked at Jared then at Jen, "whoa, you getting a little of that?" Jared smiled, "nah just going out to have therapy, was not a good day." "therapy? Like physical release?" John laughed as did Jared but he would give no details for he had no idea where the night would go. "Just to talk that's it and if anything else happens you will never know." Making his way down the back hall where all the spare stretchers were kept, Jared was tired and really wanted to go home. He pushed open the locker room door and got his coat, dropped his trauma sheers into the locker. "Don't need you tonight, will see you in the morning." He saw himself in the mirror. A tired looking soul, grey hair messed up a little, his green eyes showed some sadness. "Felt too many strange things today, have to figure this out," his words slipped out, he usually talked to himself, "at least I have someone to talk with." He laughed and pushed open the door and there she was waiting. "I thought you were meeting me at the time clock?" "You just want to walk me out the door." She said softly then pulled him to her looped her arm through his. They walked past the stretchers, some with blood fresh on them. He felt relaxed for some reason with her and looked forward to a conversation of the day. The time clock showed its wonderful numbers of, you can go home now. They placed their badges against the gate keeper. "Transaction accepted." The computerized voice, signaled all was well and they may leave. Jared looked back as Jen pulled him still with her arm looped through his. The ER was getting louder, and the ambulances were piling up bringing more than the ER could hold, but that was the nature of the beast at this hospital.

Chapter 11

Pool halls and romance

They walked outside into the fresh night air. It felt good, a little cold but good. It was December and Christmas was near. A time that used to be a happy time with him, but he didn't celebrate that anymore. Well he talked to the Big Guy, but had no one to celebrate it with. She pulled him closer to him, "I will meet you at the restaurant, don't be late." She smiled, Jared pulled her closer and whispered, "Let's go to the billiards hall, It has food and billiards and an amazing bar." "You play pool Jared?" Jared looked down at his feet for a moment then nodded, "I sure do ma'am." "Great, we can eat and play a game of pool." Jen seemed happy, and anxious to get to the billiards place. She walked off to her car parked on the other side of the ER, he walked toward his van. He looked down at his feet his black boots he wore when he was an EMT, moved across black pavement into the black night. "Now I am thinking poetically." He was happy to go shoot some pool, without the push of making money. Although it was rent time and he could use a few hundred, he would restrain himself from hustling just this once. The image of that lady sucking on a urine filled catheter didn't seem to want to leave his mind very quickly. The lady with the fracture that healed, the way his leg hurt, then didn't. The lady with the open neck and the images of abuse, his mind flew with action, his step was deliberate and strong. His old van, a 1993 Chevy Astro, EXT was perfect for him. He could fit a full sheet of plywood in the back if he took out the back seat and the captains chairs. But he didn't work on much of anything anymore. He liked the power and the size of the van and if needed you could live in it. His sister gave it to him before she bought a new car. He gladly took it and made a music system that would rock the neighbors if needed.

Jen pulled up behind his van and honked then motioned him to come to her car. He jumped out of the van and walked to her, her eyes and soft skin, dark hair, for that moment the mix of her with that smile she brought out so easily, slowed him in his tracks. "Follow me Jen, I will get us there." She backed up suddenly, and parked her car. She walked over to the now cold Jared, his P-coat wasn't keeping him warm this night. "I will just ride with you, you can bring me back to my car." Jared instantly wondered if he had a mess on the passenger side of the van. "Sure thing Ms. Jen." She pulled his arm again and looped hers through his. "You are warm Jared." She felt his strength through the jacket sleeve. He helped her up into his van, her body hidden under the camel coat she had on but Jared saw through to her skin. His imagination had always taken him to the bare in life, even with the ladies. He got in the van and still felt strangely at home with her. Many times co-workers went out after work, some married some single, all just to unwind and talk of the day. This lady was different, her spark of life found Jared's imagination, his arousal and his interest.

88

He looked at her and smiled. "How can you smile so much after the day we had in that damned ER?" Without missing a beat he said, "I am with you and going to unwind, it's therapy time." Jared nodded then drove out of the parking lot. "The pool hall is a beautiful restaurant with a huge aquarium and most importantly fantastic pool tables. You will enjoy this place." Jen leaned back in the seat and found the lever to recline. "Oh this feels good." Jared enjoyed the silence and her company. The drive was short he parked slowly and carefully, she had gone to sleep. She was beautiful and her skin in the lights of downtown Maysville was like something he had never seen. Like the shine from a billiard ball across the green felt. "Jen," he said softly, she stirred and he moaned uncontrollably. "Jared?" "Wake up nursely we are here." He had a habit of always calling the nurses, nursely. She sat up quickly, her hair fell just a little over her face and across her breasts like the sunrise, peeking out over top of her scrubs. Jared was calm and enjoyed the vision of this woman he knew nothing of as she woke slowly in his cold van. "I'm sorry Jared," she laughed and opened the door. He had already gotten out and pulled it open for her. "Maybe I should just take you home Jen, you are exhausted." "No, let's play pool and eat, or eat and play pool something like that." He pulled her arm this time and placed it into his. She leaned against him while they walked. There was music playing outside, a band was on the street across from the pool hall. "This is nice," she then proceeded to trip over the curb, but Jared had her. He lifted her quickly up and pulled her close to him. Energy was something not new to him and he felt energy with Jen. She felt right against him, but she was a nurse one of skill and money. He gently let her down. "Thank you Jared." She leaned back into him but he pushed her away and walked faster to get into the warmth. "C'mon woman I'm cold!"

They were seated immediately. The bar was beautiful with dark wood, drinks of everything and anything ever wanted flow across the counters in the back. An aquarium gave that wonderful water affect. There was even an aquarium as part of the bar. The fish swam beneath your drink. It was hypnotizing in a way. They sat in a booth, the pool tables were across the room. The center of the room had a huge black leather circular couch, with curtains that rose to the ceiling. There was a feel of elegance in the place. Jared had come here many times to make some money, but never just to relax. "This is beautiful Jared thank you." "You are beautiful." Jared stood up right after the words slipped out of his mouth. "I will get us some drinks, do you want water or?" "You pick the drink for me." He walked to the bar, "A glass of red wine and a shot of tequila." Jen watched as he ordered, one of his boots rested on the bar rail, his stance was strong, his hair grey shined in the light of the bar, why was she so comfortable with him.

You are beautiful Jen, what am I thinking? He usually wasn't as honest like this with anyone, especially someone that he was attracted to. "Take it slowly Jared." He shook his head and paid for the drinks.

"Thank you for the wine, I see you got the hard stuff." He smiled and lifted his shot glass for a toast, "Cheers.." They made eye contact and that energy that invaded him with her, hit him again. He tapped the jigger to the table then downed his shot. "So tell me of your horrible patients today." He watched her raise her glass to her mouth, to those lips. Jared turned away a little upset with his mind for taking him to a place that he would never have. And that place was Jen and those lips. "I had so many sick ones today, and they kept doubling me, all of my rooms were doubled and I had four on a vent." The nurses at the hospital are usually over worked, the patient nurse load was always high and dangerous for the patients and the nurse. "You should work somewhere else Jen, this ER is always like that, trust me I know." Jen just sipped on her wine. "No, I worked on the floors and they are boring, same thing but in the ER everyday is an adventure." Jared laughed "yea like your urine mouth lady." Jen hit him on the arm then settled her hand there. She pulled his arm closer to her breast. "Time for a game of pool." He walked over to the tables for a mere seven dollars an hour one could enjoy the perfect pool table with ambiance galore. "You play the first one I will watch." Before he could answer Steve walked up to the table. He was one of Jared's pool playing friends. "Hey Steve, how about a game?" Steve nodded and pulled out his money, a stack of hundred dollar bills. Jared pushed it away, "no no," he looked over at Jen and smiled, "I am here with a friend not here for money." Steve walked away, "later then."

Jen stood next to Jared, "I will play you, c'mon I will win." He racked the balls and allowed her to break. He stood behind her and helped her with her cue stick. He was seriously concentrating on teaching her how to hold the cue. He didn't realize he was pressed up against her. She pushed back just a little bit more. He was totally unaware of the push, continued with his explanation of proper cue technique. Jen had other techniques on her mind. Stepping back letting her hold the cue on her own, his voice fell back into her hearing, "got it Jen?" She leaned over the table once more, shakily holding the cue sliding it back and forth. The break wasn't much, she miscued and slipped off the cue ball. "That's ok Jen, it's all new to you." Jared took his shot. Each shot perfect, balanced, each stroke smooth and firm. Jen watched his hand hold the cue stick, the slide and the power aroused her. Or was it the wine. She tried to shake off the images of the sensual of all of this. But it was difficult at best. Jared looked so good to her. His hair in the light, the grey was like magic silver, his arms were strong, his hands she saw everywhere but on that cue stick. She was a little buzzed from the wine, and walked back to the table. "You finish Jared, I will watch." He quickly put the balls in, banking, double banking, jumping the cue ball. Easily handled any shot. He put the stick back in the rack and sat next to her. "This was a bad idea I'm sorry." "No, I just want to watch you play pool." She settled in to order some food, "we need to eat before I get drunk." Appetizers were the order of the night. He looked at his watch. "Are you tired? If so we can leave." "We can eat a little you play some pool then we can go." Jen wanted to take his hand but he stood just as she reached. "I'm going to play one more game of pool be right back." He set up the table and breaks. He felt her watch him, and liked the night with her.

They hadn't spoken much about work, but just the feel of her calmness helped him relax. Steve walked back up to him, "one game?" Jared agreed this time. Jen ordered some bourbon instead of wine for them both and sat back and watched him. "Tonight I will be easy on you Steve, will only take you for two hundred." Steve a tall thin, clean cut blonde business man, chuckled then nodded. Steve and Jared don't hustle each other they just out right bet on the game. Each knew the other was a good player, and each had the capability of beating the other. The game ensued, but Jared felt only Jen. He imagined her walking with him and laughing with him. He saw her hand in his, they walked through a darkness into a bright light. Jared hit the eight ball in as he fell out of the vision or daze he was in. Steve was silent and stood in shock. Jared had never run the table that fast before. Usually he allowed allowing some play back and forth, but not tonight. "Sorry dude, have a lot on my mind, wanted to feel the flush of the win quickly." Steve handed him the two hundred and racked the balls for another game. "One more then I'm gone." Jared walked over to Jen, leaned on the table and looked directly into her eyes. She looked up from her drink, "hi." His hand touched hers, she lifted it from the bourbon glass and slipped it into his hand. Raising it to his lips, he smiled just a little before he kissed it. His eyes closed and he pressed his lips lightly against the top of her hand. A flash of light moved through him opening a liquid feel of peace inside him. Letting her hand down slowly he stepped back. "I came to get a sip of wine, but decided to taste the wine of your skin." He walked back to Steve who waited for Jared to start the game. Jen sat there her hand still up as if he was still kissing it. "Winner breaks." Jared leaned and whispered, "four hundred on this one Steve?" "If I get to break, four hundred it is." "Deal." Jared stepped back and let Steve break. The balls slammed against the rails and a striped ball went in. Steve smiled with confidence. He continued to sink the balls, but Jared was not concerned. Jen walked over to him and leaned against him with a whisper, "are you going to come back and eat some of this with me, I'm lonely." "Yes, stand right here." Steve missed an easy bank shot. Jared chalked his cue, leaned and saw Jen. The cue stick smooth as he moved it, hitting the cue ball firmly he sank two with one shot. The balls fell almost before he hit them. Steve began to get nervous as Jared called the pocket for the eight ball. "Corner pocket," he tapped the pocket also with his cue stick he chalked it once more. Putting bottom english on the ball, he hit the eight ball into the corner, the cue ball rolled harmlessly to the center of the table. Steve handed Jared the money. "Next time." He turned and bowed then said to Jen, "good evening ma'am, be careful with this guy, he will hustle you to the bedroom." Jen smiled she liked that idea. Jared put the cue stick away and pulled her arm through his and walked her to the table.

94

Jared had rent in his pocket, so the night turned out to be a double blessing. He got a fix of a beautiful woman and another successful pool night. "Thank you for putting up with me playing so much pool Jen, didn't plan on it." "How much did you make tonight Jared?" He sat next to her. "Six hundred tax free dollars with two games of pool." Jen's mouth dropped open, "Do you know how long I have to work to make that money?" He changed the subject. "Thank you for letting me kiss your hand, I seem to be out of sorts tonight." Jen sipped her drink, "no, thank you, that was very sweet, but I was lonely you weren't with me." She put on a pouty face and picked up another appetizer. It was getting late and they both had to work 12 hours the next day. "It's time I got you back to your car Jen it's late." He noticed the bourbon and smiled, "thank you for the drink." He lifted it and downed it with one toss. She finished hers also and placed the glass lightly down next to his.

They walked out arm in arm again, but this time she didn't trip over the curb as they step out of the night club. He put her in the passenger side and quickly got in. "It's cold tonight, they say snow tomorrow." "Maybe we will get stuck at the hospital." Jared started the van and drove into the street quickly wanting to get it going so the heat would work quicker. "I should have come out here and warmed it up for you, I wasn't thinking." Jen hit him on the arm, "do you think I'm a wuss or what?" "A wuss!" He smiled and drove out of the parking lot, she hit him again harder.

The hospital was still very busy, a helicopter was on the pad and the ambulance bay was full. He drove her to her car, opened her door and helped her out of the van. "See you tomorrow beautiful lady." He lifted her hand to kiss it once more, she pulled him to her and kissed him on the lips. "Yes see you tomorrow handsome Jared." She turned away from him leaving him wanting more. Back in the van he smiled. "Well, well Jared could be, could be." He drove to his apartment it was only ten minutes away from the hospital. Small and simple like he was, he pulled the money out of his pocket and put it on the desk near the front door. He walked into the bathroom and pulled off his shirt and dropped his jeans. His boots came off at the door. Falling into his queen size unmade bed, he felt comfortable and very tired. He still felt her skin against his lips, her blue eyes against his soul with her kiss mingled nicely in the mix. He fell asleep with her on his mind but his dreams were of the hospital mixing with souls that were of flight from the fresh of death.

Chapter 12

If alarms where alive they would be slapping Jared senseless, but this alarm with its shallow beep, beep, beep, fell into his dreams. Everything unplugged in his dreams, but the sound was still there. Finally he woke enough to slap off the alarm. He rolled out of his bed which was on the floor without a frame. He had a difficult time standing. "I need a grown up bed." The hard wood floors were cold to his feet as he stumbled into the bathroom. "Another day another patient cursing at me, spitting on me, swinging at me, gotta love it." His apartment was comfortable and small, two bedrooms one bathroom with a shower tub and a toilet that sat facing a wall, a mere one foot away. Black boxer briefs was the only thing that adorned him this morning. He pushed his grey hair back away from his face, he leaned to look into his eyes. "Who will die today, who will we save today, how will Jen look today." He coughed suddenly and his toothpaste caught in his throat. He turned on the shower and dropped his boxers to the floor. Singing was something he did, but only in the shower. The song of day, "after midnight we're gonna let it all hang out." He enjoyed the older songs as well as the new ones, music soothed the beast.

Jen showered the same time as Jared, but of course neither knew this. She enjoyed the night with him albeit short lived, it was nicely lived. The water was hot, she was happy to be heading to work for a change. To see Jared and to talk to him of anything, of nothing it didn't matter. She just knew she enjoyed the feel of him near. The water fell down her, her mind found his hands on the cue stick, become his hands on her in the shower. She turned off the water to hurry to get dressed. Time to get to work, to get to Jared. She smiled as she dried herself, still feeling him, wanting to feel him. She tied her black hair up and away from her face. For a moment she looked at herself in the mirror. Her blue eyes, still blue. She was doing a strange inventory on her face. "Complexion still in good shape." She moved her hand across her face touching lightly. "Not bad for a forty five year old." Done talking to herself and checking out her features she hurried to see Jared.

The sunrise was beautiful as Jared drove to the hospital. "Who will die this day, do you know you will die?" His mind flashed to the many that have died in the trauma room. She was crossing the road, she was hit by a car. Her leg tossed to the floor of the trauma room. Her right arm hanging by mere tendons off of the stretcher. Her muscles spun from the tear of her leg off and away. He glanced to the shoe that still contained a foot now shrunken because the fluid had left its home with blood surrounding the once white tennis shoe. She was dead.

Another one of fresh dead entered his memories on this beautiful morning of, "who will die!" He always pondered and prayed just before leaving his home. He knew that someone that day would die and end up in his ER and his body bag. Her toe nails freshly painted,

98

young lady in her early teens was brain dead and a Jane Doe. No one to call, no one to tell, he was to draw her blood for a test. Her body still, was on a vent that was breathing for her, her hair long and blonde flowing down onto the white sheets of the stretcher. The silence in the room and the stillness of her flew against Jared, her toe nails painted red, her body in reality dead.

"Who will die today." The parking lot was filling up with the morning shift, Jared pushed his ID card against the gate box, to allow his entrance. That beautiful sunrise found his eyes once more. The Van turned into a slot and the day soon would begin. The air was colder this morning than the night, his P-coat pulled close, his hands in his pockets. Black scrubs and black boots. He watched his feet move across that familiar black pavement. Who will die today, he envisioned someone getting ready for work. Neatly applying their makeup or cologne, pulling up their hose or socks, slipping their feet into heels or boots, the flash then finds his trauma room, Their body broken, blood leaving at will, bones slipped and escaping their home. Home flashed peace into his core, for now they are dead and released to home.

"Morning Jared." A soft voice coming from behind him stopped his thoughts on death on life, on all. He turned and saw her, that smile, those eyes, that hair. "Jen hi." He felt wonderful for a moment. She caught up to him as he slowed for her to do so. "Was fun." They both spoke at the same time, the same words. They both laughed, "yes it was fun last night." She pulled his arm and loops hers inside his. "Keep me warm Jared." The morning sunrise was beautiful and for the first time that he could remember, his thoughts lifted and he felt only the beauty of life, not the thought of all the death he had seen. "Would be nice to just not go to work today, maybe just go walk the park or watch a movie." Jen pulled him closer, "are you asking me on an official date Jared?" No answer was given, the door opened to the ER and they walked in, the time clock was waiting. Badges placed against, "transaction accepted." The computer voice greeted them for 12 hours of most likely hell.

Turning to Jared, Jen pulled him closer, some of the docs and nurses from night shift looked at them as they walk in arm in arm. Jamie, Jared's favorite night shift charge nurse smiled at them, "well good morning Jared you are looking in fine shape." She winked at him as they walked past. Jen didn't know all of the people yet in the ER, she whispered to him, "she likes you." Jared pulled his arm away from Jen, slowly, as they walked down the back hall once more, the bloody stretchers still lined the walls.

"She is a wonderful lady, was abused in her first marriage, beaten rather badly now she is able to live with happiness." Jen stopped Jared as they neared the locker rooms. "You didn't answer me, was that an invite for a real date?" Jared put his key into the door, "yes a real date." He pushed it open and walked in where she could not follow.

But she answered him, "yes I will go with you!" She went into her locker room happier than she had been in a long time.

He opened his locker slowly and sat on the bench. He leaned against it and talked to the Big Guy, he asked for a good day with all working well and no death this day. He removed his P-coat, placed it into his locker robotically reached for his trauma sheers. It felt like he just put them in there, but that was a mere 12 hours ago. "Time keeps on slipping into the future… old song flew into his mind as he walked to face the ER. Jen walked out of her locker room the same time. "Shall we see what the day holds?" Jared nodded and walked ahead of her.

The assignment board was a white dry erase board where all of the action began. The charge nurse wrote on the board which room the techs and nurses would have. Jared remembered back in the day, that the tech's just shared the ER, now they were assigned rooms, created more responsibility and pushed those to work that normally just hid away somewhere. He was assigned triage in the morning and the trauma room the second half of the day. He loved early triage, usually not everyone had gotten out of bed to feel they had an emergent need. Jen was given the trauma room and as a float nurse in the ER. A float nurse helped all the other nurses with their patients.

He walked out to triage to see what trouble was waiting for him. Triage was an animal in itself. The tech sat at the front window and was the first the patient saw. The night tech was happy to see Jared, happy to get out of triage. it was not a good night, many patients waited to get back to a full ER. Not a good thing when taking over triage. All of the angry sick people would be coming up to yell at him and ask when they would get back to be seen. And of course the triage tech had no control over getting patients a room.

The night tech walked away from Jared and shook his head, "good luck dude they are angry." He couldn't get away quickly enough. The sick walk began and it wasn't even 7:30 a.m. They walked slowly with a lean toward the window. It's kind of scary at times. "Can I help you?" Jared asked as he pushed the intercom button on the front of the glass window. It only worked half the time, the other half it usually screeched with feedback. "I need to get back to see my mother right now!" "Last name please?" He asked calmly as her anger slapped him with her body language and tone. She gave the name and looked away cursing the ER to another patient that was going to sign in. "Room five, c'mon in." Jared pushed the button that unlocked the door. She walked in with anger and tossed him a look of fuck you, and walked to the back toward the main ER. "We need a wheelchair now!" A lady screamed into the microphone at the window. Jared calmly asked, "what's going on?" "My boyfriend can't walk, can't talk." He got up to try to find a wheelchair, something else the hospital was short of. Luckily on this day there was one in triage. He went to the car with the wheelchair and sure enough there was a man unresponsive to any

102

attempt to waken him. The hospital had communicators that were worn around the neck, with one push of a button you can call all of the employees for anything wanted, either to get lunch orders or for this time to get help with an unresponsive patient. Jared called immediately for help in the ER circle. Suddenly many appear from the ER, "this guy is unresponsive." Jared leaned in to feel for a pulse, "and he has no pulse." They throw him on the wheelchair while Jared attempts CPR to a patient in a sitting position.

Pushing past the small door into triage, they ran with him into the trauma room. Jared deposited him onto the stretcher and continued CPR, the docs rushed in the nurses followed. The current trauma room tech finally showed up. Jen walked past Jared and smiled. She began her nurse duties with a smile his way. Uma ran around the room, looking at Jared she was avoiding doing compressions so she just ran in a circle. "Uma!" She threw her hands up "ok ok, dis is horrible." She feebly took over the compressions. Her face showed an interesting array of expressions. Anger with pain? Yea that's what she looked like. Her body weight was not much so she has to really push on the chest of this one he was a little large in the belly lands. Suddenly she began to laugh as did Jared and the rest of the trauma team. With no disrespect but it was difficult to remain serious when doing CPR on a naked man when with every push on the chest, his penis took a flop into the air. As his chest drop occurred it dropped also. Uma laughed so hard she was barely pushing. Jared was called over to push for her. He looked at Jen she was in tears with laughter. Uma stepped away to let Jared relieve her. All were fixated on the dead mans unit. It flopped up and down with each push. Finally the time of death was called. The penis full of life was stilled. It had one last bit of flight? Uma was red she could not stop laughing. Jared patted her on the back and smiled, "You devil you, look what you did to him!' She said something in German but smiled. He walked past Jen then back out to triage.

The line at the triage window had grown and stretched almost out of the door into the parking lot. Sign in sheets were being flung through the window, as one after the other signed in and tossed it into the small opening at the bottom of the glass window. "Great," He said with exasperation, walking quickly to the window he gathered all the sign ins and checked to make sure no one was having a heart attack or bleeding to death. A lady ran up to the window and began pounding on it. "My son, my son is here!" Jared had seen death, watched the brain matter fall out onto the stretcher, but he knew most people didn't have trauma in their lives. Now the calm down moment comes, or his attempt to calm her. "What is his name?" "Tom! Tom!" He waited a moment then asked again for the last name. She gave the name and he saw he was in their trauma room. He shows her to the special waiting room, that alone could cause a freak out moment, for they just know you are going to give them bad news. He used to call them the bad news rooms, when his mother was gravely ill, they took the family into a very small room. He knew it was to keep the screaming inside the walls and not to bother other people at the hospital. He was able to help his mother find where she was to go after death. A pool hustler that helped souls what a combo. He took her to the trauma waiting room, explaining carefully that it was protocol and not to worry.

They were always in shock when they walked into the room, he turned away and walked quickly back to the ever growing hell hole called triage. They filed in as if a bus had let out somewhere down the road. The emergent nature? "I just don't feel good." The usual response. ER abuse yea that's the ticket. Jared shrugged off the idiocy of the moment and called the next patient to triage. Triage on the tech end consisted of getting yelled at by angry patients that had waited for hours to get back to the main ER, getting vitals, making sure they are not suicidal or homicidal. If they are 'HI or SI,' hospital speak for the two, then you have to make sure they do not leave your sight until security walked them to Psych. Psych patients were not always nice, many were violent and mostly uncontrollable. In the triage area it was wide open with the patients that walked through. A new patient with a new lack of emergent nature complaint, another minute another day wasted.

New patient that stated he heard voices, "you hear voices?" the young guy nodded. Jared noticed his eyes were glazed over and his body twitched. "Do you want to kill yourself?" "No," a monotone response was given, "do you want to kill someone else?" "yes everybody." Jared noted it on the sign in sheet, then with his normal humor looked him in the eyes. "Can I get your vitals first before you kill me?'" The guy lifted his head and smiled then started to laugh some. He put his arm up so he could put on the blood pressure cuff. "Sure I will wait," He laughed again and calmed some. Jared felt this mans confusion, he saw the light, the mix and the crooked corners in his soul. He looked straight into his eyes, "we will help you dude, no worries ok?" The man relaxed in a physical way and a spiritual way. But it was only a moment. Jared could feel the tension build again, he decided he wanted to leave but it was too late. "Can't let you go yet," Jared spoke slowly and calmly as he got the mans vitals, somehow he relaxed again.

He sat the patient at her desk, put the sheet down and and tells her he was HI, then looked at her with the don't let him out of your sight look. She asked him questions then asked what he couldn't believe. Not really that she asked it, but how she asked it. "Are you suicidal or homicidal?" The guy just said "no." She looked at Jared and shook her head. "Jared, why did you mark this down here!" She started to draw a line through what he wrote. Jared walked over to the guy, leaned closer to him. "do you want to kill anyone?" He smiled and raised his head, "yes, and I will kill you after she is done with triaging me." He laughed harder. Jared walked back to his desk near the window. "New nurses." He groaned at the thought and the lack of pleasure working with some of the new nurses.

There are times in triage when something from the lands of cannot believe occur. They walk up to the window. two elderly ladies with their brother in a wheelchair. "Please help us," Jared felt something was quite different with this visit to the emergency room. He opened the door, "come in ladies and gent I will help you with the paper work." They push the older man through the door. Their wheelchair barely fit through the door. Jared had seen some sick people before but this guy looked horrible. "I will get your vitals sir, what are you here for today?" He put the blood pressure cuff on the old guys arm. One of the sisters began to tell the story. "Well we just can't get him to eat." The other one of followed, to finish her sentence, "He won't move out of the chair and he won't talk to us." She stepped back and looked down at her brother, "Daniel speak to him tell him what is bothering you." Surreal was a word to describe something that just could not nor can not be a real occurrence yet it was happening in the real of time. The mans arm was stiff to a point that it wouldn't move as he tried to apply the blood pressure cuff. "How did you get here today?" "We live right down the road we pushed him in his chair." He pushed the machine to start the blood pressure reading but felt no pulse. "Um," he looked at the nurse, come here for a moment please?" She turned with a look of disgust "what now Jared can't you even get vitals." He refrained from commenting on her projection of ineptness and motioned her to quickly come over to him. She didn't budge. "Ladies could you please remain here I'm going to take your brother into the trauma room so the docs can look at him right away." They wring their hands and nodded. They touched her brother's shoulder and admonished him. "You should speak to this kind man Daniel."

He pushed the wheelchair past the nurse of no brains into the trauma room. The docs come in, x-ray followed. They looked at Jared and waited for report. "This guy is dead." One of the docs laughed, "is this a joke? "Whats wrong with him Jared?" She looked at him sitting in the wheel chair. He sure didn't look well that's for sure. "It seems he lives with his sisters, they say he hasn't eaten or talked in days." Rigor had already set in, feel for a pulse?" He stepped back and one of the doctors grabbed his wrist but it was stiff and yes no pulse. Because he had been dead for it seemed at least a few days they didn't throw him on the stretcher to try to bring him back. He was so gone that he had aged already some on the other side of life. "I will talk with the family." Jared walked out with the doc leaving Uma alone with the stiff. He would be a difficult one to bag. He was stuck in a bent sitting in chair position.

The nurse looked up to see a doctor walking in and straightened her scrubs. "I sent him in immediately I knew he was very ill." The doctor ignored the new nurse and walked to the elderly sisters. The doc and the sisters walked out toward one of the private waiting rooms to give them the bad news.

108

He sat in the chair and said flatly to the nurse, "The guy is dead and had been for a few days, I tried to get you to come over and look at him." She sat quickly turning away from him. "How was I to know?" She acted as if she was looking for something on the computer to hide her embarrassment.

the rain may find its hold

and know the yellow of gold

across the dandelions breast...

but the dandelion never hides

..always open ..always wise...

soaking the rain within

dandelion dances..through time

A moment of fresh life as security walks in with a small little blonde haired boy. He couldn't be more than four years old. They found him walking the near the garage. Lucky they did find him, this hospital is not in the best part of town. 'What is your name?' Leaning back in his chair to enjoy the fresh soul of this young one Jared waits for the answer to hopefully type in the name and find where he belongs. "My name is Joshua." "What is your last name?"

His small hands come up as his shoulders rise while his head lowers. The blonde locks curled and loose flop some as he lowers his small head. "I don't know." How could he not know his last name? "What is your Dads name or your moms name?" The boy turns some and wanted to walk back through the door where the four security guards brought him through. His index finger slips slightly into his mouth as he gestures once more. "Well..my moms name is," there is a pause as he puts his palms up "mom and my dad's name is…dad." Jared couldn't believe how innocent this one was in spirit but still couldn't understand why he didn't know his last name. Maybe he doesn't know what last name meant. "What is your whole long name Joshua?" "Joshua Dale Bennet." He typed the name into the computer. There was a Darrell Bennet in a room on the seventh floor. "Is your dad's named Darrell?" With a huge smile and an almost snap of a finger he said happily, "that's my dad." Jared tells security what room the father is in they nod "we will take him there." He walked out of triage with the four very tall security guards. Very tall to a very small four year old. He gave Jared a fresh of light and calm something needed. The fact also that he was safe and the story could have ended differently gave him another good feel. "One for the good guys."

Jen walked up behind Jared and surprised him by wrapping her arms around him. For a moment he felt the softness of her against him and was taken away from horrible triage. She let go of him quickly. "Well hello, welcome to my triage hell." She started to walk back to the main ER but stopped and smiled back at him. "Just wanted to give you a Jen hug, you look stressed." He just laughed and said slowly "yea I am." "When are we going out again, tonight after work?" Jared acted as if he didn't hear her. He was flushed from the feel of her and was suddenly a little shy. Very not like Jared. She walked back to the main ER and wondered why he didn't answer. Maybe he just didn't hear me, her thoughts created excuses for him but she sure enjoyed holding him.

Uma came running out, "I vill give you relief but for a zecond," her accent still made Jared smile. "OK Uma I appreciate it, danke and stuff." She mumbled under her breath in German then took on the angry patient at the window. One thing about Uma, she wouldn't take crap from anyone. Either in English or German you would be put in your place. Uma one day had decided to curse many of the patients. She was not in a good mood. She turned to Jared, and looked right at him and said "mother fucker." He remembered how she had thought she was cursing in a language no one understood. "Ingrid you can't curse like that at work." "Vot do you mean? You cannot understand me?" He proceeded to tell her she was cursing in English and everyone speaks English. She ran away covering her mouth. But on this day she was cursing in German as he walked away to take his break. He understood some of the German curse words and she was tossing them about.

Chapter 13

Walking through the main ER heading back to the break room Jared was pulled into a bay by one of the nurses she wanted him to help her hold a mans head while she put in an NG tube. The tube of yuk that goes down your nose to your stomach, for us to either put meds in or suck things out. She had worked in the ER longer than anyone here. Over 26 years and counting, she knew more than the docs but she would never say a word unless a life was at stake. I have seen her more than once correct a doctor on the wanted meds, telling of the contraindications of those meds if mixed.

And it is impossible to hold the head of someone that doesn't want a tube stuck down their nose. This man overdosed on something and we need to fill his tum tum with charcoal. The kind of stuff you grill your burgers with. It binds whatever is in your stomach not allowing your system to absorb the poisons you swallowed.

Jared tried to hold the rounded head of a human, as he started to thrash back and forth his futile attempts are showing and spill into the nurses frustration. "Hold his head Jared!" "Sir you have to let her put it in or they will come in and tie you to the bed with leather restraints." He then grabbed his ears to hold his head but the patient calmed some. As she put in the NG tube and with each push as the tube moved through the patients nose down his throat she yelled, "swallow, swallow!"

Jared left quickly after she got the tube down the mans nose toward the break room, determined to get his break before Uma called for him to return to triage hell. Jen saw him but she was in the middle of a conscious sedation on a patient so she couldn't leave. Conscious sedation is a horrible invention. He saw her standing near the patient as they began to put the mans leg back into its socket, another wonderful side thing of car wrecks, bones that like to push sideways or pop out of place. The docs stood on the bed, began their contortionist maneuvers with a sheet wrapped somehow around the patient to use as a pulley device. The doc yanked and pull on the leg. The patient yelled in pain, Jen watched the monitor and wrote the numbers, smiling as she looked over at Jared. "Oh shit!" The patient screams out in pain, Jared flinches a little but couldn't stop watching the procedure. The leg back where it belonged the docs were finished and they left the room. She stayed to make sure the patient was stable. "Why did he yell so much where are the pain meds?" "We gave him meds but the medicine causes amnesia, so the person feels it but doesn't remember the pain." Jared walked out of the room. "That is just not right, no way, shape or form." The patient turned on the stretcher and sat up, "you all are good, I didn't feel a thing." Jared just shook his head, how fair is that? You feel it, hurt like hell then forget the pain, not natural!

The break room was just about to be reached by Jared, but no no, one of the patients, an old grey haired man with a cane was heading his way down the back hall. "Sir? You need to get back to your bed." Jared walked toward him to help him back to his room and in one swoosh the cane was swinging at Jared. He ducked and laughed "good swing old man go on where you want to go I don't want to fight." "Damned right you don't want to fight, I want out of this place and nobody is stopping me." He turned away from him and walked down the hall swinging his cane as he went.

Jared laughed as one escaped the ER. Finally in the break room he got a cup and a diet coke. Jen walked in quickly and sat in front of him. She wanted to know of their possible date. "Jared you never answered my question." He looked into her eyes, and felt comfortable doing so. "Sure we can go out tonight, I am off tomorrow."

"Where are we going?" She touched his hand which caused him to see deep inside her. "You have a headache don't you?" "Yes, a horrible one." He touched her lightly on the head with his right hand, while his left hand still held hers. He sent light to her head, light of healing through his hands to her head. For a moment he felt her pain, now his head hurt he released her hand and stood. "Damn you had a bad one didn't you." She had no more pain it was all gone. "Jared how did you do that? You took my pain away." He smiled, "not sure, I thought I could do it, used to do it but didn't know for sure until just now with you." He leaned against the table "but how do I get it out of me." The page overhead suddenly screamed his name, "Jared you are needed in triage!" Uma tired of the break called him back.

Immediately after she paged him the Trauma page goes over the hospital intercom. Jared looked at his watch, he had seven and a half hours left. "Oh my god what a headache." Jen walked with him, "you shouldn't have done that Jared." She sighed and looked genuinely worried. Jared tried to shake it off but it just got worse. "I am ok it's gone, whew." He lied to her and walked quickly to triage. She went back into the main ER and paused to watch him walk down the hall, she liked the feel of him. She could still feel his touch into her, she smiled as thoughts of their date began to fill her now not hurting head.

Chapter 14

Jared felt separated from his body as he walked into the main ER heading back to triage. Glancing into the rooms he saw the patients, one was puking, suddenly he felt nauseated the next bay was an obvious trauma, blood all over the stretcher and one leg missing. Jared's right leg gave out on him for a moment. A lady in the last room before he turned to triage reached for him, "please I need something for pain can you get my nurse?" Jared looked on the computer to see which nurse was assigned to her. She grabbed his arm. He felt all of her pain fly at will through him, as if it was his very breath traveling on oxygenated blood cells. Invaded with her pain he couldn't breathe for a moment. She had broken ribs, he knew, because his ribs hurt like hell. She smiled, touched her side lightly then pushed harder. "The pain is gone!" she felt her side not knowing how or why it was gone but happy to be pain free. Jared walked slowly toward triage, he pulled her pain into him without knowing, he was too open. The gift came back, remembering how to tame the energy needed to come back with it. He laughed out loud at his thoughts, "tame energy from spirit is not happening." Now his head hurt and so did his side. He was dizzy because it hurt too badly to breathe with his broken ribs. He leaned against the wall to remove the pain and injury he visualized his body being healed but nothing happened, if anything it got worse.

Jen walked up to him and pulled him away from the wall, "what is wrong?" She held him close to her. His pain slowed into just a mild echo inside him. The throb dulled and finally left. His head cleared and was normal again. The sounds of the screams for a nurse and the wonderful aroma of urine returned. "Jared," Jen said his name again as she pushed his hair away from his face. He was sweating, and weak but happy to be back to the feel of normal. "Jen, you somehow pulled me from where I was, I was.." He slowed his talk and slowly pushed her arm off of him. "I can stand I know I'm old but give me a break." He smiled at her, "Jared you need to go home early you are not well." Jared felt silence cover them both, a silence that was of another reality, the air stilled and for one moment he felt her soul within his. A feel of mixing as if a cake was being made and her energy was part of the flavor with his energy. A burst of light snapped his head back as he began to fall away back to the wall he was just leaning on. "Triage calls," he said casually then walked back to the line from hell. The image of light within him was still very strong, but he couldn't look directly at it from within or it vanished. "Like chi, cannot think of it, have to let it flow." Always wanting to understand always reaching to know, his mind continued with thoughts and flight of white light as he walked.

He pushed the intercom button and asked the lady standing there, with that look of anger shooting him, what she needed. He felt her anger in a different way. Suddenly he stood and put his hand up to the window, and said, "no.." The lady was in shock just repeated his no. "What are you talking about?" Jared was determined not to feel this

118

patient in any way. No anger, no pain No! was his thought. And it worked, all of it left, as if a shield of light protected him. He sat back at his chair in a daze but glad to feel good again.

He knew he could help people, take away their pain and heal their breaks but with that gift to give he was feeling their pain and that had to stop. He must be doing it wrong or something or being smacked for closing his gift for so long. "Meditation is the key word tonight, meditation and prayer." The lady just looked at him then left the window quickly. He laughed then leaned back in his chair.

He thought of his mother who was gravely ill in the past and subsequently died from her illness. Cancer was an ugly beast that once it found a host it didn't leave. Chemo may stall it radiation may slow it but nothing killed it. Stupid infection it kills its host. Jared remembered the pain of his mother's death. His pain of her passing and her physical pain. A tumor decided it wanted residence behind her lower spine. Pushed it out created the look of a fin on her back. When it got to that point, she was usually not conscious, either from the meds or just the fever that inhabited her along with the cancer. The body didn't want it in there and it made it very hot. She died with a temperature of one hundred and eight. It could have been higher not sure, for the thermometer only went to one hundred and eight. A tear found its way down his face during this rare moment of silence in triage. "Love you mom." Knowing she was in light and love he didn't understand his sadness, it was selfish to wish to still have her in his life. Not his choice, his was to follow, live and perform. Perform, that word jolted him back to physical as he saw himself with Jen in a very sensual way. This caused a huge smile he enjoyed the banter of his mind and soul especially the visuals of Jen against him in the raw fashion and wonderful invention of making love.

The triage nurse walked up behind him and startled him when she touched his shoulder. "Are you ok?" He settled back into reality and answered quickly. "Oh yea I'm too sexy for my shirt." She slapped him on the back and sat back in her chair. "Just making sure, you seem upset." Jared nodded and sat back. Thoughts of life with thoughts of energy and thoughts of performing with Jen..

EMS brought in a patient covered in blood. He walked over to see the knife as it moved and throbbed with each heartbeat. The trauma buzzer was pushed as they rush him into the trauma room. He followed them into the room to watch the flurry of doctors and the amazement of them their eyes on the knife. Blood fell out of the wound as the knife moved with every heartbeat, up and down, drugs are pushed but he was gone. A simple kitchen knife thrust into his own heart. The docs were fascinated. Finally the heart ceased its pump its want to push blood through the body. They called the time of death as Jared watched. The rails were down on the stretcher that always bothered Jared for some reason. He always thought the dead will fall off somehow, as the doctor leaned over to see the knife. He pulled the stretchers rail up slowly not knowing the dead man's arm was resting across the rail as he pulled it up. The hand of the freshly dead man was rising up against the doc leaning over the knife. As the doc looked down to see the hand rising up he screamed thinking the dead man was reaching to grab him.

He had to control his laugh and told them it was just him pulling up the railing. The look on the young residents face was priceless. Kind of like those commercials, your dead body on the stretcher in a level one trauma room ten thousand dollars, the look on the face of the resident as the dead mans arm rose to grab him, priceless. Uma came into the trauma room ready to take over and bag the fresh dead. Jared felt suddenly an extreme sadness to his core, silence ran through him like a river flooding it's banks. He touched the man's foot but it was already cold. For a moment, for an instant, he saw the man's life. Pulling his hand back quickly he didn't wish to see anymore. His light slowed with darkness that if allowed in, would play with his soul causing him to stagnate. Like a pool of old waters, ceasing to flow was a life that gave in to that dark side. Jared removed himself from the depth of thoughts wanting the laughter again not this soul stuff.

Uma pushed him back to triage, "go back to triage vere you belong." She and her wonderful German accent saved Jared from another moment of surreal as he walked back through the trauma doors out to the triage area. Where the zoo hadn't stopped its gates opening and allowing the many kind of sick types wanting attention. He looked over to his triage window and there was another line out the door to the street of patients waiting to be seen. Jen walked through the double doors from the main ER and saw him standing there. "Jared?" She walked up to him and took his hand. He turned with a smile then dropped to one knee. "Yes angel, what dost thou wish for I will make it so on bended knee if only thou whilst let me grant your wishes."

She pulled him up to her off of the floor, "silly goose, come here." She pulled him closer to her and looked into his eyes then whispered to him. With all the turmoil around them, people on stretchers, people at the window yelling to be seen. wanting to be heard, she whispered and he heard only her voice felt only her breath.

"Jared we need to talk tonight." She smiled her blue eyes seemed darker than usual, her black hair shined in the light of triage and Jared felt wonderful by her side. "Go back to work woman, we will talk." She hesitated then walked back through the double doors to the main ER. She looked back at him and saw a light around him, a soft glow. Her hands were hot as if she had touched something on fire, but they didn't hurt. She was calm and very happy. Happy over what she had no idea but a relief flooded her and thoughts of him with her after work made the time move quickly.

Chapter 15

Uma walked out to Jared she was happy to be able to take over triage. She was done with that trauma room and wanted to sit and just handle taking vitals. Jared was ready to move around to walk off some of the energy that had been finding him. An energy that had started flowing from the patients, from Jen, and from the air into him. His mind was flying with why's and how's but he would figure it out. His cell phone buzzed in his pocket he opened it to see it was his friend John. John was an avid hustler and quite the amazing con man. "Well hello con man of the year." He smiled and walked back to the ER. He would take a break before heading into the trauma room. He saw Jen putting an IV in a patients arm and smiled at her. She didn't see him, but just the seeing her made him feel good. She was quite beautiful anyway and she was also fun to be with. "We need to play tonight, I need some money." "I can't talk now will call you in five." No cell phones allowed on the ER floor.

The lounge waited for him to rest before taking on the Trauma room again. Lunch time consisted this day of peanut butter and crackers. He didn't bring any lunch so be it. Jen couldn't take lunch yet, she had to stay on the floor for a time until some of the other nurses could cover for her. His thoughts of her did not cease. "Friends?" He said out loud as Mary, the chaplain walked past him. "What friends Jared?" She asked with a smile. Never had Jared met anyone as wonderful in spirit as that lady. She was almost a walking angel. The pain she took on from the sorrow of the family members was beyond his understanding. She would know just the right thing to say or not to say. She was a comfort to the ones that just couldn't handle seeing their loved one so injured or the fresh death of them. She took on their pain and her compassion was evident just in her smile.

He started to understand taking on pain, from the physical attacks of metal against flesh in car accidents and the motorcycle that flew into the ground, grinding flesh as if it was a lover. "Yes friends, I need some." He took a bite of his peanut butter. "Jared you ok?" He looked at her, her soda in hand but her shoulders were low and her body was tired. She was holding too much pain and it showed. "I seem to be getting that question a lot today," he hesitated, should he tell her of the way he has healed others or will she think him insane. And yet with the same thought he knew that she had healed many spiritually and physically. "I'm wonderful thanks for asking." He decided not to burden her from helping others for a moment, including himself. The trauma buzzer sounded once more she left to help whoever may need. He relaxed and enjoyed his small lunch.

*

His phone buzzed again in his pocket. He answered it waiting to hear the yell of his rant and the wrath of his wants. "Hello Johnny hows the balls hanging today?" "The balls are hanging a little to the right today, we need to go out tonight what are you doing?" Jared closed his eyes, "I have plans with a beautiful woman." John paused then yelled at him once more through the phone. He pulled it away from his ear some and smiled. "I will meet you for an hour right after work tonight at Jakes pool hall on third street." "Yes!" He then hung up suddenly. Jared closed the phone slowly he had some peanut butter on his finger and started to lick it off. Jen walked in just as he began to push his finger into his mouth. She walked up behind him reached slowly for his hand and pulled it away from his mouth. She put it in hers and sucked lightly on his finger. "Will I get a bill for these services nursely?" She smacked him on the shoulder and smiled. "Yes you owe me dinner tonight right after work." She sat in front of him and licked her lips. "mmmm you taste good." "Are you flirting with me young lady?" Before she could answer two more people from the ER walk into the lounge to get something to drink, he returned to eating his peanut butter crackers. Sampling for a moment his finger still wet from her touch. She smiled then walked out of the break room. "Tonight." Was all that was said and she left.

He was thoroughly enjoying his thirty minute lunch. Another trauma was called and he stood to go work this one. "Enough of peanut butter and crackers." He tossed his cup into the garbage can and left, ran quickly down the hall. Seven hours to go then pool with John. Jen walked into the hall suddenly right in front of him. He ran into her in mid stride. He kept her from falling back but they both fell against the wall. She smiled "well excuse you mister." She could feel an inner strength from him a power of some sort. He was also in good shape physically but his inner strength was being felt not by himself but by Jen. "Jen I am so sorry, I was running to get to the trauma room." Jared held her close and felt a warmth move through him, with arousal to the side. He let her go slowly and smiled, "yes excuse me." But she would not let him get away, she pulled him back and kissed him slowly on his cheek. "Thank you for not smashing me Jared." He enjoyed her kiss greatly but must regain his senses there was a trauma awaiting his tech skills. "I have an appointment with someone right after work Jen, is it ok if we meet after that or maybe tomorrow?" Jen would not take no, "what kind of appointment?" She walked with him down the hall back to the trauma room. "It's a pool hustle moment with my friend John, tomorrow after work Jen." He turned the corner and walked into the trauma room. Uma was busy tagging the patient with their temporary ID's for trauma's. She was happy to see him. "You vinally back vrom lunch?" Jared smiled "Vinally," using his best German accent, "go to triage Uma, they await you."

This trauma was one where an augur captured part of a sleeve and pulled the arm right into it, his arm was twisted and pulled wrapped around the pipe. The workers on site where it happened cut the pipe to the augur off, so it could go with the patient. It will have to be removed in surgery. The man was calm for what has happened to him, maybe in shock. Jared felt his silent strength and calmness. It was a

126

comfort to Jared, as it fell into him he relaxed with this trauma. He finished removing what clothing he could for the docs to see if there was any other damage on his body. They swiftly moved him to the OR, not even allowing all of the regular trauma room duties to be finished.

Immediately another trauma rolled into the room on the EMS stretcher. An explosion from a meth lab, she was badly burned as was her partner in the other bay. Jared tagged them both with identity tags and began to remove her jewelry, her ring began to slip off as he pulled harder he got more than the ring. Taking rings off of people was a skill and a gift. A little Vaseline just behind the ring and twist while pulling it off. The pulling hard is the key while continuing to twist. With one pull and two twists the ring came off of this particular patient. Interesting feel as one held a ring that was still connected to a finger and that finger was now in your hand. He stilled for a second and whispered. "Oops." Her hand was badly burned already damaged beyond, it would have come off anyway, but he didn't expect it. A sudden rush shot through him and an awkwardness began to find a home in his thoughts. What to do with a finger and a ring? He slipped the ring off and placed it in the little bag where the valuables were kept. Carefully laying the finger next to it's owner on the stretcher he walked away taking a moment to get over this surreal feeling. Once more the limits of flesh were seen, suddenly he felt a pain of burn through him. No! Was his thought and it left, he did not want to feel this burn there was nothing he could do to help these people. There is a rhythm at ER's, sometimes it is the day to die, or the day to lose a limb, this day was burn day. Hurriedly he finished his duties with the two Meth explosion patients as another burn came in.

The patient came in ninety-nine percent covered in burned skin. Not good, she was in no pain, another not good. If a patient was burned and it was not life threatening they would feel pain, for they hadn't burned through their nerve endings. But if you felt good then you would die and soon. She calmly gave us her information of who to call, she was alert and oriented. We didn't give her the chance to say goodbye to family, "we have to put a tube down your throat to help you breathe before it swells." The doc said then began intubation.

He turned away pushing away the thoughts of family that would never see her again in the way of alive. He heard what he knew were her last words. A silence shot through him like an injection into his skin an emptiness, silence. He felt her slip out of her flesh even before her heart stopped. He heard a whisper, or almost a whisper, but it flew through him caused him to shudder. Her spirit must have moved through him, for the silence was light with a lift of peace.

The trauma doors opened once more with another burn, another lady sitting up feeling no pain, another death soon. She was painting in front of a wood burning stove, some how her pants caught on fire

128

and they were attached to her skin. Jared waited for the docs to tell her she would die, but they didn't. He finished quickly his duties and stocked the trauma room. There was a moment of relief as no new traumas came in. He walked out to the main ER to help and walked right into a mess.

A patient standing on his stretcher and pulled a fresh bowel movement out of his bottom then threw it on the walls of the ER bay. He put on gloves with a heavy sigh and walked into the room. He got the person back on the stretcher and called environmental services to help clean up the literal crap on the walls, he walked quickly back out of the room. A lady walked up to him with nothing on her bottom and stood there for a moment and peed on the floor. Jared shook his head and sighed. "Ma'am you cannot do that why are you doing that?" She mumbled something and turned away from him as pee dripped down her leg. Not in the mood for this he walked the other way and acted as if he didn't see the mess on the floor.

Jen saw him walking out of the room and walked up to him quickly, "so Jared about tonight?" Jared stopped he was a little frustrated with the day and tired of the lack of compassion and the loss of life. "I have to do some work tonight Jen, tomorrow night is better," he stood in front her and waited for her response but she just stood there, as if a cold wave fell over her, the wash of his push was significant to her. Thoughts find when one doesn't want to question actions or motives. "Ok Jared tomorrow night, but…" her words fell away as another trauma was called and he walked quickly away from her. She saw nothing but confidence and strength in this man, this tech. She walked back to her charting, she wished she was going to be with him to watch his pool hustling. "I will find out where he is going," she said to herself then finished her charting on the patient.

She was dead, but they bring her to his ER, covered in blood, with a touch of a french fry on her stomach. A flash of ketchup with fries hit him as he gets her temperature rectally. Yes, one has to be dead, but warm and dead in the winter. If the body is cool, steps have to be taken to bring them back. This sad lady was dead, her blood was all over her. Jared would never look at fries again the same way. Her blood mixed with the french fries left on her body. The body bag fresh of that shower curtain smell hid the hideous blood loss. Jared felt sadness. She had kids, they came to see her while he was stocking the bay to the trauma room she just left. "Wake her up grandma, she is so cold." He closed his mind to the thoughts and the feel of their sorrow but it found him anyway. Why does he have to feel this loss, why does he have to feel their pain?

Jen suddenly needed to see Jared. She saw him in the stockroom obviously upset with something. Jared are you ok? The question was heard through his veil of temporary pain. A blessing but he felt vulnerable and didn't want her to see him this way. Too much of a wuss factor. He Answered quickly to keep her from getting too close, he was not in a place of being held or touched, not a good impression
130

moment. "Yes I'm fine Jen just busy." She was called by one of the patients near the stock room and was pulled once more away from his side.

Jared slowed his mind for a moment and looked at his watch he wished to be done with the day. Three more hours, he wanted away from the souls, the death and the reach that was now beginning to find him. The reach from the grave, or the stretcher as he felt more souls reaching, hanging out. "I don't like death." Somehow his words echoed this time across the stock room.

Chapter 16

..::time

Jared's phone vibrated in his pocket, startling him, he answered it quickly "yes!" John on the other end yelled, "Jared get off work early I have an easy mark." Jared stood still in the trauma room, "no dammit John, you take care of him by yourself." "No, it's woman and damn she is hot." Jared shifted his stance with the visual of a hot woman being taken by the con man John. "Let her go home with some money John, be nice." The trauma buzzer sounded Jared hurriedly gets off the phone, "gotta go," the phone clicked shut as the trauma rolls into the room. John shouldn't con people, it's one thing to hustle but to con people is a different animal, yes it was the same but he had rationalized it to be so.

The patient was wheeled in on the EMS stretcher, she was sitting straight up but breathing very lightly and her neck was very stiff. He waited to hear the report before starting to remove the necessary clothing. She was eating a pork chop and part of it got lodged in her throat. The guy she was with did the Heimlich maneuver but it didn't do the job. The doctors carefully examine her not wanting to push it down further into her throat. She is calm and sitting up very straight. She is afraid and the docs are being very careful as to how to proceed. They tried to remove it then decided she needed to go to surgery instead. Each attempt at reaching with the forceps pushed it further down her throat. They didn't want it lodged deeper into her esophagus or end up in her lungs. She was moved quickly up to the OR.

Jared loved to eat pork chops, "will have to chew those things a little slower from now on." Another bad thing about working in the ER, you never knew if the person survived. Jared still saw the one young girl with flowing long blonde hair, paralyzed for life.

The trauma room was empty once more but for a moment. Another trauma on the way, just as he stocked the room the doors swing open, the mans hand was wrapped but blood oozed through the gauze. One of the EMT's follows with a cooler. A cooler in a trauma room is not a sign of a party soon, or beer on ice. It's usually blood on ice or a limb. The man's hand is inside the cooler, looking a bit surreal to Jared as he glanced at it in the ice then looking up at the mans wrist, no hand as they unwrap the gauze to see the damage. Tendons, blood oozing at first but now spurted. The man was calm, Jared began to feel pain in his right hand, the same hand that was sitting on ice. He pushed the pain away with just a thought it left him. Walking quickly out of the room he needed to remove himself from this man, not wanting to know the pain of losing a hand. But the vision now found his soul and his mind, the swirl began, he was taken away into the blood and flow of life, the energy scattered in the hand wanting its attachment to the flesh it was accustomed to. The yell for a tech in the trauma room comes over the pager, and he snapped out of his place of mystery. "Jared we need you in the trauma room now!" He walked back into the room quickly with an ongoing argument in his mind. I need to wrap up this hand and get it to the OR, I want this day to end now!

The clock on the wall began to tic, sounds of triage filtered into the room, and he could hear the main ER noises, falling back into his reality. He hurried out of the room needing to talk with Jen, she seemed to know things about him or help him somehow with what was going on. But not until one more trauma flies into the room. Jared sees the man had no face, just flesh flapping across. One of the nurses throws a big bandage over the patient's face while he did his job. Somehow his face was shot off and nothing else touched. Two flaps of flesh and nothing else, bony skull showing, brains in tack, now that would suck, was his first thought as he looked at the patient. Pain meds were given quickly, and the man was taken very quickly to the OR.

There is a way to restore his face but he would never know if they did. Jen walked in looking at her watch, "Jared? Are you not leaving tonight?" He looked at the clocks on the wall then to the one on his wrist. Somehow seven hours turned into one. Time, oh yea, he remembered he is able to move with time, change time mix time. "I will have to play with this new remembrance." Jen looked at him and smiled, "play with what?" "Let me get my coat, meet you at the time clock." He ran past her and gave report quickly to the oncoming tech. Dropped off his trauma sheers once more he smiled, but suddenly a soul filtered into the locker room. The air felt heavy and a thickness was felt in his throat. It had surrounded him. "Go that way." He pointed and the soul was motionless for a moment, with its hover over the air skill that souls have. It finally swooshed, if it made a sound thats what he knew it would sound like, but they were silent in their swoosh moment. He wondered if they saw some kind of opening when he pointed but for some reason if he said go, they went. He walked quickly to get out of there, Jen waited for him at the time clock. John was buzzing him in his pocket, life was great. "Transaction accepted." the computerized voice allowed them to leave once more, "good ole gatekeeper." Jared laughed, he was happy to be off and away from the hospital on to play in the night, with pool, with John and with this new feel of comfortable with Jen. "So you want to watch me hustle?" He asked her as they walked out of the hospital, Jared saw a soul hiding in one of the bushes, it was a nasty one and began to spew obscenities his way. Jared's retort was quick, "leave now!" He then, in his mind, repelled and rebuked it with the blood of Jesus. The only way to get them gone, they were terrified of the blood of Jesus. He smiled at how many people thought he was crazy bringing the blood of Jesus into spiritual stuff, but it worked and he wasn't going to mess with those most vile evil energies without some help.

Jen looked at him strangely then laughs, "oh mighty one, are you telling me to leave?" Jared pulled his P-coat closed shoving his hands in his pockets. Looking away from her for a moment then he laughed, "just the bad stuff, you are good, so..be with me always." Jen pushed her arm through his as they continued to walk to the parking lot. "I thought you told me to leave now?" "Never." Jared replied quickly. He glanced at the bushes as he walked past the last of them with Jen. He saw other souls waiting to be guided. With a thought they were directed to where they needed to be this time without Jen hearing him converse with the unseen. "Time to play." He started to walk away from her and head to his van but she pulled him close to her again. "You are not getting away from me tonight mister!" Jen stopped walking and pulled him to a stop with her. "Jared I need a shower before we go play, come home with me real quick." A flash of her in the shower of course filled his mind. "Sure," slipped out of his mouth luckily without a drool. She reduced him to fantasy mode with just her smile. He couldn't believe he was going to her place while she showered. Walking now as if again in another realm, the buzz of his phone vibrating was ignored as he walked with Jen to her car.

*

Imagine That

They walk together with no words just feeling the night's air and the escape moment away from the hospital. "Do you?" they both say to each other simultaneously. Jared laughed Jen pushed him, "me first," his head lowered a bit hands still in pockets he waited to hear her question. She stopped in front of a white BMW. Pulling away from him she walked to the drivers door. "I will open your door in a minute." Jared stood there and admired the car a four door white, black interior automatic, though he would prefer a stick, a convertible to top it off pardon the pun.

"This is yours?" He asked incredulously. She smiled then nodded as she got into the beamer and clicked his door open. Jared looked around then up to the sky. This woman will not want to have anything to do with me, hell I drive a van and live in a little apartment. Go along for the ride, get in. A voice inside him kicked him into gear. He got into the car and smiled at Jen. She was sitting comfortably. "Now let me finish my question." Jared was quiet for a change even his thoughts were quiet. "Do you ever feel like there is something big about to happen?" They pulled out of the parking lot Jared looked at his old van as they drove by. It seemed as if it was sad that he was leaving it behind. "Big about to happen, how so?" Jared knew what she was talking about he had felt it since a very young age. But he wanted to see where she would go with the question. "This is a very nice car Jen, you have a bit of money I suppose," Jen smacked the dash then rubbed the leather lightly. "This is my baby, and yes I have a bit of money why?" She looked at him. He was so handsome to her that he took her breath with just a glance her way. "Oh nothing," he said then shifted in the seat some admiring the leather enjoying the feel of the speed of the car. "Don't change the subject on me, do you ever feel something big is about to happen?" He enjoyed the speed of the car until she sped through a yellow light and took a turn a little too fast, but the car held the turn. He held tightly to the arm rest and tried to hide his fear. She enjoyed the speed and he was obviously in for a ride. He looked at the speed limit and at the speedometer the two didn't match. "So Jen?" She looked at him not watching the road the street signs were flying past. Jared could feel the swoosh of each sign about to slap him into his own ER, lying on the stretcher looking up at Uma getting ready to take his blood. That visual shook him more than the thought of being in an accident. Uma drawing blood from your arm was like being torpedoed by a harpoon. She thrusts the needle in so quickly that usually it slips into through and to the other side of the vein. "Yes?" She asked, her eyes not on the road. The car began to veer off the road just a little. "Jen!" She looked forward for a moment lightly adjusted her line of driving, accelerated through a very sharp curve and smiled. "Jared is my driving making you nervous?" Refusing to answer this question he laughed to cover his fear and the fact that he could possibly pass a diamond right about now through his bottom. "Just jealous you have such a well manufactured vehicle, that can be driven at extreme speeds through narrow streets, barely missing street signs and somehow staying on the road through sharp, sharp turns?" They laughed as she turned into a long drive lined by trees. The lights of the beamer shined up to the trees that covered this winding road with their branches. There was a safe feeling as if one was being held by the branches or was it the night or just the fact that they were together. The flight of speed and the energy of Jen fell into him. The surreal look of the trees and the light with the sound of that wonderful engine noise as it slowed. The lights shined on a white house, more like a mansion. He suddenly felt like the male version of Cinderella and Jen was a female version of the prince. Huge white columned porch wrapping around the mansion, the lights of the car shined on a garage door. That looked more like the doors to a museum. Jen was enjoying Jared's mouth hanging open, "my little abode," she whispered as she pulled quickly into the garage. The door closed with silence. "Well, gosh Jen are you the maid here?" He asked looking deeply into her eyes. He saw no shadows of greed in her, this could not be her home. Jen pulled him to her, her hand wrapped around his head, stroking his soft grey hair her fingers slipped through and up his head. As she pulled him he gave easily to her wish. They kissed softly, lightly but more than lightly flew through Jared. She leaned back holding her chest for a moment with her other hand. "Wow." She said slowly as Jared leaned back and concurred. The silence in the garage was comforting, the feel of her kiss still flew through him slipped past his thoughts, now to answer her question.

"Yes, I have felt something big is going to happen and soon." He took her hand "Is this your home or do we have to turn in the keys to the owners and wash the dishes for a year to pay for the romp in their car?" Jen smiled, pulled her hand away from his and got out of the car quickly. "Come on in I want a shower then let's go play pool." He watched her walk through the immaculately clean garage. She waved him to follow her. Pushing the door open to the beautiful white BMW, stepping onto the concrete floor of a garage that could be his home, larger than his apartment and actually cleaner, he walked to follow the mystery lady named Jen. She pulled from his pain, she relaxed him with a smile and she kissed him taking him to a place he could never tell anyone. For it was in a part of his soul that no one had visited nor even come close to being near. "Yes a shower sounds good." He followed her through the corridor that lead to the back door of the mansion. She kicked off her shoes at the door. "Don't wear your hospital shoes in here too many germs follow them around." He untied his boots slipping them off not wanting her to see his miss matched socks on his feet. One black one white, gotta love contrast. "Jared do you dress in the dark?" She looked down at his socks then showed him into her home.

He had never seen a home as beautiful or this large ever in his life and he had only walked through the back door. "I have moments of dressing in the dark, a cool sock arrangement that allows me to be artistic in nature?" She loved his attempt to explain the mixed socks but continued to walk further into the huge home. He followed her like a little boy looking around a candy shop. Everything was beautiful but there was a comfortable feel to it. Not the normal feel of being around pure wealth. Usually a greed factor followed. Maybe Jen was married to the president of some huge oil company? She turned as if she heard his query, "I was left a lot of money from a very wealthy family Jared and yes this is my home." She walked up the stairs and turned toward him as she talked then motioned him to follow her still. "I want to work, I want to accomplish something in life, something other than just shop." She paused for a moment and stood there in the middle of the stairs. "Do you have any idea what kind of nothing life it is just to shop, go home, eat food served to you on the finest china food of the finest quality. Retire to a bed already turned down with someone waiting to undress you and dress you for the evening? Only to start the next day again just to go shopping, that is not a life so I changed it." She looked back up the stairs then down to him. "I kept the house though it's home for a bit." Walking quickly up the stairs Jared followed her closely. He saw her legs through her scrubs, he followed the line of her pants up to where he saw a perfectly shaped body. Sighing noticeably as his hand touched the dark wood railing sliding it up with each step behind her. His hand on the wood, his mind on her body, his body reacting. He stopped suddenly and turned a moment as if he dropped something. "Jen I dropped some change...I think," he was hiding his arousal, his thoughts turned to something unpleasant, hurry hurry, what what, Uma!. An image of Uma sticking him for blood reduced the noticeable arousal in an instant. "Jared just meet me at the top of the stairs to the right." She was enjoying his company and his childish feel around all of the wealth. His reaction wasn't the same as others. They usually fluffed and strutted and tried to become the wealth they were around. They become what they felt Jen wanted not who they were. Jared remained himself showing his shyness, showing his overwhelming disbelief of such wealth. It was refreshing to her and stimulating. An image of them showering together hadn't left her, not since the kiss in the garage. A flash went through her like never in her life and that image of them holding in the shower. Jen watched him walk to the top of the stairs to meet her. "About time old man," she took his hand leading him into the bedroom. He stopped her at the door, "Jen I will let you shower I can wait downstairs don't take too long ok?" John was waiting and buzzing his pocket repeatedly. "John is going to vibrate my phone to death we need to get going soon." Jen just pulled him back into the room. "Nope you are going to sit in here and talk with me about my question to you while I shower." She walked slowly into the other room. He heard the shower start while he was left standing in the middle of her very large bedroom. He thought of his apartment measuring a bit with his memory. Then talking to himself. "My whole apartment is about as large as this bedroom." Jen heard him barely as the water runs. She was in the shower hoping he walked in to take one with her but also knowing he was too much of a gentleman to just assume. "What Jared?" "I'm just talking to myself at the size of your bedroom. Heck I could fit almost my whole apartment in here."

The water was hot on her and caused an ache, "oh Jared just come in here and take me dammit!" She moved the soap over her then lifted the bathroom brush across her back. Wishing it was his hands.

"What?" Jared yelled from her bedroom. He walked quickly down the stairs as he moved down them he yelled to her. "I'm going downstairs to wait for you I promise not to steal anything." She sighed and washed quickly, he gives up so fast.

Jared could not believe the size of her place. Huge oriental rugs adorned the marble floors. Antique furnishings mixed with modern in such a natural way. He walked over to a figurine of ancient days, right next to it was a modern sculpture. "This is me," he touched the modern one, "this is she," he touched the one of old and much value.

She walked down the stairs quietly not wanting him to hear her. She was curious as to what he was doing. She watched him touch and admire the figurine and the sculpture of opposing values and times she smiled. "You like my display of contrast Jared?" He turned a bit startled and embarrassed that he was caught touching her things. "Sorry Jen just admiring your art here." He stepped away quickly, his foot caught on the oriental rug and he fell back into a painting on the wall. The canvas tore slightly as he froze in mid tear. "Oh damn, I'm sorry Jen!" Jen walked to the painting touching the part he tore. "Is ok Jared no worries, things are not as they seem." He stepped back and asked with fear, "what did I tear?" Jen stepped close to the painting and touched the tear and looked past it into the art. "it's just and old Rembrandt." Jared didn't know much but he did know that was some expensive dudes work. "Shit!" Jen turned with a shrug. "It is really ok Jared please don't worry." She walked to him and pushed him up the stairs. "Go take a shower real quick I have laid out some clothes that I have that should fit you." She paused with a smile. "I keep clothes in for company just in case." "A shower? Here?" "No down the street, yes here now go we will be late." He looked once more at the torn painting and grimaced, "damn, no cool factor this time I made a total idiot of myself and destroyed something worth.." His thoughts went away he didn't want to even think of how much money that thing was worth. Running up the stairs he looked back for an instant at Jen. She just watched him and smiled, "Hurry!"

Jared saw the clothes on the bed. A nice black blazer with a crisp white dress shirt, black leather belt with silver buckle and black dress shoes, a pair of light tan khakis to the side completes the picture of a perfectly dressed dude. Picking up the shoes he looked for the size, "yeup they fit." Jen yelled once more from downstairs. "Stop looking at your clothes and get that water running before I come up there and wash you myself." She sighed, he got into the shower and laughed he felt good he was happy, too happy, something had to give this was like a dream.

She touched once more the torn painting smiled. "Contrast of worlds, value of time, mix of real with forever." Jared did not ruin her art, he added to it, in her eyes anyway. He created a present touch with past of push and Jen was all about past and now.

Chapter 17

Play Pool

The shower was a quick one, the dressing a quick dress, He moved quickly to get back to Jen and out of the door before he ruined another work of art. He felt at home even in this wealth stopping himself for a moment, "why not I'm worth something?" He looked to the ceiling as if he talked to God, "aren't I?" A voice once more of words with no words slipped into his subconscious. "You are special Jared." He looked around to see if Jen snuck up the stairs but he saw no one. He looked at himself in the mirror and saw one dapper looking dude. His gray shoulder length hair rested quite nicely on the collar of the blazer. His eyes were green for the moment, he watched them change at times but for now they were that dark green of normal. He stood tall to make his five foot nine stature a little taller, or at least tried to be taller, he straightened the blazer. He rolled up his scrubs and ran down the stairs. He watched his black dress shoes move quickly down stairs adorned with another very expensive rug he smiles. "I like this feel." Jen was nowhere in sight. "Jen?" He walked quickly into what looked like a kitchen but could be one for a huge restaurant. "Nobody home?" Jen snuck up behind him and wrapped her arms around him. She kissed him quickly on his neck. "Boo!" Jared jumped but fell into her hold gladly. He turned to her and asked quickly. "How do I look?"

She smiled at his handsomeness. "Let's go John is waiting isn't he?" Jared quickly reached for his phone into pockets that were fresh and empty. "Damn where is my phone?" Jen just shrugged calmly looking at him flounder for a moment. Watching him pat himself down over and over again. Suddenly he jumped as the phone buzzed in the pocket of his work khakis that he was holding. "Yea John we are on the way." He pushed Jen in front of him to run. She laughed and ran ahead of him enjoying this. She looked forward to a night of pool hustling and just being with Jared.

*

John was waiting outside the pool hall for Jared. Flipping the phone open dialing his number then closing the phone almost as soon as it rings. "Jared damn man hurry this lady won't be here much longer." John was a bit cold, his jeans were warm but the white short sleeved dress shirt with hypnotizing black diagonal stripes wasn't very warm. His brown short hair accentuated a pale face with blue eyes that seemed shallow with no spark or light. A wiry build gave him the ability to run fast if needed to get away from a con that didn't work. But the lack of meat on his bones didn't mean he wasn't strong, although it wasn't helping him with warmth this night out in the cold air. This was not the safest place for him to wait for his ole buddy ole pal. John looked at the silent street, no cars, weird moment. A white BMW slowed as it approached where he was standing near the curb. The light of the pool hall was shining down onto the sidewalk, illuminating his back accentuating those horizontal stripes. An easy mark was pulling up and Jared was nowhere in sight. The car stopped in front of John, the tinted windows did not allow him to see inside and for a moment he had a flash of being shot. Stepping back quickly he flinched waiting the gun to show as the window of the BMW began to lower, he closed his eyes thrusting quickly his hands out in front of him for protection. "No! don't shoot!" Jared could not believe his friend, "hey you wuss what is wrong with you?" John heard a familiar voice and not the blast of a gun going off. He felt his body quickly to see if there were any holes. He suddenly realized he didn't feel any pain. He leaned and squinted and saw Jared sitting in the BMW, not only sitting but driving the damned thing.

Jen nudged Jared, "is he ok?" "He is just John get used to it." John leaned into the car looking past Jared at Jen. For a moment his blue eyes sparkled with a piercing look at the beautiful woman sitting next to his friend. He looked at her black hair contrasting her light creamy skin. Her eyes drew him in, blue like his but full of light and fire. His glance traveled down the preverbal path of being a pervert. Jared reached up to lightly hit him on the face. "What?" John asked then stepped back. "Go park and hurry then you can explain the fawncy car and the hot woman with legs…"

Jared sped away turning into the parking lot across from the bar. Before he turned off the car he looked around the area, "this was not a safe place for you or your car to be Jen." She pushed open her door and stepped out. "You don't know me yet Jared." She walked away smiling back at him as she crossed the street. Jared realized he was just sitting in a parked car hurried to shut it off and got out.

He felt good he liked the new clothes; he would play tonight very well. Jen put her arm in his. John looked at Jared, "Jared you are dressed a bit hot tonight definitely an easy mark good call on the clothes." Jared returned the favor quickly. "And John your shirt will blind them making my job easier." He opened the door to the pool hall leaving John behind before he could reply. Jen looked around the smoke filled room and saw some not very pleasant types. She pushed herself a little closer to Jared. "What's wrong nursely? Just look at them like they are patients. They look like most of our clientele." Jen relaxed some, "perspective is the answer to all in life Jen. Stick with me I will show you the way." Suddenly a path of light filtered into his mind, a path with lights of differing colors. Jen was standing next to him on this path, as suddenly as the moment visited his mind it left.

A woman of beauty was making her way toward John. A kind of beauty the world accepts as beautiful. Blonde hair falling across her face just allowing her blue eyes to peek through. Men love that peek a boo affect. It's the "I just got on my knees in front of you look." Nice long legs, thin at the waist and oh so much larger at the top. Nipples just peeking through the soft cloth shirt she was wearing. A skirt of matching color and cloth completes the perfect image of a beautiful woman.

148

This must be the one he wanted to con. Jared nudged Jen they both looked at her watching her movement like silk moving in the air. "Oh my my." Slipped out of Jared's mouth, Jen closed his mouth with her hand. Slipping it down his leg and pinching his thigh very hard. "Ouch!" No one seemed to hear him, the bar continued with it's commotion. Jen whispered, "poor baby." John was talking to the beautiful lady then pointed to Jared. "You will have to go by the bar in a moment Jen. I have to work. John will be with you no worries ok?" Jen loved the feel of energy that was beginning to flow through him. Lightly touching his hand she kissed him on the cheek. "I'm watching you." She walked away and up to John who was now alone. The two women passed each other. Jen looked at her and the woman looked at Jen. There was a stillness in that moment of very high intensity. John took Jens arm and they walked to the bar. "What shall you have Ms.?" "Jen." She said flatly. She was not sure if she liked this John guy. And his shirt bothered her vision. "I will have a gin and tonic on the rocks with a lime." John unable to resist replies, "well you are the gin, I have the rocks to give you a climactic tonic." Jen smiled at the lame attempt but enjoyed the humor. The bartender heard her order and delivered her drink. "Jared covers me like the gin pouring over these ice cubes, so I will have to pass on your wish to rock my tonic." John laughed then looked at Jared. "They are a might close don't you think?" Jen glanced at Jared not worried about him doing anything out of line with that woman.

The beautiful lady and Jared were talking. John told her that Jared couldn't play pool well but enjoyed betting on the game. The first moment of the set up for this beautiful lady that likes to win at her game. "John tells me you enjoy a good game of pool." Jared smiled and looked over at Jen sitting at the bar. She was smiling at him. Jen turned some showing her legs as she crosses them slowly. Jared enjoyed this distraction from the game of fake. The beautiful ladies voice came back into his hearing but he was unaware of what she said. "Would you like to play a game?" He asked quickly. She had already started to walk over to one of the pool tables that just happened to be open. John motioned at him to follow her and away the game began. Jen watched him begin the game. The beautiful lady was quite seductive trying to distract him. But he had only one thing on his mind, Jen. Leaning to break, he didn't see the neatly racked set of billiard balls he saw Jen's legs, crossing ever so slowly at the bar. Replaying her tease over and over again he pushed quickly the cue stick. With a crack the game began. The balls went everywhere but not one went in. The beautiful lady began her shoot of the game. With only one of her balls left on the table she somehow missed a very easy straight in shot. Jared was curious of this miss but took control of the game and won.

John was pissed at him for winning. Whispering to Jen, "he isn't supposed to win what the hell!" Jen just sat back watching him move. He looked good in the clothes she had for him. Very good indeed, he looked at her suddenly catching her off guard. Inhaling quickly she was caught trying to catch air. His glance penetrated her.

"Well you play a mean game of pool, thanks for the moment was fun." He acted as if he was finished. He started to walk over to Jen. The beautiful lady stopped him pulling on his arm. She moved against him slightly and whispered. "One more please." Jared felt the want in her, the want to defeat him the want to win money from him. Or more like take' money from him. "Shall we put a small wager on this game?" She asked as she racked the balls. "Eight ball or nine ball?" Jared chalked his cue stick watching her move with deliberate actions. She is playing me somehow. "Oh just a small bet," she chalked her cue stick leaned into it and smiles. "I quite enjoy eight ball."

John settled back on the stool near the bar now seeing the action would begin. After Jared loses again he will bet a large amount and then win. That's how it goes in the land of hustle. He touched Jen on the shoulder turning her towards him. "How long have you known my Jared?" Jen stiffened a little, "your Jared?" John laughed and downs another beer. "Jared and I have shared a lot in the last 20 years, so yes, how long have you known my Jared?" In a low tone of calm and sensual she slipped her fingers across John's collar. Grasping it lightly she pulls him toward her. John enjoyed this feel. "I will be with Jared into forever." John felt a tingle down to his holy socks in his poorly shined black shoes. Jen released him, reached for her drink and stood. John was left without the ability to speak for a moment as he watched her walk over to Jared. Jen stopped not wanting to get too close to him as she watched the new game begin. People were beginning to watch them play pool. One game lead to the next and the next, with Jared winning a few but the beautiful lady winning more. The wagers have grown now to a very large amount. "5,000 ok on this one?" she asked Jared after he lost one more game. Jared was even on the money up to this point. It's time to take her for some. "Sure," he said shyly then stammered some, "gosh that is a lot of money." The gosh thrown in shows a hesitance but a wish to win. Jen had been sipping on gin and tonics through the night. John had been trying to figure out what it was about Jen that affected him. He had only glanced at Jared playing his fascination was with Jen. John is the one with the bank tonight. He is carrying the money to back Jared. They still have six grand but it's time to double it or come close. John heard the amount she wants to bet and is elated. Finally we can get this woman and go party. The crowd stills around the pool table. The only noises are of glasses clanking at the bar from being washed. They lag for break and the beautiful lady wins. Lagging for break is like tossing the coin and guessing heads or tails. Both players hit a ball to the end rail and bank it to the front rail. Whoever comes closes without touching wins the break.

Jared was ready to clean the board and go home. He missed Jen and was aching just to talk with her of anything. The beautiful lady has been teasing him all night to no affect. Again his only thoughts are on Jen. The lady breaks the balls slamming many into pockets. This was a break he had not seen all night, not of this kind of strength. Suddenly he looked at John, John looked back at Jared. The room dimmed and they realized the truth. The beautiful lady cleaned the table and pushed lightly the eight ball into the pocket. Jared got hustled. John reached into his pocket to pay her the 5,000. She smiled and thanked Jared for the games. Smacking him on the bottom, "you play good pool, just not good enough." Jared felt her need to win, need for money he felt it earlier but didn't pay attention to it. Smiling he walked over to John and shrugged his shoulders, "win some you lose some." John was angry but had lost more. "Damn she had me fooled." John put his head in his hands and growled. The pool room cleared leaving them alone in their temporary misery. Jared tapped John on the shoulder, "sorry old man but I think it's that shirt you are wearing it made my eyes wiggle." John laughed and slaps his hand into Jared's they shake a firm hand shake then do the shoulder hug. Jen put her arm in Jared's "take me out of here I miss you." They began to walk out together. Jared felt wonderful even though he would have to work hard to pay the money back to John he didn't care. "You owe me buddy." John yelled as they walked out. The streets were empty and Jen was feeling comfortably buzzed. "I need some food Jared." He walked her across the street. The BMW shined under the street light. "I will drive I am the sober one here." He smiled, she smiled, he kissed her. Softly pushing lifting swirling, their tongues met for just a moment. Falling into her essence he moaned.

153

Dizzily he pulled away. Something nudged him to hurry and get into the car. Voices were heard coming from the dark alley beside the building near the parking lot. "Jen get in the car quick." He fumbled at first with the keys but was able to push the button that unlocked the doors. She got in she locked them. But he was still standing outside.

Jared felt many souls around him, ones that had passed and he had shown the path to find their forever place. He heard them, voices in his head but not a voice just a knowing what they mean, "get in the car," He pushed the button right as four huge men walk up to him. They were huge in strength not fat. Body builders most likely, was Jared's first thought. "Hello?" He said as he looked directly into their eyes. The push was stronger now for him to just get in the car. Jen yelled for him to get in. He knew if he leaned to get in they would attack him from behind. "You have some more money for us little dude." "What money?" Jared asked as calmly as he could, trying to show he wasn't intimidated. The whispers swirled around the men. Jared saw the souls appear as if to block them from getting near. He took the moment to jump into the car and lock it. They are still held back not able to reach him as he drove away quickly. "Thank you," his words slipped into the now speeding car. "Thank me for what I did nothing." Jen was afraid, confused yet calm. He felt strong within. Suddenly on the windshield he saw more than the road. He saw time moving forward, backward into forever. A place of void, a light with blue, a light with indigo. Hold onto this life as long as possible. Grow with this life your spirit is the test the flesh is the rest. Jen hit him on the arm yelling, "Jared answer me!" He shook his head and looked at her. They were sitting in her garage. It was quiet all but for the fact that Jen was hysterical. "Jen? How did we get here we just left." She continued to hit him, "you scared me, you drove so fast but nothing happened. It was as if all was silent around us. Even the speed wasn't a normal feel and you wouldn't answer me dammit!" She hit him again then grabbed him to her. "Jared what just happened?" Her tears fell onto him he was calm he felt wonderful as a matter of fact. "Jen I'm not sure but hey we are here and you have food here yes?" He got out of the car to head into the mansion. "Come on woman I'm hungry I just lost a lot of money and saw some strange stuff in my head." Jen settled a bit in the seat of the car while he got out. She looked at her watch and only an hour had gone by since they left for the bar. Meeting Jared at the door she showed him her watch. "Jared time, we were at the bar longer than this weren't we gone longer than an hour?" Jared kissed her lightly. "Jen I'm hungry let's talk about this inside." He looked back at a soul that was lingering in the hall outside the garage. His mind threw a thought to the soul and it vanished. Finding one more the way out of earth into the place we will all go. Some just get a little lost.

Chapter 18

Discovery

He was starving, never had he been so hungry. He pushed past her as she opened the back door and ran to find the kitchen. "Food! Give me sustenance!" Jen walked slowly feeling confused and light headed but still very comfortable. She could hear him going through the refrigerator. "Jared don't trash my kitchen." She turned the corner and saw him standing in the light of the refrigerator. He had a glow around him. He looked at her and laughed, "I'm so hungry I'm sorry may I?" He asked for permission but continued to pull out food. She walked up to him. "Jared please hold me for just for a moment."

His move was fast and smooth. His arms moved around her and lifted her to him. They looked into each others eyes. Jared saw a light from within her that shined out onto her face across her. He saw only love in her eyes. A love from another level of existence, a spiritual existence. "Yes I agree." They kissed slowly then hungrily. Energy shot between and through them. He gasped then wrapped her legs around him and carried her to the center of the kitchen. He placed her gently on the center counter, his hands searched for any softness he could feel. She pushed against his touch, lifted and wanted him to touch her everywhere. "Oh Jared yes…" A pan was knocked off the rack over their heads and caused them both to pull apart suddenly. A little skittish still from all that had happened they slow some in their hunger. Released from some of the passion that bound Jared since he first saw Jen cross her legs at the bar, he pulled away and apologized for his actions. "Are you crazy? I love every minute of your touch and you." "We need to eat Jen, then we can.." His thoughts went to them in the shower, on the bed, against the wall. Finishing his thought he added with a cough to clear his throat. "We can talk of romancing the flow." Shrugging he didn't know where that corny line came from but he continued his movement away from her and back to the food.

Jen pulled herself back together and slipped off the counter he so gently placed her on. She was glowing with ache alive like never before. Jared was a contrast of life, she loved contrasts. Simple yet complicated. She saw his every moment inside. The flex and flux of his spirit, the strength of his body, the total confidence that usually only people of wealth carried or they faked it. He had no wealth in the way of monetary. But he had wealth in spirit and in her heart, for her heart was opened like never before. Just being with him, walking next to him, watching him play pool ignited her. "Oh yes.. I like." Jared turned "you like some food?" Jen laughed and shook her head with a no. "Well it's all for me then." He put some chicken into his mouth and settled on the stool next to the counter. "What happened, why am I so hungry and you are not hungry?" She put some of the food back in the refrigerator. "Why did you take out so much stuff Jared?" She smiled and enjoyed him in her home. "Time is an interesting thing, it can be moved forward and backward." Jared slowed his words her way not wanting her to think he was insane.

She cleaned the mess he made and he threw the rest of the chicken away. He was done, he wanted no more. He pulled a glass out of the cupboard and drank some water out of the tap. It was cold and felt good going down his throat. He felt someone watching them suddenly it hit him on the last swallow. He casually put the glass in the sink. He didn't want whoever was watching to know he was aware. "Jen let's go talk about things." They walked into the living room off of the kitchen. It was quite large but had big comfortable furniture. The kind you could sink into. "Sit here with me on this big sofa you have here." Jared pulled her down next to him. He still felt as if someone was watching them.

He tried to shake off the feeling and looked directly into her eyes. He wanted to see her depth, her passion, her sadness her complete self without the false mask that most put on. She felt him searching her insides somehow and not in a physical way. With a calmness she was being explored way down into her core. "What are you doing Jared?" She turned her head to break the eye contact. She felt vulnerable suddenly and too open to this man that she was falling for. It was too early, too soon to want so much from him. From anyone, why does she need to be with him so badly. She stood and walked away from him and saw a shadow move past the drapes near the front windows. "Jared?" He saw it also and stood close to her and whispered, "It's ok

I will not let anything happen to you." He moved quickly to the other side of the room and pulled open the drapes to expose whoever was hiding behind them. But nothing was there but a feel of cool air that smacked Jared with it's coldness as it fell across him with an unsettling feel. He raised his right hand pointing into the darkness near the corner. "I repel and rebuke you with the blood of Jesus! Leave now!' Suddenly the shadow that seemed like just a shadow, moved past him and Jen and out onto the lawn and away from the house. Jen sat quickly back down on the sofa a little shaken over all of this. "Jared?" The feel of being watched was gone. The house had a wonderful comfortable way about it again. "We must have brought something with us on the drive home. It happens all the time with me when I leave the hospital." He sat next to her to hold her. "It's ok Jen I am here you are fine."

She leaned into him wanting more, a kiss a touch or just a feel of his energy. He kissed her lightly also wanting more of her. She was not used to shadows moving and hustlers and bars but she loved the feel of Jared. "Jen tonight something special happened to us." She leaned back into the sofa with him. "You drove so fast Jared but also very safely." Jared knew he moved them through time. Whenever he does that he gets hungry for some reason. He thinks it's his body not handling the jump right. Time traveling is something he hasn't done since he was a child. He was a little rusty at it. Maybe he shouldn't do it anymore. "And who were those men at the pool hall that said you owed them more money?" Suddenly Jared thought of John. "John! I have to go back to the pool hall." He quickly ran to the door and grabbed the keys to her car off the table. "Not without me mister!" She jumped and ran to his side. "What is wrong with John?" "Those men were watching the hustle and saw the money exchange. Not good, John is in danger." Jared knew he left too soon. Leaving him standing there as an easy mark. "Dammit, dammit dammit." He pushed his way through the garage to the car.

Chapter 19

Hustle hell-o

John watched Jared and Jen walk across the street and then return to the bar. His car was parked down the road and not in the best part of town. He still had some money on him. And decided to try his hand at hustling the beautiful lady even though she knows he was the bank for Jared. Maybe she will think I'm an idiot and horrible pool player. She sat at the bar with a very very huge man. The guy must have muscles in his eyeballs. John made his way over to her. He pulled out his last grand and smiled. "Shall we dance?" She uncrossed her legs and laughed at him. She took a last sip of the drink she had been nursing since she beat Jared. The pool hall emptied a little after the slaughter and no one wanted to play her. The giant sitting next to her at the bar looked at John smugly. "What is wrong with you and that shirt?" John looked down at his diagonally striped shirt. Patting his chest a few times he answered the now calm giant. "It's my good luck shirt." On that note the beautiful lady stepped down from her bar stool. "Leave the money with Bill, I will make it short and quick." The fresh 100 dollar bills were counted out. Her money was put next to his. John looked at her money knowing it was still warm from being in his own pocket. He sighed heavily. "Jared let me down tonight." The beautiful lady laughed once more. "Jared is a good looking young man but a horrible billiards player." She held the cue ball in her hand then laid it gently on the table. Swirling it some she looked at John. "You on the other hand are not a good looking young man so maybe you will play good billiards?" He walked over to rack the balls for the game to ensue. He didn't have a good feeling about this lady and wanted to defeat her pretty quickly and badly.

Bill the giant, sat back to watch the slaughter begin. Several men walked in behind John and then past him. They looked at him as they walked to the bar to get a drink. John was oblivious to the new giant muscle factor that had just walked in behind him. Bill picked the money off of the bar. Neatly folding it as he slid it into his inside jacket pocket. Tad too much testosterone for two grand to be out in the open. The beautiful lady gets the break and away the game begins. John called on all the luck of lady in time and history to settle onto his shoulders. He wanted his cue stick to be the one on fire, he wanted to defeat this lady worse than anyone ever in his little career of hustle. Visualizing energy stopping her balls from going in almost caused his eyes to cross. He stopped himself as he rubbed them. Damn can't see now for a minute where is magic when you need it? But something worked because the beautiful lady missed an easy shot.

He reached for the chalk to make sure his cue stick didn't slip off the edge of the ball. Lines formed on the table of the paths the balls would take. Those wonderfully clear lines seen when all is clicking in a pool players vision and game. Smoothly he stroked the cue, the motion was swift and sure. The balls began to drop the beautiful lady began to get nervous. Bill made his way behind John just as he began

162

to shoot he nudged him. The nudge didn't hurt his shot it actually helped it go in. "Hmmm, something bumped into me or is it my imagination." Turning he looked Bill straight in his eyes. Bill backed down surprisingly as John's insides were shaking his demeanor was calm and powerful.

The beautiful lady leaned over the table for a moment as if to look at the angle of his next shot. She showed John just about everything she owned under that low cut shirt she had on. But John saw only lines and positioning and money. Money that belonged in his pocket not hers. He began to call the shots just to show off. Pointing now for the eight ball to go in, the pocket called and the lean over the felt. The feel of the cue sliding in his hand with clarity he pushed the stick as if in slow motion, the cue ball hit smoothly moved toward the eight ball. Sliding against it the reaction of it falling into the pocket released pure joy in John's heart and body. He jumped up with a quick "yes!" His fist clenched his cue stick almost alive with an energy extended from his skill. "That will be one grand please." Bill looked at the beautiful lady she nodded and the money was put in John's hands. "Care for another game m'lady?" He asked with a boastfulness that made her a little angry. "Not tonight," a quick retort followed with a quick withdrawal. They are gone.

John jumped up once more with excitement, "yes, yes yes!" He placed the cue down onto the pool table and went to the bar to get one last beer and then homeward bound. He flipped open his cell phone to call Jared, or he tried to call him. As soon as he began to push the numbers a huge hand grabbed the phone from him. The huge hand was attached to a walking mountain that John saw very clearly. He tried to quickly leave the bar and the giant as he backs up finding the door. The giant just stood there with John's phone in his hand. "Can I help you with something? And can I have my phone back like now?" John was near the cue stick rack that was near the door. He reached quickly to get one just as the big guy moved to attack him. He slammed him with the cue stick and caused the giant to fall to his knees, then to the floor nice and knocked out. The other three men walked slowly toward him.

Should I give them the money now or get beat up then give them the money. John was having a battle of wits and wuss mode kicked in. He reached into his pocket and unfolded two thousand dollars and offered it to the three men moving closer to him. "Drop it on the floor and back out of the bar." Just as he was about to drop it the door behind him opened quickly and in walked Jared. More like in stormed Jared. "John are you ok buddy I had a horrible feeling and.." Jared saw that there had already been a little battle. John quickly put the money back in his pocket, "yea you abandoned me old buddy old pal." Jen was in the car right outside the door ready to drive them away to safety. "I have more money I will give it to you if you let me and my friend go without getting hurt." Jared positioned himself between the men and his friend John.

The three men agree putting their hands out and waited for the money they wanted it now. John knew that escape time had come he pushed Jared out the door as they ran to get into the car the bad guys followed very quickly. Jared got in the front of the car but John was hit from behind just as he opened the back door. Jen drove away quickly with John unconscious in the back seat. Jared had to reach to close the door as they sped away. He saw blood coming from John's head. "Let's get him to the hospital Jen." The drive was quick to their place of fun and play, the ER. The emergency room was packed. Jen pulled up at the back of the ER where the ambulances parked. Jared got him out of the car dragged him into the back of the ER and into the trauma room. He pushed the buzzer on the way in causing all of the docs to fly into the room. They recognized Jared immediately. The story was told to the docs and the work began on John. Jen had parked the car to the side. The security guard walked up to ask her to move but then saw who it was. "Oh hi Jen," "Hi Bob, one of my friends is hurt can I park here for a little bit?" He smiled and nodded, "anything for you little bit," he got on his radio telling all to allow the BMW to stay parked at the ambulance bay.

Chapter 20

Good ole ER

Jen offered to help with John but the night shift had it under control. The charge nurse shoos them out of the room making them wait in the main ER. The two seen together again confirmed the gossip of their dating. Not much got by anyone at work and gossip of who was with whom was hot stuff. The emergency room was a mess with people doubled in every room. "We are home once more." He walked away from Jen to go back into the trauma room to peek in on John. He was still unconscious not a good thing but Jared felt he would be ok. For a moment he stilled to see if he felt John's energy. Swirling inside the flesh of his body it was still very much alert and there. "You will be fine old buddy old pal." He walked back to the get Jean and head back to her place.

The ER was a mess. The aroma of rotted flesh found him as soon as he turned the corner into the main ER. He covered his nose quickly. Odors and Jared do not get along. He saw where the stench was coming from. Not a torn up body from an accident but a sweet, small frail older woman. Lying in her stretcher curled up in a ball. She had all of the central lines the IV's everything needed when people just are not doing well and fluids and meds need to be put in immediately into their system.

One of the night techs saw Jared standing near the bay where the patient was. "She was found down on straw, straw that was on a concrete floor." Jared saw the image of her now clearly as if he was there standing next to her. He heard the whimpers of her cry and felt the pain into her bones. They had to pry her from the floor. Her legs atrophied due to not moving. Her legs were drawn up to her chest, nothing but bones showing on this fragile lady. The odor was from her flesh that had rotted and broken down from the pressure of the concrete against. The skin loses blood flow quickly. When an arm falls asleep that's the first of the lack of flow. If not restored soon the cells begin to die. The skin dies then the rot begins. Just another neglected life, another mother no one loved another sibling no one cared for. Left to rot. He said a prayer for her to ease from pain, for surely God would take her soon. The odor of souls rotted like the flesh on that victim. Choices they have and had. Someone chose to do this to her. Jared saw all life as a whole of one, one light, one piece. But there was another chunk of one. That was the dark side of life. The dark side of life does exist.

He looked at her once more. Without a wish he felt her every pain saw her fear. The fear stabbed him like several spears being shot at him in a spiritual realm. "No," calmly spoken and slowly the spears stop their push. This was out of his hands or wish to help. Spirit moved through him only when the way of road was to be cleaned. Choices are made and this lady was to suffer it was her choice long before she came to this physical place of existence, as was the choice of those that gave her the suffering. Jared had to walk away from her it was not in his hands. He knew that nothing he did of helping others was in his hands. He was open to do and give whatever God wanted him to do, "I am but a servant and gladly one, to you my Lord."

Jared was deep in thought, the reality that we all still have choices in this life. We can choose the dark of energy or the light of energy. One has a consequence of the rhythm or the flow of that level of vibrations. "Vibrational beings we all are." Jen heard him talking to himself and smiled. "Vibrational what, Jared are you getting kinky in thoughts over there." Jared was filtered with a calmness as she approached him. "Yea kinky let's get out of here they will take care of John he is ok and will be ok." He could not help but gasp at her beauty. His hand immediately touched her hair moving a lose strand of black away from her silken cheeks. "You are beautiful Jen, so damned beautiful" Her eyes began that shine of spiritual of light. Pure love emanates from her eyes. Her eyes of soul.

Juan slapped Jared on the back snapping them both out of a place that was of heaven. "dammit Juan don't do that man!" Juan laughed and stepped back, "you are a little touchy tonight something happen while you were out hustling?" Jared put his index finger to his lips "shhhhh we don't say the H word here unless it is Hospital." Juan pulled him away from Jen putting his arm on Jared's shoulders and asked him about Jen. "Are you gettin some of that?" Jared stepped back and smiled. He turned back to Jen and nodded to Juan as they walked out of the ER. Juan put his thumbs up with the ok. They look good as a couple. He watched them walk away and smiled. He had always liked Jared. Many a spiritual talk they have had. He could the light they shared. On top of that they are a damned handsome couple. Juan was happy but went back to the ER. He was stuck at work and looked at the chaos and groaned, "Is it time to go home yet?" His watch said no it it's digital facial expression. Suddenly several of the security officers were running past him in the direction that Jared and Jen just went. He heard a loud yell and ran to help if needed.

The slam of time and reality mix found Jared and Jen in front of a homicidal prisoner that had decided he wanted not to be at the hospital. The officers brought the prisoners in through the ambulance bay doors and those same doors held Jen and Jared's way out of the ER. Jared was pushed up against the wall near the coke machine and Jen flung aside to the floor. He was being choked and the officers were unable to stop it and he passed out. The swirl began in his soul as he left reality of flesh. He saw another dimension of time followed the souls cries that were lost. His hand reached to escape this place, he reached for a light that was near. A voice that was not a voice found his mind, his soul. Relax Jared, that is all that was said as he was once more pushed like heaviest of weights back into consciousness. The voices were clear his vision found light. He saw Jen near him, her eyes were wet from tears and her body showed a worry he didn't want her to have. He pushed the man off with a renewed strength and stepped away from him. The officers controlled the prisoner finally as security from the hospital helped. He was thrown to the floor. Jared stood holding his throat, she ran to him caused him to lose balance once more and they both fell to the floor. He looked into her eyes as they lay on the floor. The ambulance bay doors kept opening and shutting, being triggered by their bodies so close to the sensor. "You will be with me always." His words found life and seem to push into Jen as if a physical touch flew into her. She smiled, "remind me tomorrow how difficult a date is with you." Standing slowly they were both exhausted from the nights adventures. "Let's go to my house Jared I'm tired."

Juan saw them stand and walk out. He saw more than just a man and a woman walk away. He saw light move as one. He went back to the ER and still wished he could go home but his shift was far from over. Another psych was brought in. The obscenities flew against anyone and everyone near. The nurse at triage tried to ask this person that was lost inside their own mind. "Do you drink smoke or do drugs? Do you want to hurt yourself or others?' "Yes I want to hurt you and every person in here." Security was close as were the police officers. The shroud of control was still in place false in its way of walk for no one was ever safe, especially at this ER.

Chapter 21

Denial

The night air felt good across Jared. Jen was close and walking fast to her car. "Lets go to my place please." Jared stopped and looked up to the sky. The stars were bright and the moon low. "I am going to get my van Jen, It's late maybe I should just go home." Jen didn't want to leave him Jared didn't want to leave her. The moment lasted until an ambulance pulled up and the backup signal hit Jared's reality. "I will go home and call when I get there, but will follow you home first." "Jared, come home with me please." She asked one more time exposing her soul to him her want of him. But Jared had to get away from her or he would want all of her and he felt he was not enough for her, not yet anyway. "Jen I will follow you home, please this is best the night has not gone well." She turned quickly, her heart was pounding, she missed him already. She opened the door to the car and didn't look back at him. He watched the door close and the car move down the road. His want was deep for this woman he had known for only a short time. She had seen much and heard him speak to the souls that were lost and gone. She must think he was crazy. Yea a poor crazy tech with no money and no skill, he watched the BMW drive away. The lights shined against him as he stood still in the night near a noisy ER, he heard only her voice felt only her softness against his memory.

He looked down at his shoes, the shoes she gave him and walked to his van. Thoughts flew like dust on a windy day across and through him. He felt totally alone and the silence that found his core was not one he was enjoying. "I have always been alone why is this different?" The van welcomed him with a cold feel. He sat looking once more at the stars through a dirty windshield. He watched his hand grip the steering wheel he wished she was near. He saw her sitting next to him in the van. Her smile warmed him even in a memory.

Keys turned in the ignition he saw her crossing her legs at the bar as he leaned to shoot pool. Driving away from the parking lot he felt her laughter move through him. He saw souls near the edge of the hospital walls, more like felt their presence, he ignored them. Looking straight ahead he drove slowly into the darkest night he had ever felt.

She cried but the car drove itself to her home that would seem empty now without Jared in it. She saw him walking through it the tear in the canvas of art the kiss, the lift onto the counter. His eyes as he glanced at her while he shot pool. She cried but the night held no pity or mercy. "I will see him soon why am I doing this? Why do I feel this?" Her voice echoed in the car as she pulled into her driveway. The mansion was quiet and now it was not a home. It was a place of alone. She pushed thoughts of him away not understanding why Jared didn't want to come home with her. Is it her wealth? Is she not pretty enough? She looked quickly into her rear view mirror and saw his eyes not hers. She watched her tears fall, she didn't want not to feel this rip of love for him. The car pulled into the garage that once was just a garage. Now it was a memory of a moment with a man that had her wrapped like a wrapper on a piece of candy.

The apartment felt small as he walked into it comparing it to her mansion. "Welcome to my garage." He threw his keys onto the desk near the door. The mirror in the front hall stopped him as he stood looking at himself with his new clothes. Pulling the blazer down some he turned sideways a little to look at himself. "Not a bad looking dude really." He tried to build himself up but knowing it would never happen. She was a nurse, she was wealthy, she was hot. He kicked off his shoes and walked to the kitchen. Which he sees now was not a very long walk. "Jen," her name echoed into his soul. The phone buzzed while he opened a beer causing him to drop the bottle. The beer is oozed onto the floor the phone was pushing it's buzz into his left thigh but he couldn't get it out of his slacks. He finally gripped the edge of it and pulled it up and opens it. "Hello!" He hoped it was Jen, he needed it to be her, he waited to hear her voice. But no, of course not he heard Johns. "Jared you leave me here alone in this ER?" Jared sat down on the floor in the kitchen leaving the beer to empty onto the floor. A voice of a friend a voice of.. a friend. "You were knocked out dude you needed to be there." He paused and pushed the phone to his chest as he watched the waste of a good beer. He picked it up and finished what was left of it before all of it was gone while he listened to his friend. "Jared?" John yelled into the phone, "Jared get me out of here they want to put a catheter in my unit dude save me!"

Jared started to laugh, "well pee in a urinal then they won't put a tube in your unit." Jared put his shoes back on. "I will be over there in about ten minutes John." He picked up his keys, walked past the mirror without looking at himself this time and slammed the door shut. He was in the night again and he was fine. Life was good and the day or night goes on whichever you happen to be walking in. His van drove itself to the hospital. He was off tomorrow so no worries on sleep. He would call Jen tomorrow and they would have coffee? He doesn't drink coffee but it's a thought that slipped into his maybes.

Chapter 22

Con men have shadows

Jared parked and walked, looking down once more at his shoes. Why do I always look at my feet when I walk? His p-coat felt good and the night truly was young. Maybe John would feel up to another con job because he was in the mood. It was still early and he needed to prove he could win at pool again, even if he played against a beautiful lady.

The ER had filled up in the small amount of time since he dropped off John. Jen hadn't called and he had decided not to call her. Just to see if he could do without calling or hearing from her. It's time to play some without a woman interfering with his game. He knew she didn't interfere, not sure why his thoughts were dissuading him from thinking good things of her. Denial was an ugly beast and his beast would like to be next to her right now. So a change in mindset and a flip of the switch to night and play was in order.

Walking into the back of the ER he saw a psych patient with a spit hood on and was restrained by leathers. Leathers those wonderful restraints that security puts on to do bondage 101 legally in the emergency room. A spit hood was another wonderful invention that catches spit like a screen. Keeping the spit on the person spitting and away from the workers in the hospital. Jared felt the darkness in their soul and stopped for a moment to spin his light into him. For a moment there was silence as he leaned over the one with the spit hood. "Jared be careful dude!" One of the security guards reached to pull him away from the psych patient. But Jared was firm in his stance and with a whisper he told that of darkness to fly away from the soul of innocence. The feel back against Jared was this man wanted the darkness. He had chosen to have the negative of time and a wish of evil within him. This patient enjoyed the energy so he would suffer that energy and it's rhythms forever. Forever was a long time to be unhappy.

He stepped back and away and slapped a high five to the security guard. He looked for John, the night charge nurse walked up to him and hugged him. "Do you want to help us tonight Jared?" "No way, I want to rescue a friend of mine." He saw he which bay he was in and walked into the room. There was his friend and one of time resting in the dark. He flipped on the switch and yelled, "wake up lets go shoot pool!" John jumped at first then cursed some but finally smiled at seeing his friend. "Get me out of here Jared I am fine." He shook his friends hand, "I will get the docs to write your discharge papers. Do you feel up to a few more games of pool tonight?" John smiled and reached to pull his hospital gown up over his shoulder. His face was pale but his eyes sparkled at the wish to con someone. "We have some money to make," he groaned and grabbed his head for a moment. Jared looked at how many stitches were in his scalp. "You got hit pretty hard dude you sure you are up to a night out?" He laid back in the stretcher, pulled the sheet up over himself for a moment and laughed. "Yes!" He sat back up and bragged about winning back a thousand of what Jared lost. Jared just looked at him. "You finished the con is all, I had her all set up for you. Why didn't you get her for the five grand plus five grand?"

He left the room quickly to get John's discharge papers typed so they can get the hell out of dodge. They were almost out of there, he saw Uma working the night shift not a usual thing. "Uma what are you doing out at night?" She jumped as his words caught her off guard. She must be doing something she wasn't supposed to, Jared looked around her to see what she could be hiding. "Uma did you take that patient off of the backboard?" Only the docs are to remove a patient from the backboard after examining them. Uma as of late had taken it upon herself to just get them off quickly. "Zeeze boards are too hard vor zem, I only help now go away shoo!" She smiled then followed it quickly with a frown and mumbled something in German. He watched her walk with the backboard to the place to toss them. The wonderful backboard room that was usually a mess, one should wear mask just opening the door.

The doctor came back into the room and questioned "who took this man off the board?" Uma scurried back to the break room glancing back at Jared for she knew he saw her do it. Jared smiled at her and waved, her secret was safe with him.

John stumbled out of the room ready to leave the hospital. The two walked out, passing three new psych patients now lined up on stretchers, restrained and cursing at the air. One was laughing as she watched an invisible person talk with her. Jared for a moment saw a flash of a soul there. Standing near the woman, the soul was moving as if speaking. "Not all crazy people are crazy you know that John?" John was oblivious to what he was saying he just wanted out of the place of sickness.

Chapter 23

Darkness likes to dance

Jared felt the cool of night once more as they walked to his van. It's time to do what Jared did best. He threw his arm over John's shoulders and cracked a joke about blondes and messed up the punch line. A usual with him, he was horrible with jokes. John laughed so hard it caused him to grab his freshly stitched head. They climbed into the van and headed to a different part of town to find easier targets with loose wallets. Jared drove past the bar he went to with Jen and John slapped him on the shoulder as they passed. "Stop! Lets go in there." Jared pulled to the side of the road and moaned quietly. "The people in there are young and too easy." He didn't wait for John's response and got out of the van. As he stepped out he saw his face in the van's side mirror. He saw a huge spirit standing behind him, it startled him and he jumped and turned quickly with his hands up in a protective manner then yelled, "No!" The spirit just stayed there in front of him. It was one of the light ones he would see at times. Some were dark, some had places for eyes but nothing but empty sockets. This one was of light and was very large. He walked around it carefully and watched it watch him. He closed his eyes for a moment and it vanished. John limped around the back of the van to see why Jared was yelling.

Jared walked into him as he turned the corner. "Dammit to hell John watch where you are walking!" John stepped back and grabbed his head once more. "I am an injured soldier be nice." Jared noticed some blood on the back of his shirt. "You need to change that shirt you are covered with blood." John spit on his left hand and rubbed it into the shirt. "There all fixed." He laughed and walked into the bar. It was full of people laughing, playing pool dancing and flirting. The air was thick with smoke especially near the pool tables. Jared walked up to the bar and ordered a cognac then settled onto the bar stool. John was quick to walk up next to him and order a double of anything. "Just serve me your best hard liquor and make it a twin in a glass."

The room was full of weekend warrior pool players. There were also some very beautiful women. Jared saw one that was similar in coloring as Jen, dark hair, beautiful complexion and legs that could wrap a guy tightly with that wish of push harder please. Sighing he sipped on his cognac and returned his glance to the pool players. He saw his old friend Steve there, but he was busy separating someone from their money. John walked over to a lady that was watching the action from one of the many leather chairs around the bar that faced the pool tables. He saw her point to the blood on his shirt. Watching closely Jared wanted to see how John explained this one. She laughed then he sat beside her quickly. Good ole John he still had the touch. He would have that one in his bed tonight and start a new day with four waiting. John may not look fresh as a daisy but his personality flipped the girls on their side allowing him to find their depth, and not the depth of soul.

Jared finished his drink and straightening his jacket then smiled at the image of himself in the mirror over the bar. "Let's get some rent money." Although he didn't need the money, he made enough the other night with Jen, but he wanted to try to find the normal swing of what used to be his normal night. Since his spiritual gift had begun to return, his life was turning, turning into a place out of the way of easy and simple, into a place of complicated and spiritual and those damned shadows, that so enjoy messing with a soul.

He looked around the pool hall and felt the unseen energies that easily filtered into his reality. He felt a push against his back that caused him to walk away from the bar with a feel of not wanting to look back. He knew it was not visible, he was fighting his gift but not very successfully. He walked over to one of the freshly available pool tables hoping the spirits in the land will let him play and leave him alone. Although once they knew he could see them they would come to him from everywhere. She walked up to the table, her smile was slow but turned into a very sensual one. Oh great, another woman to kick me in my proverbial pool hustler ass. "Want to play a game?" He asked already knowing the answer. The fact she was already holding a cue stick wouldn't give it away now would it? She looked over at a group of three men that were watching them from the bar one of them nodded an approval. "Yes but I would like to play for money." He finished racking the balls acting as if that was taking his full concentration. But he saw the three large men she was with and was not in the mood for another battle over anything. "Sorry, not for money just for fun." She turned on her heels slowly walking back to the men. Her body moved like, he stopped his thoughts and looked down immediately. The one man that nodded walked passed her and headed for Jared. Jared picked up his cue and acted oblivious to the large man with much anger, heading his way. I will just break the balls and hope John gets over here to play this game with me. But no, a tap on his shoulder proved to be the start of the wheel of manipulation. "Why don't you play the lovely lady?" He stood with his cue ready to be used as a weapon and answered slowly with a slight smile. "I will play her, I didn't hear her correctly." A quick game what would that hurt. The energy around the man was strong in darkness but didn't bother Jared for some reason. He motioned the lady to come back and play him. Stepping back away from the two Jared was left with the lady and a fresh game about to ensue. "Ladies first." He gave her room to shoot. She leaned to break the balls.

The dark maroon dress she was wearing did not leave much to the imagination. Stopping just at the top of her knees the eyes couldn't help but follow down that path of thigh to calf to heels. Her heels accentuated her legs as she kicked one of them up slightly when she hit the balls, she added the tease. Jared saw the one large dude smile as he watched her move. She put in several balls quickly. The only

182

thing he was enjoying about the whole game, was watching her move. I am becoming a pervert as of late. All these women and their accoutrements shoved in my face. I need to take some lessons from John in the how to get a girl in bed after two games of pool.

She stepped away from the table some after she missed a shot. Her cue stick rested against her as she leaned into it slightly. The large man walked over to her and kissed her lightly on the neck. Jared sighed at the sight and started to do what he did best. He started to clean the table. Just as he called the eight ball to go into the corner pocket he decided to miss it. A slight miscue sent the cue ball to the side which caused him to scratch. "You win lovely lady." He started to park his cue stick back in the rack to leave but that was not a happening thing. "The lady wishes to play another game." Nothing like a deep voice with anger spitting at you spiritually to create a conducive atmosphere to play pool. "Sure thing," calmly said, he showed no signs of being intimidated or even realizing what was going on. That this man was her banker and if you win you would meet the banker in a dark place.

As Jared racked the balls his memory went to a time of old. When all he saw and felt was the thrill of the con, the ease of the money, and a little bit of lust on the side as he showed off for the ladies. Pushing the freshly racked balls up to the spot on the table where they belonged. He slowly lifted the triangular rack away. Freedom on the green they became, waiting to be smashed against each other and into the pockets of luck. The lady won, so the lady would break. He looked around to find John, but he was not anywhere close. But Jared could feel him somewhere, and he could feel that he was not behaving like a gentleman.

The clock on the wall through the smoke showed time was slipping into morning hours. Jared was beginning to feel a loss from not being around Jen. He pushed that thought into the nearest pocket and watched the lady break. The slam of balls once more triggered a feel of home. The sounds of the pool table filtered through his soul. I love a good game of pool. Humming a tune from old, he waited for her to finish her turn. The light opened his eyes as now he took the cue and leaned to begin his dance, the dance of skill across felt.

She moved near him watching as he skillfully put the balls in the pockets. There was no money on the game so Jared just decided to hit them all in. On the last shot that large white spirit he saw outside his van slid it's light against the eight ball, caused it to miss the pocket. He felt as if it was laughing at him for messing up his shot. Part of Jared was trying to act like none of this was being seen or going on. Nope not happening, his minds thoughts tried to deceive but it wasn't working too well.

Thrusting the bottom of his cue stick hard against the floor he moaned. She smiled and walked to finish putting her balls in. The light spirit helped her put the last one in. Jared once more tried to act like he didn't see the abomination of cheating from the other side of reality. "Not fair," slipped out of his mouth as he walked once more to rack the balls. "Loser racks again." With emphasis on loser, he put the balls hard onto the table. Where the hell is John? Frustrated, something he was not used to feeling while playing pool and it caught him off guard. Laughter snuck into his core of silence and it was coming from that light spirit.

"Want to bet on this one?" She asked quietly and smiled at him. Jared thought no for a moment but realized maybe if money was on it he would play better. "Sure how much?" He racked the balls slowly as he watched her wave to the large dude. "Five hundred ok? The large dude pulled out the money from his vest pocket and laid it on the table. Jared checked his pockets real quick but he didn't have the money, John did.

He looked around the room for him again and finally found him. He had another lady pinned up against the wall and was not worried about showing public displays of affection. "John!" He looked over at Jared. Jared gave the need money sign with five fingers held in the air, of course meaning five hundred. John nodded his ok and away the game begins. She breaks with the same power she had been but didn't get a ball in. An opening for Jared, he sank a few then missed one on purpose. The light spirit was close to the pocket but didn't doing anything. It was just near as if it watched the game. Jared had decided he wanted her to win, then he would act upset and bet a very large amount.

She easily put the rest in. Jared did his act of upset he lost. John walked over looking disgusted with Jared but handed the money over to the lady. Another lady walked up to her and took it quickly. The large dude didn't see the exchange he was busy doing the high five with his friends and chugging some beer. Jared smiled a slight smile at the lady, she winked back at him. So there was a con going on and he was not involved, good.

John raised a thousand in the air. "We need to recoup, how about another game, please just one more?" She turned to the large man. He walked slowly over and a little unsteadily now. The alcohol was showing its affect and the large dude was not walking right. One thousand dollars lands on the table next to John's. This time Steve walked over to hold the wager. It's not a good idea for the betting parties to hold onto their own bets. Keeps people from running out of the building not paying up.

She breaks, the light spirit was behind her and pushed the cue stick as she moved it. "Not fair." Jared said under his breath but John heard him. Standing next to him with his new conquest on his arm he whispered. "What's not fair, it's all fixed just win dammit." He walked away with his woman to get another drink and gets the large dude another one also as the game ensued.

186

If darkness had a voice it would be screaming at Jared right now. For suddenly they appeared, shadows filtering, surrounding and falling next to him then slipping through him. He jumped suddenly as they passed through him. He looked over at John not wanting him to think anything was wrong. But it was time for him to battle this nonexistent supposed powerful energies. Just as suddenly as they appeared to him they slipped inside the large dude and his two friends. "Oh just great, now they mix with flesh."

The lady heard his last word Jared was mumbling and smiled once more. She leaned deeply for him to imagine those things that men do when a woman leans over. She liked this pool player and wanted a little of him later, if she could accomplish this nights work the right way, she would have him, especially if he was whispering words to her like flesh. Jared had one shot and the game was over and so was he. He wanted to go home away from everyone. He shoots he...missed. He missed an easy shot. He turned to walk out knowing she would get her shot in. It was an easy shot. But she didn't. She miscued. The large dude yelled as Jared quickly put the eight ball in the pocket. The pot theirs, he was happy it was over. He couldn't shoot pool anymore he was losing his skill for some reason. Was he not supposed to be doing this anymore or what? John grabbed the money from Steve as they walked quickly out of the bar.

Chapter 24

Jared's van looked good, "John I am going home you keep the money and get a cab to take you home I am done for the night." John pulled him over to the side of the van, "hold on a bit I have a surprise for you." The lady walked around the corner then ran over to the van. "Hurry lets get going. The other lady that John had pinned up against the wall earlier in the night followed the lady he had been playing pool with into the van. The sliding side door shut, they yell at Jared to drive.

Now it all made sense, they were in on the scam. She flirted, she got him to put up money, she fooled him into believing she could beat Jared, tada. "If I had told you Jared you would have messed it up somehow." Jared just wanted to be alone. Never again would he shoot pool with John. Looking back in the rear view mirror he saw the light spirit following then slipping into the van. A voice of calm without a voice settled into his mind. "Call on the light when you need help Jared." As soon as he heard the silent voice it left. The white light fell away and the sounds of a shrill girl voice kicked him in the ears. "My name is Sheila." She pulled on the front seat to move closer to him. Then she sat back in the seat to show off her legs. "You see anything you like?" John had moved to the back bench seat with the other one and had begun his dance of hands and tongue.

Sheila took advantage of John leaving the front seat open. She moved slowly up and sat next to Jared. Thoughts can escape into forever in moments like this, and Jared's did just that. No interest in the people in his van which was under attack with the wants of flesh and the wills of boring. She was showing her legs, and a little bit more. He just kept driving, his eyes looked into the rear view mirror just as John was about to plunge into the softness of her heat. The moans moved across Sheila which caused her to open her legs even more. She wanted Jared to touch her, she took his hand off the steering wheel and put it on her leg.

The crawl began, the slow crawl of darkness. The sound was of a something not of this world. Not of the world of those with eyes that only see the one level of life. Bad energy lived and thrived and demanded to take over anyone that was weak enough to allow its filter inside. The choice always the holders, but what can one do when choice becomes invisible. They have been labeled emotions and normal, In reality they were the swirl of darkness that robbed so many of their light, of their forever that was waiting to be lived. Hidden behind fear, lust, envy, jealousy zapping into the core of the ones of weak and familiar complacency.

Jared could feel and see the dark entities. They had entered his van and moved with skill through is friend and onto the women. Powerful thrusts of lust circling the hunger of human tendencies became visible. He needed to get them out of his van. Even his friend John needed to go. He stopped at the next gas station and yelled as he pulled his hand back away from Sheila. "Everyone out of the van Jared wants to go home!" John's timing was impeccable as he exploded into her just as the van stopped. The woman screamed as if being attacked, which caused those at the gas pumps to begin to pull out their cell phones to call the police. Jared waved frantically and laughed, "no, no just my friend getting lucky back here!"

The darkness slipped to his mind, the visual, the feel, the smells of sex entered Jared but he had no want of this type of connection. Jen's beautiful, blue crisp eyes found his memory, pushing all the thoughts of quick satisfaction and darkness away. This was how it happened, the rationalization began in most. Everyone did it, it's natural isn't it?

Sheila pushed her way over to Jared. He saw the bits of negative black inside her. "No Sheila, no thanks." He pushed her quickly away, she smiled but he saw pure black in her eyes. Why do I see this? She was not an evil person. He got out of the van and walked away from all of it. Leaving his coat and everyone behind, he walked into the night's air. Refreshing yet cold he shuddered at the feel. "Jen.." His head lowered as he watched his feet, those nice dress shoes, step across the black pavement. The ocean was where he needed to go. It had been too long since he had felt the refresh of it's air and the fill of his soul. He ran through the night and heard his shoes hit the ground but looked straight ahead. As if flying he could hear the oceans surf. She was my only love, "when an ocean becomes your only love you are in deep shit dude." His banter into the void was a way to remove the serious of the night. Finally he arrived at the beach, the sands were dark with a few flood lights from the hotels near illuminating the surf. He stood at the edge of the cliff and watched the crash of waves although calmer at night they still had a stilled energy that filled him and helped him.

Chapter 25

The hospital was alive with patients that were not all surviving. Every room doubled and not enough staff left the patients not cared for and the staff on duty exhausted. Donna was the charge nurse on this day from normal chaos. She began to call people in to work. Jared was on the top of the list of techs. Donna was a slight of build lady with a feisty energy. She was a good nurse with frustrations on how the ER was run, just like most that work in the world of medical. It seemed time had shown that more and more people are falling ill and more and more are visiting Mayvilles ER.

She gave up quickly on Jared and called a couple of the other techs but nobody answered. She blocked the number so they wouldn't see she was calling from work and called again, It worked Jared answered with a voice of slumber and comfy. "Jared this is Donna we need you can you help today? Maybe work a few hours please please?" Jared sat up in his bed he still had on his clothes and his shoes from the night of walking and shadows he chuckled a bit. Donna knew he didn't want to come in. "Jared just nod yes and get in here as soon as you can I will be waiting for you." She hung up not giving him the option to reply. Although she had no right or way to make him come in she knew he would. Jared was one of those special ones that helped others. Even at the expense of himself.

Donna called Jen to see if she could come in to help. The chaos around her was getting even to her and it took a lot to get Donna unnerved. Jen was not quite awake but was willing to come in for four hours but that was all. She had not heard from Jared. After a night of not sleeping well she was ready to do something to try to remove the missing of him. "Yes I will be in for a four hour one Donna but that's it." Donna marked the body count of fresh troops and was happy.

*

After dressing slowly he had to call a cab to take him to work. He had no idea where his van was and he hoped John took it home to his place. He would talk with him later, right now he wanted to just get to work to kill some of the day. Then he would call Jen. He missed the hell out of her and needed to see her soon.

Jen walked into work. Waiting to get distracted from the thoughts of Jared, maybe even find someone else to remove the feel of him from her thoughts. She slowed her walk into the day. Maybe there was a new resident or doctor she could flirt with. Just maybe she should find someone that would mean nothing to her but allow her to enjoy time moving through the night not alone. The ladies locker room was beside the men's. She looked at the door of the men's, remembering when she walked with Jared. As she was looking at the door it opened and there was Jared. His face was there, looking at her, full of gentle full of hello and calm. "Well hi Jen, did they call you in also?" Jared liked seeing her. He didn't want to admit that he was missing her as badly as he truly was. "Jen..I.." his voice trailed off as he attached his trauma scissors to his black cargo pants. The scrub top of black also showed a crisp white shirt underneath. She could smell the fresh of shower on him and fresh cotton. She wanted to fall into him so badly, she sighed as her key automatically pushed into the lock on the door to the locker room. "yes Jared, why didn't you call me?" She asked not expecting an answer. Pushing through the door she wanted away from the feel of a fool. He followed her into the locker room. She saw him follow her, "you can't come in here!" Jared pulled her to him. She looked into his eyes, he looked into her soul. The kiss slowly found rest upon her lips wanting this taste of his kiss. Someone walked right past the two of them as they were locked in this sensual embrace. Smiling at them it was Michelle, the young nurse that Jared admired. She finished her use of the locker room and hurried away. They continued to kiss. He didn't not want to let her go. She didn't want the kiss to end. "Jen I had a horrible night you have no idea." She didn't want to hear of his night. Hers was horrible and she had no reason to feel this. They just met but the connection he had made in her soul was deep. Thoughts tried to find a reason for behavior when it just didn't fit into the normal mode. He let her pull away from him. "I had to walk home Jen, I fell asleep as soon as I got home or I would have called." "Jared you could have called me." Everything that happened flooded his mind, the image of Sheila, the darkness, John plunging into that woman and the run to the beach. But she wasn't listening to him. He felt her anger and pain. He left the locker

194

room and left her to get over her anger. "I am here if you want or need me Jen."

He was trying to get a grip, get something of a grip of reality. His soul hurt. If that was at all possible. He saw patients in their bays, he saw blood orders ready for him to do his job. But it was through a fog. Like a silent window with noise crowding his mind Jen was there. In every part of him she was there. Walking past him quickly she saw one of the residents. He was the one resident that has had his eye on her for some time, ever since she moved to the ER. She stopped to smile at him and wrap her arm in his. Knowing that Jared watched, she moved against him. Her hips found his as they walked. He pulled her closer not knowing the game she was playing.

Jared moaned loudly then slammed his fist into the closest wall. A patient across from him laughed. "Having a bad day young man?'" An elderly lady sat on the edge of her stretcher. She wanted to go home, he smiled at her. "What is the saying? Women can't live with them can't live without them." She smiled then asked to go home. "Why are you here? What is wrong?" She moved with animation and a bit of cuteness. Her white hair wrapped up in a bun on the top of her head but it was a mess up there. Jared felt she must be a psych patient for she didn't seem to be ill of flesh. The conversation grew as he used her to distract him from his jealousy. Why was Jen doing this to him? Because of one night? One night of not taking her with him of sending her home? Why are women so damned mean.

The patient saw the frown on his face and laughed. "You want to go home too I see." Jared listened to the rest of her story. It seemed she had a drinking problem and fell somewhere outside her home so she was now in his wonderful hospital. "Have to take off your clothes ma'am you are on a hold because you are drunk." The old lady shifted and then stated "No," as her reply. Jared nodded along with this. "She hasn't done anything…" The charge nurse shot a look at him and he shut up pronto. She left him to the task of removing the drunk ladies clothes. Jen was making it very clear for him to see that she was blatantly flirting with the resident who was soaking up every attention she was giving. Suddenly the charge nurse called Jen over to her. Jared saw her pointing her finger at her as Jen walked away and also away from the resident. "One for the good guys." After a battle of wits and conversation he removed the clothes of the old lady. She was allowed to keep on her underpants but that was it. As he began to take off her jeans she just lay back and spread her legs. Her very dry legs. The dry skin flakes off as a dust cloud formed near his face. Security had been there to help with the removal of clothing. They suddenly step back away from the woman and outside of the bay. Jared left quickly holding his breath. He would not breathe in all that dead skin.

Jen saw him pulling off the pants. With the removal she saw the horrible look on his face. "Serves him right the turd." She walked back over to the resident to flirt some more with hopes that Jared would see her. Learning to not breathe temporarily in the emergency room was a gift. One never knew the odors that would find your nostrils. Jared ceased his breathing hurried to bag her clothes and rushed out of the room. Taking a gasp of air he saw Jen still pushing herself against the doc. He didn't like the way it made him feel. He tried to act casual as if the day was normal and his flow was cool, he walked over to talk with the secretaries to kill some time. Katie and Liz were working this day. Two of his favorite 'sexytaries', a nickname he used for secretaries. They were usually sexy and all made up beautifully to present to the world their skill in typing arranging and being 'sexytaries'. He got confused on their names though usually called Katie Liz and Liz, Katie, they were used to it.

"Any cool phone calls today?" He leaned against the counter and waited to hear another odd call to the ER. "A lady called in saying that we took her ability to do her wifely duties, because of the irritation due to a catheter we put in." Jared waited for more stories of weird calls and made eye contact with Jen. She was giving the resident a piece of paper, most likely her phone number. Shifting his stance he tried to make the pain he felt not exist, he groaned unable to hold in some of his emotions. He listened as stories were told by the secretaries, but he heard nothing. He could only feel a pain so deep within him it almost killed him.

He looked back at Jen she was walking over to the nurses counter with a patients chart in her hand. He dropped his head once more trying not to hurt. Jen walked up to him wanting to hear the story. Jen

197

laughed as she finished and touched Jared's shoulder but then stopped in midair. "Dammit Jen what are you doing to me?" Both of the secretaries looked at him then wait for the answer. "You didn't call me, you made me go home, you went back out without me." She walked away leaving him leaning against the counter. He looked back at Liz and Katie. Liz flashed one of her, what the hell expressions his way. Putting his hands up in the air he walked the other way. Away from Jen and into a room to clean it. She saw him across the hall cleaning one of the rooms. She watched him move with a sadness. Yes she felt he was sad. Maybe this game she was playing had gone too far. She had to give one of her patients some morphine then she would go talk with him.

As he finished cleaning the room a patient was brought in. He had to put him on the monitor and remain moving to distract the pain he felt. Jen looked at the resident and smiled then walked toward Jared. The resident was watching her and smiled. Jared turned away from her feeling she would tell him she was done with him. "Jared," she said softly. Not wanting to face her he continued to act as if he was cleaning the counter in the room. She walked up to him and pressed against him. Katie and Liz stopped what they were doing and watched, their heads together as they leaned to look over the counter and across the computers to watch the two. "Jen I'm sorry I didn't call, the night was..." She stopped him turning him to her. "Kiss me you fool." He saw Katie and Liz looking at them. He smiled at them then pushed hard against her to taste the kiss that he knew was the one he wanted to feel forever. They moved with light moans as the kiss began to get a little too hot to be at work and in a bay in the ER. Suddenly a patient was wheeled into the room. EMS had a bit of a laugh, Jared and Jen pulled apart with a feel of pain from the separation. He looked into her eyes "we need to have a real date tonight," pausing he waited for her answer. Looking around her he smiled at the patient waiting for them to finish their extra-curricular activity. "Kiss her for me, it's been forever since I have kissed a beautiful woman." Jared kissed her again deeply. Katie and Liz clapped their hands as did the EMS worker and the patient. The resident frowned deeply and walked over to the two. Pushing his way past the patient he pulled her from him. "Excuse me tech, what are you doing to this nurse?" Jen pulled her arm away from the resident. "He is kissing me, he is arousing me and he will be taking me out tonight have a problem with that?" Jared stood there still feeling the heat of the kiss. In a daze was a good way to put it, "yea," he spoke without knowing. The resident was pissed that a tech had the attention of this woman that he wanted. "Fine enjoy your tech," with extra emphasis on tech, he walked out of the room but tripped over the stretcher that the patient was on. Almost falling into the secretaries counter, the resident regained his composure. Walking quickly over to pick up a patients chart he acted as if nothing had happened. But Jared was a happy camper. The patient asked calmly, "can I get an EKG now to make sure I'm not dying from voyeurism?" He laughed as did

Jared. Time was good again in his walk and his soul. Jen finished working with her patients. Her walk was light and is full of true and no games. She wanted to be with him to know him, to find his calm and know his pain. She wouldn't play the jealousy game anymore. The patient's stretcher was moved into the room. "Thank you for the enjoyment of you two." Jared connected the leads to the monitor in the room. "It was my pleasure, sorry though not very professional of us." "It was wonderful." "How do you feel?" "Not good my chest hurts worse now." Jared didn't feel a push to heal this man. Something caused him to pull away. Sometimes a person was supposed to go through their pain, just was their path. Jared got the nurse for this room to tell him of the history of the patient. Linda was a good nurse and another person he enjoyed working with. She was fresh back to work after having a baby and was ready to work. She enjoyed gambling at the local casino and betting on Jared's pool playing on occasion. "This guy is hurting Linda, check on him." She walked over to get his history. Jared went to talk with Jen, all eyes were on them now. He moved away as Uma walked past him. She was carrying something that just didn't look right. "Uma?" She stopped for a moment but looked very confused. "Jess?" Which he assumed means yes, "what are you carrying?" "Zis looks like a leg, I found it on the floor near zee patient but zay say it isn't zairs? I just don't know vut to do Jared." Two bays down from the room she found the leg was a man that was frantically looking for something. He hopped around with much energy. "Uma look it is his take it to him."

200

"Oh my goodness I veel so dirty." She walked quickly to him he was happy she was relieved. Quickly washing her hands she made an ugly face. Jared smiled at her. "What a trip she is."

Katie and Liz called him over to the counter. "Jared!" "What, what," he said with a smile. Killing some more time with them. "Congrats on the Jen hookup she is a good person!" Jared smiled and lowered his head. "Aw shucks." Katie chimed in with a want for all of the details and when the wedding was. He was saved from this conversation of weddings and such as one of the patients ran out of their bay and also out of their gown. She flew past Jared with a look of glee and giggling, naked as a jay bird in flight. Uma ran after her with a sheet hoping to catch her and cover her. "Stop! Stop! Vou must stop, vou cannot do zis!" Jared looked at the visitors expressions while the naked patient ran wildly through the ER. "This is a good thing." The whole ER laughed as she ran past each bay finally coming to rest on the hip of the large and in charge nurse, Stephen. He was a big man that was a plus to have around. He usually helped handle all of the violent situations in the emergency room. This time he tackled the naked giggling jay bird. Falling to the floor he pulled her down but she ended up on top of him. Uma caught up to them and threw the sheet quickly over her. Flying past her it covered nothing of her but totally covered Stephen's head. "Oh my goodness, zis is not right!" Stephen shifted his weight causing her to fall to the floor. The sheet lifted and wrapped around her quickly. The scene slowed to an end and the ER erupted in laughter.

Jared smiled at Jen, she looked back at him with such a look of gentleness it almost knocked him off his feet. He turned away to absorb or try to absorb the feel of her energy and move it away from his lungs he felt elated but unable to breathe easily for a moment.

He was only working for a few hours on this extra day at work. His phone buzzed in his pocket and startled him. He was enjoying Jen, he closed his eyes and saw her, "She is beautiful." Liz heard him and laughed. "Get a room and get it over with Jared." He walked quickly out to the hall outside the ER to take the phone call. No cell phones were allowed in the emergency room, which meant, everyone kept them on vibrate and everyone had a cell phone. "Jared where the hell are you?" It's John and Jared was not in the mood. Closing the phone he then turned it off. "Not today John, nobody tis home."

Jen snuck up behind him and wrapped her arms around him. "How did you get into my heart so quickly Jared?" He leaned back against her feeling the silence in his soul. It was one of peace and slow. No voices of pain no dark shadows slinking around his thoughts. Those old souls lost and watching for a moment, left him for this time of peace with Jen. The hall outside the main ER led to the back doors out of the hospital. The ambulance bay was seen from where they were standing. It was empty, the morning light moved across the dirty carpet that lay on the floor. Dark in color it still showed dirt, like a soul of light showing its darkness. The choice to drop garbage on the carpet, the choice to pull darkness into that light we were all born with. Mixing it, destroying the peace we were meant to have for eternity.

Jared's time of silence left quickly as a slam of darkness filled the hall. Jen stiffened behind him and whispered. "What is that Jared..what?" He turned to face her and walked her back into the ER away from the black swirling cloud that hovered near the ceiling over the ambulance bay. "It's nothing Jen just get back to work and stop goofing off. We only have a couple of hours and we can talk of the ways of Jared and Jen." He paused and a pressure on his back but he didn't want her to know. She smiled and was comforted by the calm of him. She didn't see the darkness anymore she must have imagined it. She looked around him and there was nothing but the light on the dirty floor. "That floor needs a good vacuuming, I will page Miriam." She kissed him quickly and pushed her badge against the magnetic lock on the door.

Jared watched her walk away he didn't want to turn around to see what was pushing against him. He lifted his head and straightened himself. He shrugged as if to shake off water that had just fallen like rain onto him and pulled light around himself. The gift of old was beginning it's damned whirl of opening that gate across the physical plain into the place where only spiritual eyes could see. And only eyes that were open saw the true of energy in life. "Damned dark energy." He turned quickly, he was ready to face whatever was there. He had good on his side and light was stronger than darkness or evil. "Evil is weak."

It suddenly attacked Jared with a sword? He pulled what seemed to be an invisible saber from his belt. It was a broad sword with a sharp blade. He saw the battle but it was in the eye of spirit not flesh. He slashed the invader across the midsection then finished with a slash across the throat. Blood covered the white shirt he wore, in this place of spiritual he was wearing a white shirt with black pants. Looked like a pirate in his mind's eye. "A pirate?" Jared could see both planes of existence, the spiritual one, the one of swords and blood and the one of flesh of real of life known to most. The ER was still the ER. Patients were moaning, some screamed some puked. The splash of the vomit always hit the floor with a repetitive rhythm. Odors of the unnatural kind were always wafting in the ER. Jared was tired of the whole nine yards. Once he floated among them at the ER touching them, helping them with the old Jared charm. But enough was enough. Another spirit walked up to him and another attack began. It waved a sword at him. He had to again slice them across the chest finishing with a slice across their throat. The blood once more fell away from the spirit and once more it covered him. He wondered if this was just a fall back memory of all the blood he had seen. The next spirit came up to him. Jared spoke quickly to this spirit, "wait, I don't want to do this anymore!" The spirit stopped then said to him very clearly. "You have to or we will kill you." Jared lifted his broadsword slashing once more dropping the blood to the floor from the spirit. The blood splattered across him once more. Just as quickly as it started it stopped. He stood there motionless as the spirits stopped their attack on him. Interesting is the visual of two worlds, interesting but very distracting. The sounds of the patients fall slowly back into his ears. He began to doubt his sanity and laughed suddenly. The blood of spirit gone from his chest for his scrub top was black. His pants were black and his t-shirt was white. Underneath the black scrub top, thankful that the white pirate shirt was gone and the visions of men attacking him with swords. He saw Miriam smiling at him. "What are you doing Jared you look silly standing there like that." She pulled out the vacuum cleaner from the closet near the door. He saw the dark swirl above the door but it swirled away and vanished. Miriam started coughing some then grabbed her throat. "I have a bad cough today." The vacuum was stubborn coming out of the closet. Miriam started to laugh, "Jared?" Waving her hand at him, she gave up trying to get that silly look off of his face. She vacuumed the dirty carpet and smiled the whole time. She did enjoy her Jared even though he was just not right.

Chapter 26

Jared was not right, not normal he had heard that his whole life. What was normal? Was it the walk to work with briefcase and following with a nod of zombie at the boss? Was it the picket fence with a wife that didn't love you? Was it the boring lift of a day that had only a wish of getting finished with work? He knew what they said was true, he was not right or normal. The shift and remembrance of his gift opened him to the evil, the darkness in life and in time. But he also saw the light and goodness in life. He was to walk this path for some reason and would not question anymore God and His wisdom. "Forever surrounded by light of true love is not worth losing over anger and hatred and greed." He walked into the trauma room to escape for a moment the ER. Silence was there but not for long as the souls that had died found him. They slowly moved toward him, some of light, some were the boring dark nasty ones. The ones that gossiped to ruin, to steal or to kill their friend. Now with this test he wondered if he would do the right thing. "Always the choice huh Big Guy." He spoke into the air and walked out of the trauma room. The battle began and he would win. For he would trust and have faith in the light of soul and of good. "Let's get it on." He whispered as his head lowered once more. The walk of his feet across the tile floor opened to him forever in a moment. A flex of time and he was away, away from the emergency room. What he saw was beautiful lights bright and very blue mixing with white. A voice with no words told him what to do. "They will come to you, you will know who they are." A stop in walk caused a loss of balance, he sat in a nearby chair in the ER. Jen found him once more. He saw her walking toward him. "A vision of angel tis true tis true." words slipped from him as if he was under the influence of alcohol. But he was under the influence of an awakening that would not cease its want of his walk and way. He turned his eye away from the souls that were lingering. Shutting them off from vision of within he walked that line of reality known to most and spirituality known to a few. Jared was remembering the way and the walk of his spirituality. His gift to see souls to move with time and to heal was just part of what he knew he had to do and would do now that it had returned. Jen pulled him up to her off of the chair he sat in. Oblivious to the people around he whispered to her, "I need you tonight." She could not believe nor understand the feel she had with such simple words. If a heart could melt, hers would have at that moment. She pushed hard against him and pulled his kiss to her mouth. The patient in the bay across from them just smiled. "Nice," he said with a smile and a grab of groin. He was a psych patient and would use this bit of sensuality to spur his want to jerk off. It seemed he had a bit of a sexual addiction. Jared and Jen felt the energy of lust fly at them from the side. He was jerking off to their left. "Talk about ruining a moment dude." He suddenly stopped but it was too late, the patient's orgasm was complete. They walked away and tried to act professional but smiled as they walk into the privacy of the trauma room.

The trauma room was the busiest room at times and also the room where people complained and compared notes on the good looking ones in the ER or the gossip on the new person or the old one that didn't do their work. Jared kissed her once more as a trauma decided at that moment to intrude. "Gunshot wound to the abdomen." EMS began giving their report but Jared heard nothing but a pounding of his heart. Light filtered through him from her glance, he was in love. How can he be in love? He had never been in love. Wait a minute what the hell is love. Immediately he argued and denied the feel of weakness and possible pain. She was wealthy and a nurse she won't.... "Move it bud we need to put this patient on the stretcher." EMS had landed and Jared and Jen needed to get out of dodge.

They walked quickly away. "Let's hide in the on call suite." One of those little rooms where docs have to sleep when they are on call. She had a twinkle in those eyes of hers and Jared nodded with agreement on hiding in a small room that had only a bed. "Sure!" Located in the glorious back hall of the emergency room therein lies the room. The door opened easily for some reason it wasn't locked. "Tonight there was no one on call it's all ours for the day and night." "Jen I am just..." she pushed her finger against his mouth "shh," they kissed gently, softly, slowly.

A pounding on the door shot a rip of adrenalin through both of them. Jen covered her mouth as Jared stood quickly to turn the button the door to lock it. The handle began to turn. Jared stood her up quickly turning her away from him as the door opened he acted as if he was untangling her hair from an invisible necklace. "Jen I cannot get this thing untangled," he said as seriously as he could. He knew the door was open behind him but no one had said anything yet.

"What are you doing in here?" Stephen the charge nurse pulled him quickly out into the hall. "You too young lady!" Stephen tried not to smile and used his best authoritative voice. "I was untangling her necklace, we both wanted to see what the on call room looked like and…" Jen just stood there and tried to untangle her invisible necklace. "Oh well of course," Stephen said and walked away from both of them. "Clean these stretchers Jared and Jen your patient in bed 12 needs some pain meds." He turned the corner and stopped for a moment. They thought he had gone back to the ER. "Whew that was a close one." He looked around the corner and yelled, "gotcha!" He walked back to them with a more serious look. "Jared, don't do anything of out of line at work in this room." He feigned a look of innocence. "Just last week we found two nurses in here doing the dirty, they were fired immediately do you want that?" He smiled then whispered, "but I don't blame you, you two make a great couple." Stephen walked back to the ER and without turning around said, "behave!"

"Jen I need to talk to you about some things." Suddenly whispers surrounded him. The light around Jen shifted. It wasn't her it was one of those lost souls wanting to mess with Jared. He wanted to tell it to leave and do the in the name of God thing, but somehow he didn't think it would work. And with that small doubt came the strength of darkness to begin its filter into him. His soul was a prize, he loved God and helped others to light. If they could get him to fall they would be able to rest for a time. He had spoken to the women of evil, they never slept unless they pulled someone away from God. The part in the bible, no rest for the wicked, was talking about the true beings or angels of the devil, that didn't get rest or the reward of rest unless they caused a soul to fall. The pod head humans just didn't realize it walked beside them daily, waiting for them to fail. With that moment of doubt a feel of depression and defeat was dragged through his body.

He pushed her against the wall and acted as if he wanted to take her there and smiled as she giggled. He ignored the entity the best he could and summoned all of his energy of light to push it away. Encircle it with light that will destroy it. Suddenly the back doors to the ER flew open and crashed against the wall. Jen jumped and leaned into Jared. He was calm he knew he just pushed the entity somewhere. He didn't know where but it wasn't around her. "I don't want you hurt in any way Jen." He leaned to kiss her and felt her trembling. I am strong Jared don't worry about me." She looked around him at the doors. "Why did they open like that?" "Most likely Stephen trying to get us to work," he said, she smiled. "We have a date tonight yes?" They walked back into the ER, he nodded. "We have a date in a couple of hours." He slapped her on her bottom just as the resident that had an interest in her walked past. She smiled and walked away to the patient to give pain meds, but the resident didn't smile. Jared felt his anger and just shrugged his shoulders.

The resident stopped for a moment and look him dead in the eyes. He pointed his finger at Jared and made one last attempt to get him to leave Jen alone. "You are not good enough for her c'mon man let the real men have her, she deserves the best." With a smile and another shrug he walked away from the frowning resident. Who suddenly looked very small in Jared's eyes. He had always felt less than for so many years because of his choices in career and play and he finally saw, he was no less than or better than any of these doctors, nurses or anyone in life.

One of the nurses called him over to help her with combative patient. It was Kim, she had long dark hair that she wore back in a pony tail. And a humor that he enjoyed and she had also done a rare thing. She had given birth to five children. "Help me Jared!" The patient was an older woman with eyes of wild and crazy. She was obviously out of her noggin either on drugs or just mentally not right. Kim had to put an IV into this wild one to give her some meds. "Calm down you are in the hospital we are trying to help you." He held her left arm with his right hand and her leg with his left hand. He felt like he had this side of her under control. Uma ran in to help and held the other side. Suddenly the feel of fingers of steel began to rip into his right butt cheek. He yelled out with a "Youch!" and moved his hips quickly to the left away from the patient and started to laugh. "She just tried to rip most of my bottom off!" Uma laughed so hard she let go of her arm. Kim was on the receiving end of a right cross that floated across and caught Jared square on the jaw. He fell back some but couldn't help but laugh. Kim joined the group in laughter as the patient just squirmed and sat up then dropped all the time her wild eyes seeing what she perceived were her enemies. They finally got her under control, the IV was in and away they went to another adventure in the ER.

Jared was floating this short day at work. A float turd doesn't have a team of patients but helped with the small jobs. Stocking the bays, helped where needed. An elderly lady was lying on a stretcher as he walked past. "Hello ma'am we will get you off that hard board in a little bit." Every patient that fell anywhere would be transported by EMS via neck brace and hard back board. She smiled at him and was very calm. "Thank you young man."

The very next room held another elderly lady. "Anything I can get for you?" She smiled then started to stand up. Grabbed the right side of her hip in pain she sat back on the stretcher. "Whoa sit down feisty one where are you going?" She shifted a little on the hard stretcher, "I

212

want to leave I'm ready to go I thought you were coming in with my discharge instructions." "I will check on it." Kim was her nurse. "Kim is she ready the lady in bed 7?" Kim still laughed at him getting goosed nodded with a smile. "Do you know she is 99 years old'?" "No way." He walked quickly back into her room. He always wanted to know the whys of life he asked his question that was always asked to the elderly patients. "What is the secret of life? Have you figured it out yet?" She smiled a little then spoke quickly on her likes. "Well I never drink any of that pop, that is not good for you." Jared always enjoyed his pop he didn't like hearing this. "I walk a lot and eat red meat." She grabbed her hip again. "You don't look comfortable let me help you back in the stretcher." She was no bigger than a minute. With one lift and slight pull she was sitting better in the stretcher and looked much more comfortable. "Thank you young man you are very nice." "I will check on your papers."

Kim stood right behind Jared with her instructions. She had a broken hip, but it wasn't not enough of a break for her to need surgery. A broken hip and barely a complaint, a generation of strong types that didn't exist in this day. Jared walked back to the main ER very impressed with her. Jen walked past him quickly moving toward one of her motorcycle trauma patients. He was not doing well. He was doing over eighty miles per hour on his bike and crashed. "How is he Jen?" He leaned on the stretcher rail as he watched Jen work the meds for the patient. She was genuinely concerned and genuinely frustrated.

"He is not doing and won't do. I have to get him up to the OR immediately." Blood from the patients left ear poured down onto the stretcher. A small pool formed at the base of his head. His eyes were swollen shut and purple was the color of his eyelids. "He is paralyzed from the neck down he has a head bleed and I have no idea what they will do with him at the OR but they want him now." Jared got the portable monitor to put with the patient for transport. "I will help you Jen calm down some you didn't do this to him." Jen continued to arrange and push meds through his IV. Calming some she looked at Jared. He was strong in so many ways. She had so much respect for him and she felt such a love with him. She shook her head then looked back down at the syringe she pushed the meds and sighed. "I know what you feel Jen I feel it also, that's why we need to talk."

A shift once more of those invisible types moved around Jared. He ignored them wondering why they appeared at times and at other times they were gone. He looked at her to see if she saw them or felt anything. She shifted some then looked outside the bay then back to Jared. "Do you feel that?" "What Jen? Feel what?" Jared was still resting on the stretchers railing. The blood oozed faster out of the mans ear. The feel of not comfortable grew. Jared could see them as if they were drawn like casper. But Jen only felt them. "Jared suddenly I feel very uncomfortable." Jared walked over to her. "Jen it's just your patient and your compassion," he pulled her hand to his. "You have too much compassion ya know." She relaxed with his touch and smiled back at him. "You are right let's get him up to the OR." The entities floated around him, they whispered obscenities into his ear, he heard words that were not words, knew what they were saying. Not one bit of fear was within him. Casually moving to prepare the trauma patient he visualized his light from his own soul wrapping the casper's up and tossed them out the door. It didn't work. "Damn." Jen heard him "What?" "Damn I wish we were off of work I want some alone time with you." He satisfied her yet still was confused on how to make those left over's go away.

Suddenly one of the docs walked up to him. Dr. Mack patted Jared on the shoulder. "You do a fine job son." Jared saw Dr. Mack look at the area where the casper ghost things were. They were suddenly wrapped up in a blue light and flung away. Dr. Mack smiled at Jared then walked back to his little desk near the nurses station. Jared was left standing there in dismay. He knew, he saw them. Jen was ready for them to go to the OR with the patient. Jared continued to look back at the doc. Respiratory showed up to bag or push air into the patients lungs as they traveled to the OR, the vent would follow.

Not often was Jared at a loss but this time smacked him to his core. In one part of him he was confused yet the other was ecstatic. There was someone who could help him get rid of the leftover souls that followed him around. Suddenly Jen threw a curve his way. "Jared I see something around you it is clear but liquid in movement." Looking quickly behind him there was a new one. A lingering leftover soul, but this one just needed help to find it's way out of this plane. "Yes I see it also Jen." She whispered something and it moved quickly up and away. "What did you say?" She winked at him. "I will tell you later." The doc looked at both of them.

They finally got the patient to the OR. "Alone at last now tell me what you said to those ghost thingies." He pushed the stretcher faster and winked at her. "We will talk of such things on our date if we ever get on a real one." Jared passed one of the OR techs. She smiled at him then started to walk with him while he pushed the stretcher back to the ER. "Hi Jared haven't seen you in a long time." Jared looked at Jen quickly and tried to act casual about this ladies advances. "I have been busy Mary I'm sorry about that." 'Well call me sometime I miss watching you hustle pool." Jared turned the corner to the elevator, Jen turned away from him.

A woman can cause silence to feel as heavy as a million pounds of pressure on your lungs. "Jen?" She didn't turn. Pushing on the elevator button in a repetitive manner she was showing her jealousy. "Jen? Are you not speaking to me now because of one woman's comments?" The elevator door opened and there stood the resident. The one that wanted her, the one she used earlier to get Jared jealous. "Great," was all that came out of his mouth. Jen lit up once more and seemed happy to see him. "Hi Jen what are you and the tech doing?" He asked as he looked down her then back up, blatantly checking out every part of her body.

216

Before Jen could speak Jared answered quickly and calmly, leaning against the wall of the elevator he crossed his arms tightened his muscles for a moment and attempted to calm down. "Falling in love." The resident stood back and allowed the stretcher to be pushed into the small elevator. Jen was pushed a little against him due to the lack of space. The resident liked this a lot and took full advantage of it. Turning slightly acting as if he was just adjusting for the small space, he pushed against her. "Falling in love you say, well, well congratulations." His arm went around her shoulder as he pulled her into him further. Jared turned to face the door he didn't want to see this exchange. Not wanting to see that she was not stopping his advances nor did she acknowledge his words of love.

The elevator moved like molasses through ice water. Jared just wanted off the elevator and as far away from this feel that he could get. He needed to toughen up or something. Being around her was making him into a total weak idiot. "What was I thinking?" His words shattered the silence and slammed into Jen. She knew she needed to do something, say something quickly or she would lose him.

"Well techs don't have to do much thinking Jared that's why you don't make any money." The resident laughed at him then pulled Jen closer. Jen couldn't move away there was no space to move away. Jared had his back to the two of them. "Do you play pool?" The resident asked with a cocky tone. Jared turned and saw them together it caused his stomach to turn. He grabbed quickly at his gut and

217

doubled over. The resident smiled, "yes I could even beat you at a game of pool." "Jared are you ok?" Jen asked and tried to push the resident off of her. But he wasn't budging he enjoyed this moment. Jared felt as if something was literally punching him in the stomach. The elevator door opened finally allowing him to leave quickly. He left her with the resident and the stretcher. He had to get away from the resident. Something was attacking him physically and distance was what came to mind, away from that space and that resident.

Jen could not get him to let her pass. He pulled her harder against him. The elevator door closed but no button was pushed so it remained on the first floor of the hospital. "Let me go Jonathan I need to see if Jared is ok." He pressed his lips against hers and slid his tongue deep inside her mouth. She bit down on his tongue and pulled away falling onto the stretcher that was still in the elevator. His eyes seemed dark with no light. The darkness folded in on itself wrapping and looping. She tried to fight him off but he was on top of her. Jared felt a pull back to the elevator. He could hear Jen calling for him. Her voice was in his head as clear as if she were standing in front of him. Still holding his stomach he pushed the button on the elevator to cause it to open its doors.

He saw the resident pushing her down and he began to unzip his pants. Jen looked at Jared her eyes screamed for help. "What the hell is wrong with you get off of her!" The resident heard nothing but the moans of Jen. Jared shoved him against the wall off of her. His arousal was evident and hanging out for both of them to see. Jen rolled away onto the stretcher then out into the hall. Anger was an interesting animal, giving the holder of this emotion a couple of options, extra energy to pummel the one that created the anger or extra energy to close the doors in the soul so the pain of anger being spewed would not harm. Jared had the pummel mode kick in. His fist was finding the depth of this residents stomach cavity. Along with ribs that began to crack as he continued to introduce his fist into his frustration and jealousy with the resident

"Stop Stop!" The resident covered his head and body but to no avail. Jared was in the land of lost heated anger. There are times when anger was no longer justified and there is the rub. Darkness had shifted and found Jared's light of soul. Filtered with clouds of negative thoughts of negative feel. Feeding the anger frenzy Jared heard a voice of calm. A voice telling him to "stop." He slumped forward against the resident for a moment then walked away. The elevator doors had been trying to close but the stretcher was sticking out some causing them to stay open. Jen was there her eyes full and wide with shock and pain of the whole affair.

The resident slipped down the side of the elevator and fell unconscious. "Jared you have to help him!" He looked at him on the floor. With an inhale he pulled his calmness back to himself. With an exhale he moved the dark spit of anger away from himself. His hands rested upon his chest where he felt the broken ribs, sending light he began to heal him. The pain filtered into himself and it was not a good pain. With a moan he continued to heal the resident that he had just beaten. Moving his hands down to his stomach he saw internal bleeding and a torn liver. Jen stood at the door and watched all of what was happening. She felt the heat of light but there was no light. She saw it with her soul. "How do I see this, feel this." Jared heard her but continued. He must fix the damage he had done. He was wrong to have hurt this man this badly, very wrong.

The resident began to awaken, something interesting occurred when Jared healed others. They knew he was the one that healed them. They felt his energy they saw his hands like light move through them fixing the breaks and the bleeds. The resident knew what Jared was doing. No words found their way out of his mouth or mind. He just relaxed in the hold of what felt like pure love. Jared doubled over in pain he was finished with the healing but must make it leave himself. Still unaware of how to heal others without hurting he stumbled back out of the elevator. Jen stopped him, held him. "I love you Jared." Suddenly the feel of agonizing pain left him. There was a loud noise against the wall across from them. He saw darkness that swirled churning as if to regroup but then it was enveloped by light.

This light was not like the light we see from light bulbs and candles. It was seen with the eye of the soul and it was pure light stronger even than that of the suns heat brighter than that of the suns brightness. The resident also saw the light as the darkness exploded away. Jared turned to walk back in and help him to a standing position. He pushed the stretcher back out into the hall. He motioned for Jen to help him with the contraption so they could get back to work. Jared expected nothing from the resident no words were needed. "Jared....I.." He walked toward Jared his entire being had shifted in stance and in stature. "I have been a pretty arrogant son of a bitch I want to thank you for.." Jared nodded and continued to push the stretcher. "No problem dude see you in the ER." He paused then added with a smile, "God did it, thank Him."

Jen smiled at him as she pulled the front of the stretcher guiding it. He smiled at her watched her move and felt more alive than he has ever in his life. Looking down he watched once more his feet move across the floor. The resident didn't follow them instead he walked outside for a feel of the air and to think about what just happened.

"I love you too Jen," he said but the stretcher creaked as he said it and there were two phlebotomists walking past them that smiled at him followed it with an "awww." "We have two more hours here then we are free to talk of the Jen and Jared events." "Events huh, we are just events?" His hair was unruly and flying out of control more than ever. "My hair is acting like static electricity is pulling it away." A voice once more fell into his mind. "You did well." Faith was an interesting animal. Jared found that he liked faith much better than anger.

Chapter 27

They walked into the ER and find several traumas occurring. Three teen age types found pushed into the back of their cars, no seat belts worn, no way to tell who the driver was. Since Jared was floating he helped with the many trauma's. Jen pushed him into the room blowing him a kiss, her mouth moved with the words I love you. "I don't feel a pulse, we need CPR now!" Jared pulled the CPR stand over to the stretcher. It allowed the pusher to be above the patient. His hands on the chest of the teenager pushed to pump the meds that were being delivered through central lines. He pushed to pump the oxygen that was being given by the respiratory therapist through the bag valve mask. He pushed to become the heart and do what it does so easily every day every second. His sweat began to drop on the young one. "Stop compressions." The docs looked to see if there was any rhythm, if the heart was beating on its own yet. "Continue compressions." Jared felt the spirit of this man leave slowly. It seeped out of him like a leak in a rubber boat and the air was finding escape. He pushed harder and faster. Suddenly two ribs broke, a common occurrence while doing CPR but he kept pushing. He heard them call TOD, time of death, of the other teenager in the other trauma bay. He pushed harder and faster he began to yell "'No!" to this fresh of life, but nothing worked. He was too badly broken inside he was bleeding out. He was bleeding internally everywhere and his heart had stopped. They told Jared to stop compressions but he couldn't. "No!" He was gone for a moment into the feel of the young soul. He heard him cry to be still alive, just as suddenly as he heard this he heard a whisper of "'release me." He stopped immediately, sweat fell freely from him, his arms were pumped from the compressions. He heard a silent "thank you for trying," floated into his mind with that way of voice with no voice. Suddenly he saw the soul of the young one move across to the other bay. There was a liquid feel of peace, "he was a good kid," he said as they closed the kids eyes. Jared had two bodies to put into bags. He watched as the soul of the other one lift and move the other away from the flesh. It was used to being in skin and muscles, of mind and blood, that the soul sometimes got confused, and didn't leave.

He saw darkness move into the room and filtered around the other teenager. It seemed to infiltrate him pulling on him. Jared pushed a thought of get lost to the dark and caused it to stop and moved across to him. But Jared had such a light it could not touch him. The docs snapped their fingers in Jared's face. "Bag em Jared, wake up son." Everyone left the room after the call of death occurred. Some of the nurses stuck around to do their paper work. But he was left alone with the bodies. He called for Jen to come to the trauma room. She quickly came in to help him. "I need you to turn this dead kid so I can put the body bag under him." "Oh just what I wanted to do today." She rolled the body over to her she smiled wanting a kiss from Jared. Jared smiled while pushing the bag under the freshly dead kid.

Suddenly without warning the kid passed gas. Now Jared had learned to stop breathing in rooms when odors found their way, this was an immediate cessation of breath. No one wanted to breathe in the fresh gas of a dead person. He pushed the bag under the kid and moved away gasping for air. Jen could not stop laughing as she held the dead boy.

Jared walked back to the dead boy. "We share such wonderful moments together Jen." She felt time slow to a stop while she looked into his eyes. Whispers found them both whispers of soft and of light. Suddenly there was a swirl of light that fell in the center of the trauma room. Jared moved quickly over to Jen to protect her. No one was in the room but the column of light and Jen and Jared. It was pulsing with a vibration that caused both of them to have a little trouble breathing. The column of light flexed and fluxed mixing with blue it was a blue light flowing pulsing. Jared had his arms outstretched to protect Jen. They were lifted to a time away from the emergency room. They saw souls fall into darkness with screams of agony. They saw souls lift with a light that covered pulling them close with that aroma of life and love. "Where are we?" He asked the light but knew the answers were inside him. As suddenly as it started it ended. The bodies of the teenagers were there still cold and Jen was still holding the one.

"Jared?" She asked and lets the kid roll back onto the body bag.
"Jared we need to talk darlin what are you involved in?" "There is a
224

line we will walk Jen, we will walk together." She closed her eyes to hear him. "You belong with me as I with you, we have something to do I don't quite know yet but we are to be as one." Jen liked this feel of being with Jared. Looking at her watch she moaned. "Will this day never end?" She walked over to him pulling his face into her hands and looked into his eyes. "We are one Jared I have waited for you," she paused when two docs walk into the room. One of them was the resident that Jared saved after he nearly killed him. Jonathan stammered a little then spoke, "Hi Jared and Jen need any help here?" He was afraid of Jared and Jared didn't like his fear. "Jonathan everything is ok dude please relax." Jonathan began to cry. The other doc had already walked out not wanting anything to do with the fresh dead bodies. "I see everything differently now I don't know how to thank you, both of you." He looked at Jen through his tears and whispered, "I am sorry Jen so sorry." Jared reached to shake his hand. "We are one Jonathan and Jen is mine." He smiled at him he and waited, he laughed nervously, "yes she is yours and you are someone very special ..I" Jared stopped him in mid-sentence. "No Jonathan you are a doctor you are special and gifted. Follow the feel and the flow of this new way of thought Jonathan and you will be ok at the end of time."

The child that found a toy of fresh and new holds it carefully waiting to discover it's special gifts of pleasure. Jonathan had been given a new life and a new path his eyes would look for the good not the negative in souls and in flesh. Jared saw this in him, nodding at him he pushed him out of the trauma room. "Go and learn how to heal people doc, as they say down south, get er done."

Humble was a wish that most wanted a doctor to be. This man would now be humble and treat with his heart not with his ache for money or his want for easy fixes. "Jen go back out to your patients I will take care of this." Jen had always had some kind of knowledge of the other way of time. The spiritual realm that walked beside, but she had never seen it so clearly nor felt it as she had with Jared on this day. Do I want to know this? Her questions followed a wish to run away with him. To pull him to her mansion gather her monies and run off to play on this planet, this life, before their souls were pulled from their flesh to serve into eternity. "I don't want to go. Let's run away Jared lets go play." Jared smiled as he zipped up the body bag slowly stopping just at the boys neck. The family will want to view him. "We have things to do first Jen then I will consider giving you the honor of my company." She hit him on the arm hard, "you are being a jerk." She went back out to the ER and looked at the clock once more. "Almost time for a real date!" Jared answered quickly, "Oh baby, oh baby, oh baby yea."

Chapter 28

He listened as she walked away. Looking down at the boys face, he lowered his head with a wish. "Guide me because I'm just a pool hustler and a tech." A low growl was heard but he ignored it thinking it was his imagination or maybe his stomach growling. Putting a sheet over the body bag he began to cover the evidence of the medical attempt to save their son. Family was ok with seeing comfy blankets and soft white sheets but not the plastic of a white body bag covering their loved ones face.

The day was filled with sunlight. Warmth followed the sun and the play in life began. Job security for hospitals, people don't play safely. Jared wanted to be out in the sun and away from this old visitor. A gift they say more like the curse they also say. When a body of life was given vision to see the altered reality in life called the lands of spiritual, the plank of normal walk was removed leaving the one of gift alone with only their faith.

Circling in his thoughts was Jen and a bunch of dead people bothering them both for the rest of their lives. "Bunch of dead people," he mumbled and went back to the ER.

A shrill scream from the ER created a visual of a haunted house. Walking back into the mess of bodies, ill and screaming he smiled seeing Jen leaning to give a patient some meds. Her black hair and contrasting skin of that velvet kind caused a heat to move from within him. Another contrasting moment was the feel of anger from a restrained patient lying on a stretcher in a room as he walked past. Balance in life. She was restrained and talked with slurred speech. Needing help so she screeched. Jared leaned into the room, "what do you need ma'am?" She looked to see who was walking into the room. Lying flat on her back legs stuck open from the leather restraints on her ankles she was in very much a vulnerable state. Her hands equally bound by the restraints completed the picture of a normal out of their head patient in the ER. One cannot walk around half naked in the emergency room. If one does one will be tied down to bed. "Come here I can't see you." She said with a slur to Jared. He leaned over her to let her see his smiling face. "Why don't you feel my titties while you are in here?" Her eyes were glassed over but the point was made. "I don't think so ma'am that's not in my scope of skill as a tech." He got out of there quickly not wanting to be accused of accosting her. She had a spiral of dark types falling into her every thought. Jared wanted no part of that. Her nurse was Darren, he was one of high morals and just a plain ole good guy. Darren patted him on the back as he walked past heading into the room with the wild lady. "Be careful in there," Darren smiled, "hey Jared." He finished mixing some meds for the patient and looked at him. "Be careful with these meds? Oh heck I know what I am doing." He walked into the room. Jared waited. Looked at his watch as just a few seconds went by before Darren walked quickly back out of the room. "Told you to be careful

228

in there." Darren looked a little bit pale, "you ok?" "I just vomited in my mouth." She asked me to do some pretty nasty sexual things to her. I will never be the same." Jared smiled at him, "you will forget it soon," he passed his hand over his head and acted as if he was doing the Jedi thing and caused his mind to forget what just happened. With a zombie walk away from Jared he nodded and repeated in a monotone voice. "I will forget it soon."

"I can lift my legs for you," the large patient says quietly as he walks into her room. She needs to be cleaned and has requested her tech to do this duty of non-pleasure. She comes to the ER to get touched, not to get treatment for any illness, just her perverted illness to be touched by medical staff. He started to refuse but a new tech walked up "I will help you Jared." He stepped to the side, he didn't want the soon to inhale the odor of lost lands from between her legs. She said quickly as the wash rag approached her, "I can lift my legs for you," with one quick movement, she moved like a contortionist. Her legs literally beside her head, exposing what was the most expansive amount of flesh with matching odor, that he had ever witnessed or had the honor to smell. He stopped to breathing and watched the slow motion of the other tech wiping this patient of weird. "You are very flexible," Jared stated flatly trying not to gag. The sheer size of her vagina was at least a foot long from top to bottom.

It was not the size that was disgusting, it was her legs planted neatly at her side with that look of glee on her face that was disgusting. She lowered her legs with the same speed she lifted them as the other tech finished the task. He tried to get out of the room but the doc stopped his motion of walking away as she walked up. "Jared assist me with this pelvic exam." He contorted his face with the loudest silent look of no he could conjure but it didn't work. "Certainly," he said with no enthusiasm.

He stepped to the side of the patient and waited for the words, the doc informed the patient the need for pelvic because of her reasons for being at the ER. The patient smiled as the doctor began to lean to get into position to slip the speculum into the ladies vagina. "I can lift my legs for you." Swoosh, with one swift movement of an acrobat, the legs rise and stay in their place of trained. The doc just said " well, well," as the speculum went in, the doc visibly gagged.

Ending the exam quickly she left the bay. He left the bay, they all left the bay. Jared felt like he was traumatized for life. He may never want to touch a woman again. Smiling at that thought he commented out loud, "nah." The day continued as he begged the doctor to discharge her. Her visit was a bad moment that would take twenty thousand years to remove from his mind.

Patients have at times accused nurses and docs of doing some nasty things to them. It's usually a good thing to have someone come into the room with you with those types as a witness. But sometimes an accident occurred and something may be construed as a sexual act. A doc struggled one day with his procedure, he needed to check the ladies bottom for blood. Which involved putting a finger up the bottom. The doc needed a female to witness the exam not male. Jen walked past the room and was pulled in by the female tech to help assist. A few minutes later a very red faced doc walked past Jared out of the room. Jared looked into the room and saw Jen laughing that silent laugh. Her shoulders moved but no sound was coming out. "What Jen?"

The patient was also laughing, while doing the exam, the doc turned the patient on her side and proceeded to insert his finger into the wrong opening. As he probed she quietly stated, "you are in the wrong hole." He said his apologies put on new gloves and finished the rectal and walked out quickly. Hence the red face. Jared began to laugh as the patient told the story. "Woohoo, I haven't had sex in three months I'm going to tell all of my friends to come to Mayville's emergency room!"

After the patient was discharged the staff began the humor. "We will have doctor long finger see you next time." On and on it went as the light of a bit of sleight of hand and slip of finger found laughter in a place of usual sadness. The flight of duty the way of need found Jared once more as he had to help with a procedure, holding someone's leg so that the ortho people could put a screw through it to hold it in traction. It's on the kind of cool factor meter. But holding an obese man with legs three feet wide so the nurse could locate his very small penis, or 'unit' is what he called them at work, was not fun. This day with much effort he had to hold a thigh that was as big as Jared's torso, as the nurse tried to find the smallest piece of equipment Jared had ever seen. The body shouldn't by the laws of life be allowed to grow as much as it does. Why does nature do this to human kind? He couldn't figure out the reason for obesity. To cause people to be trapped in these huge vessels. Why? Was it a punishment from past lives? The mans unit was found and the catheter was inserted with a result of wonderful urine. Walking quickly out of the room Jared had no judgment on this one of large, just compassion. As he walked down the hall too many thoughts of the why's of things pulled him into its chamber.

Borrowed?

This breath of air we so easily pull inward without pleasure of giving back the wish of thank you. Clothes are borrowed as well, the books upon the shelf, the car we drive, all borrowed. Is it too fresh to say we borrow this birth of life also? Of course not, we know we are mortal and our flesh so easily ages with time of smiles and frowns, ups and downs, etc...

Why do I trample among the leaves, pushing a foot into the reality that they were borrowed by the tree? Now we see the beauty of colors and gasp, oh so wonderful this plethora of colors and shapes. But we witness the end of a life, albeit, not of the flesh that we are accustomed to, but life nonetheless.

So, do we find that life when ending its borrowed function, has a beauty unlike its lifetime? But I have seen the end of life across the trauma table at the emergency room. And that is not a sight of beauty; it is barely something that can even be witnessed. So we find the beauty of the end of life has to be seen with different perspective.

The beauty of death from this life, is the belief that the energy, or soul that we hold within this shell, is magnificent and now set to fly into the place of real birth. Yet, the shell does not have the beauty that nature gives for our pleasure, when death occurs with humans. The opposite occurs, almost as if to show us, this is not the life that we feel to our depth, it is just fragile meat and bones. We grow accustom to

233

the sight of eyes with soul behind, the walk of our muscles through our emotions. When the body is emptied of the energy of the stars, we turn away. Closing the shell up into a bag, or burning with flames.

Borrowed time they say, borrowed life, is what we explore. When something is used, we take it to its limit. Enjoy the flavor of the peach and the texture of the ground beneath our feet. Every item we use or supposedly own it is just that temporary and borrowed.

What does this tell my thoughts? Borrowed, they are also, to grow into another and yet another. To witness the change of seasons with nature is beautiful, even with the tree's trunk. As its bark ages the depth of valleys cause us to look and almost see and taste the history this tree has witnessed. How often have you leaned against a tree and wondered at the sights it has been allowed to have move across its bark?

We have energy surrounding... within   without .... always, and very much...borrowed, or could it be said, should it be whispered, the only thing not borrowed, is our soul...

Chapter 29

He was wanting to play some pool, kiss some Jen and relax under the stars but alas not yet. His continual thought on life and ways of walk was subdued. The gloves came off his hands quickly as he snapped them from a distance into a garbage can. "Two points," one of the chaplains came up to him and pressed herself against him. The feel of her breast was very obvious as his arm was the object of her affection. "Well hello Laura and how is your day?" She continued to hold his arm against her breast. Walking away quickly from her, he had no idea what that was about. But his walk away was too late, Jen moved right up to him. "Come here Jared I need your assistance in this room." "What patient needs help Jen?"

The smile was already there. "Damn you Jared why are women all over you all the time?" She pulled him hard back to the break room. "Jen calm down, I did nothing wrong." Jared learned at this moment that telling a woman to calm down was damaging in all arenas. "Don't!" there was a pause between words. If time could still now Jared could possibly escape the next word but time doesn't sit still. "Tell me to calm down." The feel of her breast was against his arm he liked that very much. "Jen I.." No words mattered, the jealousy god had been dinged like the bell on a counter at a hotel. The summon was loud and the path unfolded. He knew he was in for a bit of her energy to be thrown at him like rain on the street. "Jen..I" She stopped him once more. Not with any physical movement, just with her glance. "I am innocent," he said softly waiting for her wrath.

A woman's wrath doesn't mix with a way to prepare. She flew at him with anger at that woman's touch. He watched her words fly at him but felt only love from her. The break room was empty but for a moment. The filter of people was not of real, those damned dead people found them again. They were wanting to feel this jealousy she had, they swarmed around both of them. Jared wondered if she felt the souls that were pushing pretty hard against him and her. She suddenly slowed her words, she felt the push of those souls that wanted in on the energy. "Go away you are not wanted here!" She said to the not welcome entities, but Jared for a moment thought her words were aimed at him. "Damn Jen I didn't do anything wrong she pushed up against me, damn!" He started to walk away from her and the feel of anger, he was confused. She let his arm go with a sadness suddenly filling her. "No," she felt a pull from her core as he walked out. "Jared?" He was upset with her games and her lack of trust. But was it he who was not trusting and he who was playing the game?

Insidious was dark in life. The ride was on the dark side as Jared walked quickly away from her. His anger was out of place and made no sense but he still felt it. Thrusting, slamming his fist against his locker door he was not a happy camper. "I didn't do a damned thing wrong yet she is upset with me?" Talking to himself was a normal occurrence. Anger with himself was not a normal occurrence. A growl was heard again this time he knew it was not his stomach. He saw the black of anger in the form of a misshapen animal. One leg and very unsteady it stood behind him. The voice was in his mind not in the walk of reality. "Great it's time again for a visit from you." The entity growled into him with words of disgust and berated him slowly. Slamming his fist against his locker once more Jared began to slowly break down. Tears found his face, tears found his soul. " I cannot live this way!" "You can be with us Jared, just follow us." His fist hit the wall, he ignored the beast that stood behind him. He repeatedly hit the wall putting a hole in it. Jen was the last thing on his mind, Jen was the only thing on his mind.

Chapter 30

She stood in the break room and missed him, wanted him to come back, needed him to know she loved him. Not understanding why he left with so much anger. She straightened up and wiped a small tear off her cheek and looked at the time. Almost time to leave with "Jared," even his name comforted her. She wanted to find him. She left the lounge quickly and would get him to snap back to reality. He seemed to have shifted somehow and she wanted him back to his normal of gentle and kind self.

The souls of black she felt around her, but with one slight hand raised they moved away quickly. The push was strong and fast away from her. They found him, they fell against him, they knew him. Jared suffered this day because of another woman's advances. What was he to do? The ER called him back he didn't want to see Jen. She caused him to feel less than, made him feel worse than he already felt about everything. The hours were finally closing and he could leave work soon. He turned on his phone and waited for John to call, he wanted to get away and play pool. To hell with the date with Jen. He was not in the mood for games or to be made to feel the fool. He needed to know where his van was, hopefully John had it.

The entity reached with long fingers of leathery feel complete with nails long and dirty. It touched him slightly and caused him to shiver with disgust. Fear followed quickly and enveloped him. Darkness was only strong when fed, fed with fear, anger, jealousy. Jared felt a whisper inside. He wondered how he could feel this but it was there. With this whisper was love. Gentle in touch and word. "Love." Just saying the word caused the entity to withdraw it's touch. Shriveling into a ball of black it fell away to the floor then under the door of the locker room. It roamed the halls to invade whoever had a weakness that would allow it in, he was left alone.

Circles are continual; they surround and grow but are always circular. Keeping something inside or keeping something away. Jared had a circle of darkness around him. Put there by his own will. "Is this a test once more?" Memories went to the past and the dance of tests. When one was enlightened and eyes were opened to the supernatural. Faith had to be and would be tested. Would you still remain humble, after you healed a person, would you remain humble, after you saw into the future, would you hold onto the light in life or gather the darkness of negative around you to use at your bidding. For, they wait for you to call on them and therein lies the rub. The power and the knowledge of power on earth given to the one, if just a whisper to the way of dark found it's mark then that place of tease began. Difficult to let go of power, that power to hurt someone if they messed with you by sending a thought to the ones of dark to flip the motorcycle they were riding, or to cause their bike to mysteriously get hit by a car. Yea, it was real but so was the light. And sometimes just sometimes, people would be protected by God. The mark against the soul would be on the user of the bad guys energy. Jared knew the tests but this one had him for a moment. Somehow a piece of darkness had found a resting place inside him and he was unaware of it.

Jen walked up to the men's locker room door pounding on it. "Jared open this door now!" Without hesitation he opened it and faced her. He was angry playing the part of angry but didn't know why he felt this so deeply. "Jen I can't live with this constant ache and pain then anger and love you drive me crazy!" Light was an interesting thing. It opened the eyes with warmth it also heated the body if light from the sun. But light from the soul was stronger than any light known to mankind. He, for an instant saw her soul. Light from her eyes shined like none he had ever felt or seen. A thousand words of love and calm began to remove the anger. A thousand silent words being carried by the light of her soul through her eyes, found him. She saw his shoulders drop, his whole body relaxed. "Jen I love you." He pulled her into his arms. The world was a place of noise and dark, their world felt right, it was an easy wonderful feel. Her lips slightly opened caused him to hungrily reach but slow his push against her. Calm down some Jared, talked to himself trying to control his want for her. His arousal was evident and he cared not that she knew. She leaned into him wanting the feel of his kiss, the taste of his mouth. She felt his want against her, she softened and began an ache like she had never felt. She could fall to the floor at that instant to allow him to move inside her thrusting into her depth. Just as they began to touch lips Uma walked out into the hall.

"Oh I am so tired I must go home!" She walked to the ladies locker room, smiled at Jared and Jen. "You two need to get a voom oh my goodness you are both droolink." They pulled away but still felt the twist of each other's wants. "Uma hush you kaluk sheizer!" Uma opened the door and walked away from them.

"There you two are!" Stephen acted as if he didn't see them holding each other. "Jen your patient in bed four needs some pain meds and Jared stop distracting the nurses." He went back into the ER waited for Jen to come back but smiling at the two. "A good match." Jen straightened herself as she touched Jared's arm sliding it slowly down finally letting go. She looked at her watch and whispered, "almost time for our date." Jared answered quickly, "yes our date." They turned away from each other walking to different ends of the hall to enter the ER from different doors. He reached to adjust his arousal trying to think of something to make himself relax it some. "Baseball, billiards, Uma!" He immediately began to slow in his arousal with the thought of Uma near him.

Jen had to remove her ache it was almost difficult for her to walk. "Oh my goodness." She grabbed her head trying to stop the spin of his touch of his glance. The sound of a patient vomiting erased all ache immediately, her walk became easier. The splatter of this vomit was heard as it hit the floor with amazing skill and loudness. She made her way over to the nurse's counter to mix the drugs needed for bed four. The very loud very distinctive sound of a skull hitting the floor was heard throughout the ER as everyone ran to bed nine where the sound was coming from. Jared and Jen arrived simultaneously. The patient was on the floor her heels hit the floor with every shake. She was seizing. Stephen shook his head. "I told her to stay in bed but she kept standing up." Jared watched the flow of the nurses and the control of a situation that would scare many. The lady would have to be restrained to her bed for her own safety.

Jen leaned against him while they both watched the lady seize. With that simple touch against his hand Jared began to find arousal once more. He glanced down at his cargo pants, he wouldn't be able to contain composure much longer. "Jen I have to go help Darren over there." Pointing vaguely into the main ER he moved away from her touch. Jen just smiled feeling a heat once more in herself. "Contrasts I love and he is a contrast with me." Thoughts were alive created more thoughts that invaded reality causing action. Jen's thoughts would cause much action when she and Jared got off work. A smile of sensual escaped but not unnoticed. The phlebotomist was there watching the whole exchange. "Well Jen you and Jared have a thing... goin on.." She sang a little of the song then gave Jen a smack on the arm. "Better grab him up before I do, he is a hottie." Jen's daze carried her into visuals of making love, of laughter and long nights with talking of everything and sitting doing the nothings together that couples did. She wanted to take him everywhere. Show him the world. She had always had money just never someone to share it with, someone to care for, to live with, to love and sleep with. "Contrasts, yes we are a contrast." She watched him move through the ER, he was unaware. There was fluidity about him, every motion was smooth. She felt dizzy suddenly. The air around her felt thick and not good. She felt as if she was hyperventilating but she was breathing normally. The phlebotomist walked over to her. "Jen you are as white as a sheet are you ok?" Jen started to nod that she was fine. The phlebotomist grabbed her as she fell to the floor. "need help here!"

Everyone in the ER was used to this cry for help whether it was a prisoner running away or a combative patient. This time it was a co-worker unconscious on the floor. Jared looked over to see if help was needed not knowing it is Jen. He felt a shot of pain through his chest followed with a lack of air. He couldn't get his breath. Immediately he envisioned light wrapping around himself dispelling any dark that may be hiding in this invisible thrust against his literal throat. He saw a face with no eyes, empty are the sockets surrounded with black. This was a familiar face from the past, the past of demons and gifts and reality of the supernatural.

Still clutching his throat he gasped for air, he whispered, "I walk with the light and with God leave now!" The face turned away letting go of Jared's throat with hands of no hands. The only visible part that was barely human was a face without eyes. Moaning loudly the entity slammed through people while leaving the ER, Jared watched as the wall bowed just before it moved through it. Black covered the wall for a moment like an ivy that had no green. "Jared we need you over here!" A yell across the ER was finally heard by him, Jen was still unconscious. He inhaled deeply covering the air that filled his lungs with that taken for granted touch of oxygen. He recovered quickly and wondered why no one saw that he was in distress. "Jared!" He rushed quickly over to the commotion and expected to see another patient on the floor seizing. "Jen!" He pushed all away from her and knelt on the floor and lifted her into his arms. "Jen hear me, come back to me." He saw with the eyes of the other lands, an entity held her tightly and squeezed the breath out of her. He looked around frantically there were too many people to say anything of the spiritual nature. "Get her to the trauma room!" Jared lifted her from the floor but the entity remained on her. Away from some of the people finally he whispered for it to leave. With every spear of light he could muster he threw a blanket over her. "God help her, stop this thing please." Immediately there was a flash of bright light that caused him to stumble, he closed his eyes it was too bright. He fell to his knees he couldn't see. Jen began gasping for air. She opened her eyes to see him there with his eyes closed. Everyone was around them watching and yelling orders, wanting different meds to be thrown into her veins but she felt and saw only Jared. With a glance to her left she saw a small amount of light like a ball slowly dissolve around something black. "Jared open your eyes what are you doing?" The nurses and docs swarmed around Jen and pushed Jared away. "We have her now Jared go get a stretcher for her." He was always pushed away, never the one needed for the final anything. Good to do the grunt work not good enough to finish. Having a pitiful moment showed not good timing on his part. He sat back on the floor his eyes still closed he was very, very tired. Weakness was all that was in his every muscle. Slumped against the counter, left alone on the floor, he opened his eyes slowly. Jen was lifted away to a stretcher reaching and calling for Jared but the drown of everyone's yells removed him from her. He watched them take her to the trauma room. "Now if I can just stand up."

Religions teach us many things, some about God some about mans beliefs thrown in there mixing with fear and damnation. God had always been part of his life. Born and raised a Catholic Jared later in life learned that God was in everything and everywhere. No need to believe what men preach, trust in your heart and in love. Another wuss factor in him, love for life and for people. God saved Jen today now somebody save me. The x-ray tech saw him on the floor and hurried to his side. Her blonde hair fell against his face while she tried to lift him. "You have to help me a little here Jared." Her hands wandered some to his arms and felt his muscles instead of helping him up she decided to slip down to the floor next to him. They were behind the phlebotomist desk and the counter out into the main ER. So none of the patients could see them. "Stacy I will be ok you don't have to help me," he struggled to stand but this weakness was something very new to him. Battling this dark stuff was wearing him out. Stacy leaned against him pushed her breasts onto his arm and part of his chest. Why do women do this to men? Knowing he felt the softness of her round firm young breasts she giggled a little. "Let me help you up Jared or we could just stay here it's very comfortable don't you think?" Jared leaned away from her and stood on his own. Pushed once more another set of breasts away from him. Never thought I would be doing this. "Stacy I'm fine thanks." The other x-ray tech called her back to their cubby in the back of the ER. "Jared here is my phone number next time you go shoot pool please call me," she kissed him on the cheek but he pulled away quickly. The pull caused him to lose balance and fall against a rack of blood tubes holding full samples of blood. "No harm all is good," he quickly blurted out not wanting any more attention his way. Stacy reached to pull him up once more from the fall pulling him on purpose tightly against her. Without hesitation she dropped a kiss right smack hard on his mouth. Jared pulled away as gently as he could not wanting to hurt her feelings. "Stacy you go back to work we will talk." Reaching to trace his arms again she whispered, "call me tonight," she walked sensually away.

The phlebotomist watched the whole exchange. "Jared you are going to get in some kind of trouble if you don't balance your women at least see two that don't work in the same place." He leaned against the lab counter. Still weak and dizzy, Stephen called him over to him. "Jared you need to go home you are not well you cannot even stand up." Most of the ER was still in the trauma room with Jen. He agreed and limped slowly to the locker room. He stopped and asked quickly, "I get full time today yes?" He nodded. "Go home I will see you tomorrow." He was weak, It was the spiritual battle stuff again, It wasn't going away. The locker room was quiet. He sat on the bench in front of his locker and leaned against it. He closed his eyes and wanted his strength back he wanted happy back in his life. "I don't know if I can walk this path." Silence was his companion. He saw nothing in the spiritual realm or the real realm all was just normal and silent. His phone buzzed in his pocket but he ignored it. "I'm going to go sleep some." He knew Jen would be ok and that she would call him when they let her out of the trauma room, he relaxed in the thought that he did care for her very much. His P-coat felt heavy but also felt good. It was something real and it was his. It had never hurt him nor had it turned into a nasty looking entity. "My baby blanket," he patted it on the sides and walked past the mirror. He saw a weary old man. His phone was buzzing again in his pocket. Reaching it he turned it off. "Enough for today I'm going home." Silence was an interesting visitor.

Chapter 31

Jen fell asleep from the meds they gave her to calm her. There was nothing wrong with her all of her vitals are good. The docs put her in a bed to watch her for a few hours and did a cardiac work up. She tried to talk but nothing was going to be spoken from her mouth for hours. She was drugged, a perfect answer, when in doubt knock the patient out.

Dreams were interesting and scary and wonderful. But what are dreams? Jared was riding home in a cab. His van was still somewhere with John. Jen was dreaming of Jared. If thinking of someone can materialize them then it was working with him. He felt Jen sitting next to him in the cab. She leaned against his shoulder her hand reached and found his, perfect in time and imagination. "I could get used to this." The cab driver heard him, "get used to riding in a cab are you crazy?" Jared lowered his head, "no comment." His apartment was quiet. It seemed he was being given a break from the noise of dark and light and emotions. Sleep was what he would do. After dropping his clothes off at the door he enjoyed the feel of his skin against the air. He sat on the leather sofa which was cold but also felt good at the same time. "Ah contrast. "Jen loved contrast. Jared wanted to meditate, "time to clear the pipes."

Relaxing into the fresh silence given to him he immediately saw lights moving through and across his vision. Eyes remained closed but he was beginning to see with his spirit. Blindness was not a good thing to have in life. Blindness in sight or in that special place of vision from the soul. Even his thoughts created the knowledge of depth of mucho crazy stuff.

He saw Jen standing next to him. There was an endless ocean behind them. The sky was illuminated by lights with colors that don't even exist in the normal plane of existence. Colors washed over them, whites and blues, crystal blues surrounded both of them. Many smaller lights were rising above them lifting into a vast blue opening. It all fell into darkness and silly dreams as he fell asleep in the middle of his meditation. He began to snore, a loud snoring filed his apartment. The sofa held him as he fell over and curled up on the black leather temporary bed. Naked as a jay bird he slept. In his sleep were visions of Jen.

Chapter 32

John tired of not getting Jared on the phone jumped in the van to drive it back to his apartment. It was almost noon so he had to be home, he wasn't working and he wasn't answering his phone. John knew he wasn't with anyone. Jared hadn't gone out with anyone since Lori broke his heart. He always felt he needed to teach him how to bed a woman in five minutes without guilt. If a woman wanted to be taken give her what she needed no matter what she looked like. John grabbed himself, "gotta love the feel of that heat." The way to Jared's was past a lot of pool halls. Unfortunately for John he couldn't resist a pool hall. Especially one where there were beautiful ladies standing outside.

Reaching into the glove compartment he grabbed a thousand dollars and shoved it into his coat pocket. Looking into the rear view mirror he ran his fingers through his brown hair straightening it some. He stood outside the van and looked back inside it quickly to check out the back bench seat. "Ah memories." It's time to play pool and get some lovin. John called Jared one last time. The phone went directly into voice mail. "Ok Jared I'm at the pool hall on 4th and Wagner get over here as soon as you can." Flipping his phone closed he walked his cool walk over to the pool hall. He saw two blonde beauties waiting for him to show them a good time. At least in his mind they were. What he didn't see was the dark energy that filled them and surrounded them. What he didn't know was that they want him in more than a physical way.

Jared woke up freezing, he was curled up in a tight ball but that didn't help warm him. "'John! He yelled as he woke up. "John why am I yelling his name?" He slipped on some black sweat pants and a black cable knit sweater and tried to warm up some and get his bearings. Last thing he remembered was being weak from the spiritual battle and Jen being hurt. Now he wakes up yelling John's name. Picking his pants up off the floor he looked for his phone, it was shut off. I have to get in touch with John. Why such an urgency to get him? Why not more of one to get in touch with Jen? Damn questions circled in his head. The silence he was given was falling away to much noise. The phone took forever to power up. It showed he had a message from John. He put on some tennis shoes and called for a cab to take him to the pool hall. He tried to call him but John had his phone turned off. "Great John good timing there dude."

Jen woke up and wanted Jared, "where is Jared?" She asked the nurse, she was. getting ready to take Jen's IV out of her arm and send her home. "Jared went home sick it seems you both fell ill at the same time." Her mind shot thoughts of his safety and his wellbeing. "Get me out of here I need to find Jared" "You two have really hit it off haven't you Jen." Jen felt wonderful just thinking of him. "Yes, it's really strange he isn't even my type, but damn I can't stand to be away from him." She took out her IV. "Well I hope he feels the same I saw one of those x-ray techs all over him after you were taken into the trauma room." Jen stiffened hearing that and grabbed her chest, she tried to control the heat of pain that just found her heart. "It's those silly crushes those young kids get with the male techs." The nurse nodded a little and smiled one of those smiles of 'yea right.'

Jen rushed to her locker, she was still weak but was worried about Jared plus she missed him badly. Her phone was dead she couldn't call him. Her car never looked so good as she ran toward it. The drive to his apartment was short. He lived close to the hospital. Pulling up she didn't see his van. She remembered he told her he didn't have his van. She had never wanted to see anyone this badly in her life. His face, his eyes, his hair soft and just touched his collar. Even the way he carried himself. She wanted all of him and she wanted him now but where the hell was he? Knocking on the door she yelled his name, "Jared let me in," repeating that for a few minutes proved to be futile. He wasn't home. She needed to get her phone charged and call him, find him. She rushed back to her car and looked frantically for her phone charger. It wasn't in the car. While driving home she reached to feel him, from within. She knew somehow she knew she could talk with him with just a thought.

Jared suddenly felt a heat move through him as the cab pulled up to the pool hall. The same heat Jen created in him when she was near. His van was parked across the street. "Thanks for the ride," he tossed the dollars to the driver and got out but now wished he went to Jen's and not to the stupid bar. "Why the hell am I here?" The cab driver laughed, "son you have a problem you called me and wanted me to take you here." The cab drove away fast leaving him standing there in the sun. His sweat pants blew some in the wind, a wind that seemed to be getting pretty strong.

The pool hall looked different in the daylight. Jared usually went at night. It wasn't very crowded during the daylight hours. The types that were there were just young ones that were killing time. He saw John playing pool with a blonde lady. Her clothes told Jared she was one of the easy ways. "John!" he called from across the room. John kept shooting. "John!" Jared made his way over to him. Stopping suddenly he saw the reason why John couldn't hear him. He was surrounded by black. The energy was not good here. "Here we go again." He acted as if he didn't see a thing and pulled John away from the pool table stopping him from shooting. "Hey ole buddy ole pal what's up and where are my keys?" The conversation to all around concerned keys and nothing else. Jared saw the ones of dark all around them but with ignoring them he created a wall they couldn't penetrate. He didn't know why that worked but it did. John finally came out of his game mode face. "Jared, damn boy where the hell have you been it's good to see you!" He pulled Jared into a semi hug. John was not happy something was wrong. "I want my keys dude where are they? John took them out of his pocket "right here but.." he put them back into his pocket. "You need to play some pool with me for a while then we can leave." The lady that was near him walked away. A low rumble began or was it a growl, either way it was a sign for Jared and John to leave. "No pool right now I like playing at night John let's go." John was in an easy going mood so he immediately agreed with Jared. "Tonight is a promise yes? We play pool?" Jared walked John away from the table, "yes tonight, say goodbye to all the lovely ladies John."

Distance to a door was an interesting thing. Sometimes it was nothing like a walk in the park. Other times, like now, it was a forever walk. When a man the size of a mountain walked over to the door blocking it, time seemed to do its stand still thing. "John why do you always get me in these predicaments." John looked down at Jared smiling wryly. "It's what I do ole buddy ole pal." John broke free from Jared's hold and pushed his whole being into the walking wall blocking their escape. Jared had no idea why the mountain was stopping John but he was following with the flow. He slipped around behind the mountain man and opened the door. John slipped past also around the slow moving man and they escaped into the sunlight. Running to the van Jared yelled at John. "Remind me why you are my friend?" John laughed as they jumped into the van. Jared was happy to be behind his steering wheel again and drove fast and away from the dark little pool hall with shadows trying to follow, but just not able to stay with them. Or was Jared being given time to regroup. He was not worrying about the gift but was glad they were not following them he was still worn out from the previous attack.

John was wearing nice black slacks with a rich black sweater. Underneath was a white t-shirt with the collar just peeking over the black of sweater. Even his shoes were black dress shoes. "John? What are you up to dressed like that so early in the day?" John smacked his thighs and laughed at his friend. "I was wanting some afternoon delight since my ole pal, ole buddy, ole friend was either working or not answering his phone I figured I had to do it alone." Jared drove John home. "You need to go home and rest some my friend." Jared may be projecting a little there. The little bit of sleep he did get was a very cold sleep. He wanted to see Jen and start their real date. "I have a date with a beautiful woman so you need to get home and get your own wheels."

John shifted in the seat and stared at Jared. "John stop it you know I hate it when you do that." John said in a flat tone, "I am at a loss." He sat back in the seat and began to smile the smile lead to a loud laugh. "You have a date!" Looking outside the window then sticking his head out he yelled. "It's the end of the world as we know it, Jared has a date!" Jared laughed a little but he was not liking the feel of this. John turned then with a new tone of serious he asked a blunt question. "Why have you not been able to win at pool anymore Jared? What has happened?" The image of the big light spirit that kept his shots from going in but helped the ladies to fall easily, captured the moment in his mind. Jared couldn't tell John that ghosts weren't letting him win, he would think he was crazy. John was the least spiritual person he knew. John followed his question with another question. "Why didn't you want to take that hot thing that night. She was open and ready for you to have your pleasures across her fields of glory."

Pulling up to John's house at a good time Jared didn't answer either of his questions. "We will talk all about my lack of's and such later I have a date, get out." Bluntly said but with an understanding of friendship. John got out quickly slamming the van door. He looked at Jared once more. "You are turning into a mess Jared, shape up boy or I may have to find a new partner in crime." He watched him walk away and up to his front door. His slacks were catching the sunlight carrying the sheen of the black. Jared saw dark around his friend. Something he didn't want to see or know about. John turned to wave goodbye and for an instant there was a red glow from his eyes. A creature in the spiritual place of different stood behind him. Jared turned away driving fast down the road. "I will just act like I didn't just see that."

Visions have life and voices have tone. These spirits he was seeing had flesh of soul waiting to capture the light from the unsuspecting. John was one of them. "Watch your choices ole buddy ole friend." Needing to see Jen he flipped his phone open while driving toward her house. The light of day was beautiful. The air was fresh but cold and he wanted to be with Jen and soon. The road was smooth as the van moved quickly down the road, the road to his pleasure and the woman that had filtered into his soul. "And she is beautiful ta boot!" The window of the van slowly went down as he rested his arm outside. Ignoring any negative trying to find his thoughts he wanted her and soon. He turned on the radio, a catchy love song was on and he snapped his fingers to the old tune and pushed harder on the accelerator.

Chapter 33

Her phone rang while she was holding it and pushing the numbers to call Jared. It was Jared calling. Quickly pushing answer she hit the web browser button by mistake. "No dammit!" She canceled then hit answer she pushed the phone to her ear. "Jared?" "Hello Jen are you home?" Everything that was worrying her, everything that hurt stilled immediately. The cliche words of you make me complete, settled into her like the morning sun against the grasses still holding the dew of night's touch. "Jared I need to talk with you," she paused, "yes I am home." The sound of music in the background filtered through the phone. The wind from the window being open was heard by her. "You are driving? You have your van back?" "Yes I am on my way to your house, is that ok?" She straightened her hair quickly smiled, "yes, yes, please hurry I want you here." Jared felt wonderful this was what they write about in books. The rear view mirror held a shadow but he looked away from it still holding onto her voice that filled him somehow. "I will be there in a few minutes Jen talk to you then?" "Yes Jared I am here." The phone was put on the seat next to him. Time swallowed its pride and slowed to a surreal moment with Jared. Everything was beautiful in life even those of dark have light in them. He enjoyed the ocean, a good game of pool and the feel of ecstasy with the thought of soon being next to Jen. Opening his heart he waited for her to fill it with her own light of love. "Yes love," the music from the radio lifted him into a place of fantasy and romance.

"Yes love.." He tapped on the dashboard and continued to ignore the darkness that had tried to circle him and remove the feel of love. But light of love was too powerful and this was love.

Jen looked out of the windows of the large front room trying to see his van. Waiting to see his van. "Jared.." She kept playing with her necklace fiddling with it while waiting for him to show up. She paced from the front of the house to the back near the driveway she was like a crazed animal needing to be fed. Finally she saw the maroon van pull up into the drive passing the house and into the garage. Running through the back hall she pulled open the garage door.

He stepped out of the van and smiled with his arms open. "Jen, dammit woman come here now!" She ran into him pushing him back against the van. "Lets go inside Jen I have something to tell you." She pulled some from him but he didn't allow it to happen for very long. When a kiss becomes almost a moment of orgasm the two people involved in this kiss were in trouble. "Jen," he whispered her name just as he found her lips. Soft was the touch but the way her kiss found his core sent a shock through him. Immediate was his arousal. Standing hard against her his ache had just begun.

She opened her mouth to pull his tongue inside teasing it with a soft sucking motion. She felt his want pressing into her. Swelling with ache she lifted her hips against him letting him know, yes letting him know. "Oh hell Jen." He lifted her in his arms carrying her into the house. The stairs held them, he lowered her to the steps carefully and lifted her legs around him. She leaned back into the carpet on the stairs wanting her ache to be filled by him she opened easily. But Jared just teased her. Hard but gentle he rubbed lightly up and down against her lace panties. Moans filled the mansion that had been silent of any pleasure for years. His hands reached to lift her to him away from the stairs. Pressing harder, his breath hot against her neck, he lifted and dropped against her. Still teasing her he lifted her to carry her up the stairs. Jen held onto him her legs around him. Moving slowly on him wanting him to need her, to release himself from those sweat pants. "Jared I love you..I," he kissed her filling her gently with his tongue. Time does not exist nor does gravity as he carried her easily up the stairs to her bedroom.

Amazing how fast a pair of sweat pants can come off and a cable knit sweater. Leaving flesh that had a need to be against another one of flesh. Her bed was a king size bed full of those fluff pillows that just take up space. Jared pushed them off the bed as he lowered her down to the bed. Her clothes slowly came off while kisses of slow, warm and wonderful lifted her against him. Does anyone ever know how clothes seem to fall away when passion takes the stage? "Jared." she whispered while pulling him close to her she felt her breasts against his chest. He felt her breasts against him. Finally breasts that I can keep against me and enjoy. The visual of Stacy's breast and the chaplain's breast for a moment took hold. Slowly with a gentle thrust

260

he found the swollen heat of her ache that he had wanted since he first looked at her. "Jen I need you." Her legs pulled him wrapping around him in rhythm of each push she lifted riding the waves of his hard yet soft want. He looked deeply into her eyes finding only light there he moaned. "More Jen I want all of you open more for me." Easily she lifted quickly she gave. The air held their scent, Jen held his soul. She grabbed the headboard opening all for him to have. The feel of her sliding against him was overwhelming. His right hand slipped under her to lift her to him so he could find more depth. "Deeper I need to be deeper...." Her mind was shattering with pleasure, lifting her hips allowing him to explore every part of her she could not keep her moans quiet. Escaping into the air surrounding them Jared's moans matched hers.

He lifted her as time found it's measure of release. Gripping her he kissed her deeply with sucking pulsing tongue thrusts matching his thrusts of hard into her softness. "Jen!" he yelled knowing she was with him feeling her swell and surround him he climaxed with her. Visuals of light pulsating with them completed the mix, his soul with hers his release with hers. She fell away from him as he lifted above her locking into her with one last long thrust.

Remaining in her he lowered himself to her. Kissing lightly they teased each other as the heat continued to build once more. She began to swell again against his hardness that never ceased. "More Jared I want more of you." Jared not needing to be asked twice began to move once more into her. "Harder!" She arched giving him her breasts to do with what he wished. Hard inside her, tongue finding nipples he circled then sucked completing the rhythm. But he could not hold on long. Release was soon she aroused him too easily. Jen also couldn't hold on, as she folded against his push wrapping him tighter with her legs. "Yes, my Jared yes!" His muscles flexed as he tightened once more arching with a push deeper than he had ever found. She pulsed around him pulling him into her. Relaxing into the bed they fell against the softness of the sheets. The light in the room was soft while they kissed lightly, tongues touched and slipped into each others mouth, both wanting more. Both would get more after they rested. Jen relaxed into his arms.

Jared was at peace. For the first time in his life, he felt he had found peace while not standing near the ocean. The oceans pound of energy had been the only thing that had ever released his burdens, his pain, his darkness. She moved slightly leaning into him. Her skin felt right with his. Her beautiful soft skin. She nestled under his arm. His hand moved a strand of her hair away from her face. She fell asleep.

He relaxed falling into the feel of complete satisfaction. In every part of his being he was satisfied. There were no whispers to remove him from a smile, no doubts because of lack of skill, no shadows from the stir of the past. He slept.

*

Dreams found him immediately. He was with Jen in a place of waters with colors that change with the lift of the waves. The sky held lights and darks and circles. They walked along a shore of a soundless sea. The air was liquid but silent. The breeze was a constant soft flow across them. In an instant they were near a tree with branches that reach to where he cannot see. There are tall grasses behind this tree and a lake of warm waters. A glance to the waters and they transported into the wet of its hold. Making love slowly by the tree, the air once more fell across them. The silence was not quiet, it was full of the feel of love. The expanse of this place was in the feel of never ending. As if it was a complete universe just for them to enjoy, a universe of beautiful colors of the touch of light, the feel of air the never ending rhythm of making love.

He awoke suddenly his eyes opened quickly. Jen was shifted and awakened with him. "Jared?" He sat up quickly feeling the need to protect her. "Jen," his voice was calm but his gut told him something was wrong. Looking around the bedroom he saw nothing that was out of place. Sweat was forming on his body. "Jared what is wrong?" Pushing the covers away he stood naked in the bedroom. Ready to handle the intruder, seeing his sweat pants on the floor he put them on quickly. Jen looked around the bed for her clothes. Giggling for a moment at the disarray of clothes on the floor caused Jared to look at her. "Stop giggling this is serious." He smiled though then flexed looking over the room once more but nothing was there and he heard nothing. "Jen do you feel this?" Sitting down on the edge of the bed near her he pulled her close to him. "Now I am getting paranoid." "I feel something is bothering you but that is all I feel." She traced his chest lightly with her fingers. He smiled as the familiar way of her found his core once more. "Jen stop we need to find out what this is." She sighed. "Fine then you stand there and be all spiritual and warrior like, I am going to get something to eat."

Jen got out of bed slowly enjoying the seriousness of Jared and the feel of her own sensuality. She felt beautiful with him, beautiful comfortable and safe. Feeling safe with someone was a new experience for her. She watched him look around the room while she moved past him to go to the kitchen. "Come and get a snack with me my warrior." She was wearing only a shirt, her legs captured his attention causing him to relax. "Yes my baby doll." Turning she laughed "baby doll?" He stood next to her as they walked down the stairs. "I don't know what woke me up Jen I felt someone was in the room but no one was there." Jen put his hand into hers, "lets just eat you made me hungry." Jared without his shirt on was a little cold. He looked at the canvas that was still torn from his first visit to her house, her mansion. Still feeling as if something was with them he realized it was a spirit. Because he saw no real flesh types around. "Go away ghosts." He mumbled then caught up with her. She was already pulling things out of the fridge with abandon. "Pick something and enjoy it." Jared looked at her chewing on strawberries, then a carrot while reaching for more pieces of veggies and assorted goodies in her fridge. The sun was shining through the window filtering with the silence and comfort of this place with her near him. "I like this Jen." She chewed loudly on a carrot. "You like carrots? So do I, yum." "No this, the peace of this time with you." He sat at the small table that was near the center island. Motioning her to sit with him he wrapped his arms around himself, "I'm cold woman." She sat with a plate full of assorted veggies and cheese, white wine completed her snack. "Want some of my wine it will warm you up" He sipped some from her glass. He saw a figure reflecting in the glass it appeared to be standing behind him. Jumping he turned but nothing was there. "Jared stop it you are scaring me to death here." He sat hard in the seat.

"I think we have a visitor from the hospital Jen, something followed us home." She munched louder on a piece of celery. "Nonsense I told all to stay there." Her casual attitude calmed him. You told them to stay, how did you know to do that?" Jen sat back at her tray of munchies and crossed her legs. Jared looked for a moment at the line of her legs, the way of their softness to where he was beginning to want to explore once more. Snapping her fingers in his face she saw and felt where his mind was wandering. "Jared talk to me of you and of your gift." She chewed on a piece of celery waiting for his answer knowing he was surprised she knew. He reached for a carrot and sat across from her and shook his head. "How did you know what do you know?" Chewing still and talking Jen felt like a teenager with no worries and very much in love. "I have a gift also and I see yours." Jared looked into her eyes wanting to be able to talk with someone about his worries about the ER about the gift all of it. "What is your gift?" "Don't distract me tell me of you." She walked him over to the sofa in the living area. The sun was shining through the large window across her art and onto both of them sitting.

He told her of the times he could see the future and play with time. Making it speed up so he could get out of school. Jen just listened and chewed. He had never seen her eat so much and so fast. "There is a time coming Jen when time will fly away from the normal lift and create vibrations destroying…" he paused not knowing why these words were falling out of his mouth. Jen slowed her chew on the carrots and celery. She stilled but wanted more. "Tell me what you know Jared please." He was being spoken to by a voice of calm. A voice of no voice telling him to let Jen know. "Know what?" He asked the voice out loud. Jen reiterated, "Tell me." Her hand lifted his into hers. "I can heal people but only if God wants them healed." He shifted not wanting her to think he was bragging but she knew he was just stating the facts. "There is a time coming soon where people will be judged by their spiritual level of growth." Sounding a little too adult he slowed his thoughts or tried to. The speed at which they were flying was out of control. Jen listened more intently than before. He was telling her, confirming to her what she already knew, but thought she was the only one with that knowledge.

Jared stood still looking around the room as if something was there with them. Of course something was there the creator was always with all. "Walking the line of reality and spiritual is a difficult one Jen." Jared had lived in reality for the past 20 years of his life but the gift was alive again wanting him to walk both paths. Jen pulled him back to the sofa trying to calm him. She felt the battle inside him, the pull of dark, the pull of reality and a pull to be complacent in his life and choices and just exist. The battle to do what one was supposed to do in life was a hard one. Jen knew this walk she had lived it also her life alone. She could not find the right man that could understand that would understand the spiritual side of life. "Jared I know of this walk sit and tell me more please." Jared calmed just by her touch, he sat next to her and looked once more into the beauty of her eyes that lead him to a soul that was brighter than the sunlight. Hearing his thoughts turning poetic he shook his head to remain away from the silly wuss factor of poetry and romance. "Jen I don't know what I am to do, I just know the spirits at the ER are getting stronger with their attacks on me and my ability to heal people has been making me sick with their pain for some reason." Exhaling as he seemed to be throwing words at her without a pause he smiled to make a quick joke. But she stopped him. "Jared I see them also and feel them. They have been around you they attacked us today at the hospital thats why we are here away from that place and in my bed." Smiling she looked at the sofa, "or my sofa," he laughed then kissed her lightly. "You help me Jen, in more ways than you know."

There was a crash at the other end of the living area. Nothing was out of place and both of them remained calm on the sofa. "When one sees into this other world Jen the spirits on the other side see you." Jen closed her eyes for a moment and whispered for whatever was there to leave that it was not wanted. The crash occurred closer to both of them this time. Jen was lifted from her feet and thrown against the wall across from the staircase. Jared jumped to reach with his energy to surround that entity that was attacking her. Relaxing with the light he was surrounding himself with he created a sword of light, throwing it at the darkness that had Jen. The dark entity dissolved immediately away from her then re appeared above her head. Jen slid down the wall and passed out. Jared had no anger just calm. He had learned that anger only fed the darkness as it lapped it up wanting more of that energy and that vibration. In a language unknown to the human tongue he threw words at the darkness while raising his hand and called on the blood of Jesus to cover what was attacking them. It was blasted literally away and out of the window.

He rushed over to her and held her, he could feel her heart had stopped and the blood had slowed with no spread of oxygen, it wouldn't be long before she became part of the spiritual world. Lifting her close to him he leaned his head against her chest. He was waiting for spirit to bring her back by working through him. His faith was being tested, Jen was being tested, but neither knew this, a test of faith. Would Jared allow spirit to move through him? Would Jared remain growing with his gift or shut it down again finding complacency in his life just waiting to end existence.

Jen was in a place of light with no sound. Her eyes saw nothing but she could feel Jared was close. There was also a feel of complete love with no fear. She had no hands or body as she tried to look down to see where she was. The movie began or a show is what it seemed. She was watching Jared hold her limp body. She saw a bright light move across Jared and enter him through the back of his head and down into her body. Lifting suddenly he pushed his head deeper into her chest and against her breasts. Her inhale was a full deep one, Jared knew she was back. He was calm but she was still not all the way back to him and to the physical life. "I need you with me now, Jen please come back." With those words she was thrown back into her body. Her eyes opened quickly her arms reached around him pulling him to her breasts even harder. "Jen I can't breathe!" Jared laughed but tears fell from his eyes. Never had he felt such love never had he wanted with his whole being to bring someone back to fix them of their pain. "Jared we are meant to be together, the dark cannot beat us when we are together." Jared lifted her to a standing position, "we are together now and you were brutally attacked." Jared was very tired and had to sit on the sofa. "You are wearing me out woman and not in a good way." Jen continued with her wish of them together to find what they are to do. "Maybe we are like a team?" The day had gone by too quickly, for the light was low now on the windows. "Where did time go just then Jen?" Jen did not remember the light and the vision or the visit to the place of between reality and spiritual. She just knew she wanted to be with him and she knew they had a path of difficult to walk, but they would walk it together. She did remember the entity attacked her but that was all. She felt very close to Jared. In a way she had never felt for or with anyone.

Jared had a strength inside him he was unaware of. But when he felt attacked he did not retreat nor was he afraid that was the first step in the path of a long walk into spirituality and darkness. One had to know how to battle the dark or you could be killed. Your spirit may live with light and go to a place of love but your flesh would be torn away and discarded.

Jared walked to the window to see the sun fall near the edge of the horizon. "We both have to work tomorrow Jen." She walked up to him pushing a carrot into his mouth. "You need more crunchy veggies in your diet and more of me." Kissing him she pushed against him wanting to feel every bit of him against her. He inhaled her kiss pulling her air into his lungs. "Stop woman I'm tired, give me a second." The carrot mixed with their kiss giving Jen a taste. She crunched a piece of the carrot she had taken out of his mouth. "Then tell me more Jared." Jen acted as if the spiritual attack was nothing. Maybe she was used to it he didn't know but he did know it wasn't over nor would it be for a long time. The place he saw in his dreams of liquid air was place he knew where they could go spiritually and rest in safety. "Jen do you ever dream of a place with an ocean, a tree, and air that is…" "Liquid." She finished his sentence with a smile and a chomp finishing another carrot. "You will turn orange if you keep eating those things." Jared walked over to her kissing her on the cheek. "You have had a dream of a place with liquid air?" Jen stopped eating and lifted a water bottle to her lips. Before she took a sip she closed her eyes. "I can go there now, but now I see you there with me. We are walking the oceans edge." She gulped water down. He couldn't believe someone else knew of his place, of his forever place he called it. A place he saw when he was young and visited often. But when he closed his gift away he lost it.

Jen motioned him to go take a shower pointing up the stairs while she continued to swallow the water emptying the water bottle easily. "You shower, I will come up in a minute and visit, we have much more to talk of before going to work tomorrow." He walked up the stairs watching his bare feet move across the carpet. A memory of resting, Jen there while wrapping her legs around him caused him to smile. Running up the rest of the stairs he wanted to feel the water across him. Water always helped release him of any covering of the day. "Time to wash the day away."

*

Jen put the veggies in the fridge. She felt wonderful. There was no more fear or worry or lonely in any part of her thoughts or being. "He is the one, I am home again." The light was now gone from outside. The mansion felt like a home for the first time. She cared for someone, she realized she had never cared for anyone in her whole life.

Chapter 34

The water was hot on Jared. His back was to the flow he allowed it to fall from his head covering his face. His mind was gone to a place of conversation with God. It was time for him to fully embrace his gift and grow with it or be lost. He had a choice to close it again and ignore it but he also knew with that choice he would be alone with the dark entities that lived beside all in life. He opened his mind. Some people meditate while sitting. Some cross their legs while sitting in the lotus position but Jared could meditate in the shower or anywhere if he just stilled himself to the flesh and movement of his own body he opened to the voice of God. Meditation was truly just a type of prayer.

Sometimes a meditation would just clear the mind and soul of clutter. Sometimes there is a voice not heard in the mind but in the souls memory. In those times visions find your heart. Trusting what you see. Having faith that the good and love of life is what was filtering into you was the ultimate test.

Jen opened the shower doors to join him. "You startled me." The water became the sensual touch of a voice not heard. He explored her with his hands and pulled her closer kissing her as the water slipped down to their lips. The way of light into the bathroom from the sun had slowed to a dimly lit room. The waters fell off both of them. Steam rose from his hand as he touched her lightly on the shoulder.

She was leaning into him in a way of gentle with love. He closed his arms around her swaying in the water with her. He saw more than steam from his skin he saw his want of her lifting into the air sensually. Time in this moment altered its flex removing him from her for a visit to the place of no sorrows. A man with white robes and a long white beard stood in front of him. Looking back over his shoulder he saw himself and Jen still swaying in the hot water of the shower, holding each other peacefully.

The man spoke to Jared but without speaking. Jared just understood what he said. This man had been a constant in his life. He didn't know if he was God or just spiritual helper but he did know he felt very at peace when in his presence. The light in the room, a room of white with a single column in the center seemed familiar to Jared. He watched the man walk with a very large book in his hand. Within a vision one can look at details. It is the eye of time within our souls. But this vision cannot be driven or manipulated, or everything will fly to the way of invisible. With crumbles of thoughts dashed into reality. He felt Jen once more as he returned back into his full of self. Letting what was seen speak to his heart within he relaxed back into the feel of her love against him.

She lightly kissed his neck he lightly, slowly moved her against him. Kisses are the wet of the shower. Flight occurred for both of them. They lifted into the place of forever while the waters held their flesh with warmth and safety. They walked the oceans waves. No words needed to be spoken they had escaped into Jared's forever place. The skies were colors that shifted with their glances. A mere thought transported them to the far reaches of this forever place. They could walk on the waters, be covered in the waters while making love all with no effort. Everything flowed easily.

Suddenly they both felt the weight of their bodies surrounding them enclosing them inside their bodies of birth. The water of the shower had turned cold. "Yikes!" Jared quickly turned to shut off the showers water. "Nothing like being ripped from forever back to the way of freezing cold water." Jen pushed close against him. "I'm freezing Jared." He lifted her out of the shower and wrapped her legs around his waist. "Then lets go get warm." He looked into her eyes and still saw the forever place there. She smiled putting her arms around him harder. "I love," she paused then finished with a quick, "forever place, let's go there again." Jared carried her to the bed, his strength seemed to be complete when he was with her.

Jared stopped at the top of the stairs lowering her slowly to the floor. "What are we going to do Jen?" He reached for her hand while they walk naked to the bedroom. Jared's hair was dripping wet down his back causing Jen to bite her lip lightly. An image of her nails pushing into that water against his skin was tantalizing and distracting. Her thoughts are of the pleasure kind. Jared carefully turned to watch her sit on the edge bed. His hair dripped cold water across her stomach. Jen lay back stretching wanting him to see that he

275

could have all of her. He had never loved a woman, he thought he had but he loved her down to the depth of his soul. He lay next to her and slowed his breathing and his want for her. "Do you feel the shift Jen?" They lay in the dark resting beside each other both aware of the energies that had found they were in love. "What should we do Jared?" She pushed against him then felt the need to cover herself. She put on a cotton robe and got under the covers away from him. He picked up a towel and dried himself then put on a shirt and boxers. He looked at her covered with a look of dread in her eyes. "We will rest and talk tomorrow." He pulled her into his arms and they fell asleep. Both aware of the energies and the shift of attention to them. He pulled light around them and they were safe, for the night.

While they slept the dark began to surround them. It carried a want that was closing in on the mansion with an eerie silence and covering itself with the wind. It hid among the bushes then to the trees leaping to the roof of the mansion. This thing was of the evil in time. The energy that wanted to destroy all of light and feed the souls to the place of the damned. The flesh without flesh of dark energy were surrounding them. Their light taunted the demons with the bright of it and angered them. The demons of earth were running out of time and Jared knew this as did Jen for both were given a gift and both were discovering they would have to learn to fight or they would perish.

Jen heard something or was it that she felt something wasn't right. The window near the bed had no shades and in it was evil looking in on them sleeping. Jen woke Jared and looked to her right to the window where she felt the chill of something wrong. He was not fully awake and thought she just wanted him, he was not aware of the demon watching them. Jen pulled him closer as if to kiss his neck and whispered to him. "There is something dark watching us through the window Jared." Like the night the demon could be wherever there was a shadow. Choosing to slip through the glass as if it was nothing it slid along the floor near the bed. Looking only like a shadow on the floor it was hoping to catch the lovers by surprise and enter one of them.

Vampires may or may not be real in the world of sucking blood. But vampires in the soul world do exist. Draining one of their energy and literal life force by invading a sleeping person. Jared felt it but it was not at the window he felt it near the edge of the bed. Jen stiffened under him as fear filled her covering her she began to shake slightly. Jared was not afraid nor concerned. He wrapped light immediately from God with just a thought. Surrounding both he and Jen with this spiritual blanket he rolled away from her to stand, full of strength both physically and spiritually Jared saw the demon slither up the wall. It was trying to make itself large to frighten him. He had not invited it in he wondered why it was able to come into the house.

Jen covered herself with the blankets and curled up watching Jared stand there to battle the thing. She felt something cold touch her. Looking over her shoulder at her pillow she saw dark slipping onto her hair and across her face. "Jared!" She screamed but as soon as she made a sound the black moved into her suffocating her for a moment. Jen was thrown into visuals of a place of dark and pain. People were screaming in agony from their choices in life. Those that hurt others, those that killed, were there reaching wanting her to be part of the suffering. Jared's face was seen. He was moving toward her flying over the one screaming. Moving her to safety away from the hold she awakened back in her bed. But the sun was just coming up. Jared kissed her. "Jen I didn't know it had you, I was battling the one on the wall." Jen grabbed him and kissed him hard. "Don't ever leave me Jared." He settled near the edge of the bed. "Jen this is why I closed off the gift. I got tired of fooling with this nonsense of good against evil. I just want to live and play and make love to you." He finished the last word by kissing her again softly this time. "Jared I have to tell you something." She sat up still holding the blankets over her to cover her naked body. But Jared sat there in all of his glory. She smiled at his confidence.

Jen began a story of her life and choices and ways of lust and greed. She was born into wealth. Never had to work. She despised those not cultured. They were lesser beings in her eyes. She would awaken at night sweating after being invaded by something as she was sleeping. She was opened and raped nightly by a dark entity that continued taking her at it's pleasure. She never knew if it was male or female or if that even exists in the way of entities. She also didn't fight it. She welcomed the intense orgasms. She enjoyed it's touch rationalizing it as just a dream. Her anger grew daily and her rage also never slowed. She was visited at night the first approach was through the window. She was sleeping but not deeply. A voice found her in what she thought was a dream but it was real and asking her to let it into her room. He was handsome, dark hair with bright blue eyes and as she thought it was a dream why not. She invited it in and from that night until just recently it took her. Even during the day it would attack her. Throwing her down on the floor raping her. She still did not fight it. Always finding a way to rationalize it away as a day dream. Her parents walked in on her during one of the episodes. The entity threw itself into her parents suffocating them. She watched and did nothing while it killed both of them. She inherited the rest of the wealth. Listening to the cause of their death as both suffering heart attacks. Not one word was ever said nor anything questioned as to why they both suffered them together at the same time in the same place.

She began recruiting people for this entity. Bringing home men for it to turn them into the dark souls that lose forever. These men would make love to her then sleep. She would feel them the demons, move into her dates. Pulling their life force from them. Every morning when they would awaken they would leave almost lifeless. She would then let it take her over and over again. Pulling her soul away also causing her to grow weaker and weaker.

She was close to death when a voice of calm found her thoughts. Telling her to push the darkness away and pull the light of God to her. She would have to go to nursing school. She needed to pay back all of the harm she had caused. And to build her soul to the way of light. Souls were energy and energy never dies. Her spiritual level of vibration was in the place of suffering forever. But for some reason God saw some good in her. She began school, she listened to the voice of calm and gentle and pushed all darkness away. With each day of light entering her she grew to understand this evil and it's walk. She battled it still daily but would not allow it to enter her. It couldn't without being invited.

"Jen I know all of this in you, I saw it long ago." Jen kissed him once more. "Now you see why I also work in that horrible ER, and why I also see the dark in life." He rolled over on the bed and lay next to her. "We have a lot of work to do, shall we do it together?" Jen pulled him this time closer to her. "I guess the invitation is still alive how do we close it?" "See this is what I hate about having gifts from God, you never have a day off." Jen kissed him then they fell asleep for the few hours they have before they must enter the ER again. Both of them aware they would be attacked and both knowing they had to fight it or they will be killed. "Drama 101." Jared whispered as he spoke once more in a dream state. Jen just snuggled closer to him.

Time had it's way of holding memories in the minds of lovers. This was a time of forever that would fold them into a place of calm,

280

a place of real monsters with real fangs. A place of calm was defined as strength in the core of Jared. Nothing could hurt him. He was of light. He was pure within stronger in light and depth and it grew daily.

Chapter 35

The alarm clock woke Jared immediately. He felt Jen near him he kissed her lightly on her neck and tried to forget the battle with the entity the night before. "This damn line I walk will drive me crazy." Words sometimes fall out of ones mouth when thoughts couldn't contain them. Jen heard him and moaned reaching for him to push against her harder. "I want you Jared please." Jared was a man of wonderful traits would never pass up the opportunity to make love to a woman especially one that he happened to have fallen in love with. He looked at the clock and knew they had to leave soon which left him not much time to make love. She reached for him and he pulled her against him. They fell onto the bed as he pushed deeply Into her. She wanted him to envelop her completely wrapping quickly her legs around him she lifted off of the bed. His hands controlled her every movement. Every movement against him.

Kisses were fire and the rhythm of push with sweat forming. "With me baby, with me please," His voice trailed off into moans mixed with hers. Thrusts of ache were cleansed with love easing into each other they rested with each pulse.

The sun shined brightly upon their skin and Jared knew they needed to slow this reach or they would be in bed the whole day. He looked quickly about the room and saw no darkness or felt no demons on this morning. They were giving them a break. He kissed her slowly, softly. "Jen we have to get up baby." She pulled him closer, kissed him with those light kisses from a place he knew was from heaven. Comfy wonderful warm inviting wet hot....his thoughts slipped back to reality. He walked to the shower, away from the heat of her, she was driving him crazy.

She fell asleep as he walked toward the shower. She would not be away from him long. She couldn't resist the waters on him with her against those same waters. The water was hot and felt wonderful. Jared found that perfect place with her, if time stopped and he ceased his breath he would be a happy camper. Suddenly a face filled his mind and a voice fell slowly against his thoughts that matched the waters fall at his back. The steam rose, he relaxed. "It is time to grow Jared." He saw the visuals of the many spirits near him. the ones of light. "Please I am trying to take a shower here!" He relaxed into the water but smiled. He turned off the water and began his step into another world and place. He knew that God would give him more signs and push him to be what he was to be and what he chose long ago before birth ever found his voice.

He was in love with Jen, felt like was she was in love with him. So in all reality this should be the perfect of life. They needed to marry soon, to make it all right with God. He ran back up the stairs to the bedroom to awaken her for work. "Jen we are going to be late wake up woman!" Jen stirred some but reached for him. Her arms encircled his neck pulling him closer to her. "Hi baby...." A kiss was found as is the arousal factor that happened once more with him. "Jen please darlin don't do this to me you are killing me." She smiled then lifted to her elbows resting. "Ok but tonight I want more of you." She paused then added a very sensual "c'mere baby." "Jen stop please." He turned to find his scrub pants and scrub top. Yes he was aroused again, scrub pants with tent factor just didn't look right.

She slowly got out of bed. Reaching for her scrubs of red with low waist and low top he shook his head as he watched her dress. A fight was brewing and it's of his want to just be in bed with this woman on a constant. Exploring her every moan, her every bit of skin, her body responding to his touch and want of her. "Jen dammit what am I going to do just the thought of you and I get aroused?" Jen walked sensually over to him. Her index finger found his lips then traced the front of his east. "Handle it my love." She turned away from him and moved her hips in that way that women drive men crazy with and they knew it. He slammed his hands down on his groin to push the arousal away. "No," was the only word heard by the universe and by the air.

The pair finally got into her car and began the drive back to the emergency room. "Stop by the beach before we go Jen." She slowed the car to make the next turn that would take them to the beach. Jared watched as the sun was rising, putting the color of it's touch across the beach and the ocean. The sunsets were what was beautiful here the sunrise was way off to the west. His thoughts as usual in the morning of "who will die today," still found him but with Jen close he was

284

very comfortable, she looked at him. He looked at the colors of the sunrise hit the day. The expression on his face caused her to lose her breath for a moment. He had a light inside him that fell around him down to his toes. He turned to say something to her and saw her staring at him. He startled her with the sudden glance her way. "Jared you scared me!" Jared just looked back quickly at the colors of the sun hitting the morning. "Well I am sorry my face scares you." He said with a smile as he reached to feel her hand in his, It was warm. A flash of a fresh dead hit his mind. The many hands he had moved that had become lifeless. "It is not natural what we do Jen." The waves were doing their crashing against the beach filled the moment as Jared smiled. "I love it here, I could be a hobo easily and live on the beach." Pulling her hand to his lips he kissed the top of her hand lightly. "Walk with me Jen on this ocean, this is where I feel eternity and used to be the only place I would feel at home." He looked into her eyes and kissed her. "Now I am at home with you." She reached to kiss him deeper. Complete comes to mind again as Jared moaned during the kiss. "Lets walk." The waters were alive with a wild surf this day. But the pacific coast was always alive. Unlike the beaches on the east coast that could actually be flat with boring slight rolls of water that touched the beach. The pacific ocean was always reaching, lifting, pushing itself toward the beach. As if it was a lover wanting and craving every bit of sand to mix with it's flow. At least that's what Jared thought as he walked on the beach with this lady that seemed to be part of his soul. He began to feel weak suddenly, looking at Jen he saw she was unaware of what was going on with him. His legs began to shake some. "Hold up Jen I'm having trouble walking." She turned him to her and looked at him then spoke in a calm low voice. "Leave him now you are not wanted here." Jared saw the darkness that had attached itself to him spiritually he saw its tendrils reaching, slithering onto him. Just as she spoke the words it flew away to the beach then off to a person walking near them. He was oblivious to the touch. Jen held him close to her for a moment. "You need me you know." Jared was still weak from the attack. "Let's get to work I'm beat." He looked back at the ocean and smiled he felt its touch washing him from the attack but also taking him back to a time of youth and freedom.

"It doesn't like me not allowing it inside me anymore Jared and that is my burden in this relationship." Jared just smiled and flexed. "Bring it on it's time to rumble." He threw his fist into the air. Deep inside him though there was a worry building. He sensed the battles would become more violent and more frequent. Time on earth was changing. It was time for the darkness to walk alone and be thrown away from earth. The battle would be messy and he knew he would be in the middle of all of it. Was Jen a good in all of this or a bad? His questions caused a moment of doubt. He looked at her and saw nothing but light of the spiritual kind around her. "Nah.." Jen heard him and smiled, "Nah?" "Nah what Jared?" The ocean pushed with it's wind against them. "We need to get to work." Jen leaned against him as they walked. Whispers always did find Jared in his sleep as he walked through his days in the ER and now with Jen. Those whispers of calm that tried to guide him, helping him, but sometimes confusing him. Whispers from the other side of life sometimes spoke in ways not understood immediately by the mind. That was why he must pray daily. His prayer was simple he just close his eyes and relaxed into thoughts of God and talked to Jesus like He was his friend, He was everyone's friend. She drove faster, she does love to speed. Jared held the handle at the roof top near the window on the door.

"Slow down woman." Jen was unaware of speeding. She pushed the accelerator down harder just for a second to scare him. Jared smiled but was tense refusing to let her know she was making him not very comfortable. She pulled quickly into the parking lot. "Safe and sound." "No comment." Jared said as he turned away pushing open the door. She grabbed him back to her to kiss him hard. "That would have to keep you for a time." He got out of the car and walked lighter than ever. Watching his boots move across the concrete he felt the morning air and was happy. She slipped her arm into his as they walked toward the back of the hospital. It was towering in front of them like a huge beast. The ambulance bay doors opened and closed quickly as EMS continued to bring one too many patients. Jared saw the doors like they were the mouth of that same beast. "Jen we need to get out of this hospital soon." He stopped walking suddenly and pulled her closer. "It's just too damned dangerous physically and spiritually." Jen heard him but pulled him along with her. She couldn't leave, not for a while, she had to pay back what she did and what she was involved with in the past. She kept those thoughts to herself. But she could not leave this hospital until she felt she had paid her due. She pulled harder on him, "come on Jared you wuss let's go to work."

*

The walk into the ER found Jared still uneasy. He also hadn't heard from John and that was not like him not to call. Speak of the devil as soon as his thought ended the phone buzzed in his pocket. Jen walked in front of him and into the hospital. Looking back at him she saw he was on the phone. Hoping it's not a woman thinking it may be John she waved him to come in to work. Jared motioned her to go on in without him. John seemed frantic about something. "John what the hell is wrong with you?" John was talking in circles about hustling and where Jared's head was and that it's not in the game. Blah, blah was all that Jared thought listening to his rant. "I have to work dude I will call you in a bit." The phone put back into his pocket he looked to the skies. Tired of where he was not knowing where he was going in his life, he walked to the back door of the ER. The double ambulance bay doors still opened and closed creating more patient load and bringing in more patients. Jared did not like the feel of the day at the ER. Looking down at his feet while he walked in he saw the times of past when life was easy to the point of being boring. He was in love with a woman that was magical, to his core. He wasn't looking forward to playing pool. All he wanted to do was run away with Jen and make love. "Well not always make love." One of the nurses walked in beside him chuckled. "Not always make love huh?" She smiled and walked past him into the hospital. He watched his hand reach for the handle. "Just go in Jared and git er done." The sounds of the ER were immediate. He could hear a drunk yelling that he wanted to leave and he stood in front of the time clock. The night shift was oblivious to the man. People could be made to disappear it's a gift when working in a hostile environment of redundant nature. A drunk could stand right in front of you and you could smile and walk around him. This one was not going to let Jared walk around him. He immediately swung at him. Jared ducked then pushed the man up against the wall. "Calm down old man." He said to the patient but his words were not being listened to. Security came in to take over and allowed Jared to clock in. Jen watched the whole exchange as was all of day shift standing in line to clock in for the day. Jared turned and saw them. The applause began "good control there Jared!" Jen said then turned to clock in. Jared just smiled and wished he was not at the hospital.

Chapter 36

Demons Hiding in Flesh

The gatekeeper, time clock once again seemed happy it had Jared captive. Transaction accepted, "I'll show you accepted." He grumbled and headed for the locker room to get his trauma scissors. Jen was busy talking to the night nurse that had already started giving her report. Walking past one of the bays he saw one of his most familiar patients. She enjoyed swallowing razor blades and putting glass up her rectum. Or anything she wished to put up there. "Hello Sally, you are back to visit us?" She was not a tall woman, and the hospital gown barely fit over her stomach. But Jared saw that light inside her. She had demons messing with her mind twisting thoughts. Everyone was visited by these demons at one time or another. Some of them hide reality so one can continue to walk in the flesh. Maybe these are not bad demons. Jared hadn't quite figured that one out yet. But her demons stem from abuse during her youth. That and the chemical nature of humans, delicate was the balance with the brain.

Marks of self-mutilation covered her arms and her neck. Her blonde hair just touched her shoulders but she smiled when she saw Jared. She knew he didn't judge her at all she also saw into the others. It was far down inside her soul but the light of life was still finding moments in the sun. That sun was being able to just walk with the normal pod people on earth. Jared always saw the normal ones as blank stare, pod people. Their minds had gone into complacency mode lost in nothing, searching for nothing just circled in the air waiting to drop into nonexistence.

Her bay was empty nothing but the stretcher was in the room. All of the counter equipment and the suction canisters were removed. She was known to put anything up her so it was a precaution. The docs won't do anything to help her, they talked at her not to her and whisked her to the OR or to psych. Whichever seemed the most needed at the moment. Jared had an affinity for this soul. Maybe she was a test for others to check their humanity and not check it at the door. Maybe she just chose this path long before birth. Or just the consequences of horrendous abuse left her mind shattered. Whatever the cause, he treated her with respect.

"Hi Jared," she smiled brightly when she saw him. Leaning against the door of the room she held the back of her gown together and looked to the floor. "We have to stop meeting like this Sally." She smiled, he touched her shoulder and asked in a whisper, "are you ok today?" "Yea just wanted to swallow a razor or two." She smiled again and giggled. "I am about to go off in a little bit you better leave." Jared walked into the room, "sit down on the stretcher with me for a bit Sally lets talk." She moved slowly still holding her gown closed so as not to show her naked back. She was on a hold, so her clothes were locked away. Jared saw the halls of dark in her mixing with twisted corners of light. He saw the cry for help from a small girl deep inside her core. The small girl that was alive at one time before abuse. One of the docs came in to talk with her, Jared just sat and waited for him. "What did you do this for Sally and why do you keep doing it?" She looked at Jared and smiled. He felt the energy shift within her. He got in front of the doc just before she tried to hit him. Jared caught her fist but the spew of vulgarity had found its mark. The doc was being cursed at in a language unknown to man. Jared held her arm then made eye contact with her. "Sally...come back out and play." She immediately relaxed in his hold. Her slow smile began once more. The doc was gone, gone just as she raised her fist. "So do you feel better now?" She sat on the stretcher lowering her head. But her smile had not left. "You are a good person Jared but you better leave I'm going to go off again." Jared walked out of the room but looked into her eyes before he did. "I see you in there Sally, don't give up ok?" She giggled again then her face changed to a frown. She sat then lay on the stretcher, she was quiet and wanted to sleep. He left her there feeling the presence of the many forces enjoying the play in her mind. He was not able or allowed to help her away from the demons she had chosen to live within her. She had the path, it was in the hands of all around her to allow her light to be seen.

His walk to the locker filled with those thoughts of wanting away from this ER. Too much darkness, too many falling into a place he wished to not be around anymore. The ocean was where Jared wished to be. The ocean, walking the beach finding agates and panning for gold. Contrary to popular belief one can pan for gold on the coast of Oregon. He smiled at the thought of this and his step was lighter. His locker awaited the deposit of the outside things, wallet, keys, phone, and the withdraw of the ER things. Scissors to cut clothes off of patients. Some already dead, some paralyzed, some just wanting to die. With that flash that could find a mind, he saw the many patients he had used that pair of scissors on. Dead with blood still oozing, paralyzed with silent tears from the face of the body now unable to move. She was young, he was old, they were someone's love, they were dead. Tossing the flash back into his ever filling pan of memories he straightened himself to stand as tall as he could to begin one more day. "Enough of this drama." He smacked his head to remove the thoughts of redundant negative. "Everything happened for a reason, so get your ass to work." He hadn't seen Jen but felt her, yes felt her love. "Now that is beyond corny Jared." Many years of being alone may have caused this interesting convo mode with Jared and Jared.

Jared was back to the land of OZ, the ER. He reached for a pen to place it at the top of his scrubs. Time did its thing, It shifted and slowed. The feel of all spiritual was clear to him. He felt the entities talking to patients pushing their vulgarity into their ears, into their souls as he walked through the ER looking for the night tech to get report on his new day of interactions and duties of bedpans and blood draws. Shaking his head he wanted away from this visual. Suddenly one of the spirits walked up to him. Invisible but visible in a not comfy way. Stepping through the energy he pushed his step past the non that wanted to distract him and drain him. The dark ones had an agenda. Jared was not in the mood. He also felt it turn to look at him. Following his walk with its glance Jared did not turn around to give it satisfaction. He had to arrange the levels of concentration within his core to control his gift and the negatives of life. Energy flowed, gotta have the right current to handle it. Demons were real, angels were real, so pick which one you want to party with. These energies enjoy invading the rooms with a heavy feel of fear or sadness. Inundating the innocent visitors with that feel of doom and fear but there is also the ones of pure love. They find and surround the ones who chose in life to give and show compassion.

Once in the burn unit, the feel was of very, very bad. One of the trauma nurses told him of a black entity that left from a freshly dead patient. The black entity moved quickly past the nurse station, then slamming open two magnetically locked doors. She spoke of how the doors bowed first, then the magnets gave way.

He stopped at the phlebotomist desk. The bay across had a patient struggling to lie down. Wanting to rise to sit up. Blood fell away from that person. A pool of blood was beside the stretcher. His clothes were covered with blood and torn. The patient was lying in a pool of blood, there was that blood again. Turning away from it he walked to the next patient. She lay there, he had a blood order to pull from her blood that would tell what? He did not see the reasons behind this futile moment. She was dead but alive. A Jane Doe, her wallet contained a will stating where and to whom to give her things to, she was prepared to die. He looked at her lying lifeless on the stretcher with the vent breathing for her. Her hair golden, her nails were freshly painted with a red that shined. "We hang on to life so hard or was it the body just didn't want to let go of it's fleshly life?" His thoughts were finding voice. Walking past the next patient. Jared looked at each one this day. He was trying to find a reason to continue working in this place of blood with spit thrown at your face in an instant. Death walking with life, entities were near waiting, a virtual portal for the afterlife. As soon as that thought flicked its way into him he saw a patient whose eyes had that shine within that almost knocked him over. He would die soon, he had just been diagnosed with lung cancer. His family was calm. Jared tried to help the man to a more comfortable place on the stretcher. "Need anything?" The wife smiled at Jared the children were grown. "No thank you sweetie." She answered him softly. Her eyes were read from crying, her hand was on his. The man had a strength unlike anything Jared had ever felt. With a wish of light across this mans soul he surrounded him. The man looked over at Jared the very instant he did it. Which caught him off guard, "thank you." The man said calmly as he pulled his wife's hand closer. He stepped back and away. The grown children looked like the man of soon death. They reached with silent eyes wanting him ok, needing him ok, but allowing the moment they were there with him to be special. The docs were in a room with another patient. The patient had somehow swallowed something metal accidentally. The x-ray was held up for the guy to see the piece of metal half way down his throat. The ENT's were excited, "this is one for the books." They said to him excited and happy to have something new to do to a patient. The man was having trouble breathing. Contrasts, a team of happy young docs and a scared man hoping he could breathe. The young docs were ready to get him to the OR. He was ready to feel normal again.

Jared was in a fog of the world of two times and two places, but they existed in one time and one place. Knowing the reality of reality was non, finding it daily with every walk, his steps showed the lack of life in life. We are in a place of tests and growth of levels. He was in a place of entities and final destinations. When the grim reaper takes your hand, was it going to be clean so you could go play with the fun boys? Or was it dirty, with ugly of choices in life? Shaking his head at the thought of the waste of so many people's lives caught up in material things. Was having money and a home and a shiny car worth taking your forever away? Forever in a place of dark and cold and scary just to claim the physical of a moment, a slight moment of pleasure here on this place of non-reality. "Yea they like their stuff enough to kill you for it."

Chapter 37

He left the ER to walk outside and away for a moment. Jen saw him walk out but was unable to leave her patient. She also felt him and he was in a place of sorrow and anger. She had never felt this from him. It hurt her, and was very unsettling and frustrating. The patient in the room stirred and began to awaken from the procedure. She had to wait just a little longer then she could go to Jared. She put the vitals on the chart. Numbers fell out and onto the sheet but her thoughts were with her duty, her desire to do what was needed, in her life and path of life. She was to help others in this ER until her job was done. He needed to be gone from this hospital soon. It was dangerous for him here, but she had to stay. The many memories slammed back into her. Reliving the thrusts of the invisible time. She pushed the old thoughts away and thought only of Jared and felt his love. "Wake up sir your shoulder is back in place." She tried to get the patient awake enough so she could go to Jared. The nature of the beast with conscious sedation, the RN had to stay until the patient was awake and vitals were healthy.

The resident that attacked her walked into the room. "Jen is Jared ok?" He was genuinely concerned. He looked down and away from eye contact when she looked at him. He couldn't look into her eyes. "I saw him standing in the middle of the ER just staring blankly ahead but I felt an energy," he paused then looked at her, "I see things since he healed me." He stammered some finally finishing his thought.

He is struggling with the negative stuff here.." he stopped again and Jen interrupted him to calm him. "Yes you are seeing more in the spiritual plane. You see it does exist." She stood next to him and looked into his eyes. "You can relax about Jared he is a very old soul. He can handle just about anything thrown at him." He turned away from her to leave, he said nothing and just nodded. His walk was slow, his step was cautious. He was in a new place of life with the gift or curse, of seeing the real of energies dark and light. "He is young, he will be able to help many find their way back to God." Jen remembered the first time her eyes were opened to the spiritual side of life. She chuckled a little then added, "hold onto your hat doc the ride is just starting."

There is a time in all lives when the blank stare would become a wide eyed moment into the literal place of our birth. "We are stardust." She looked around the ER to see if he had come back. She relaxed and waited, she knew fear was a waste of emotion and smacked any prayer right out of God's hands. She continued with the monitoring of her patient, but her arousal for Jared had not left. She wanted some of her Jared soon. Smiling to herself this relaxed her even more. They would have to marry soon and make it wonderful.

Chapter 38

Jared tried with all his heart to let go of this new pain. He started to cry and released some of it through his tears. God gave us tears to let the explosion of pain fall out and away. He buried his head in his hands. He began to weep and his sobs were heard inside the ER, he was standing just outside the ambulance bay doors. He walked away from the hospital, toward his car. The ocean was where he wanted to be and right now. He was shattering inside with fragments of past knowledge of past ways of thought falling away then dropping like razors against his skin. His phone buzzed, automatically he answered. "Hello," he watched his black boots move across the pavement. Realizing he did not have his van he came to work with Jen. He walked back to the hospital still holding the phone to his head. "Hello?" There was only someone breathing on the other end no words are said. "Hello!" he closed the phone. He wiped away his tears and pushed his ID against the door and waited for the beep that would allow him back into the crapper. "Yea the crapper that's what I will call this hospital." He needed to get her keys or shoot some pool or make love or anything to get this feeling away and out of his mind and body. As soon as he entered one of the docs called him in to help roll a patient off a backboard. Jared hesitated but followed the doc inside the room. The man was restrained to the board naked and full of stun gun torpedo's. Security followed Jared into the room. They would release him while the doc removed him from the board then would secure the patient to the bed. Jared saw leaves all over the naked man's body. The man was angry but obviously drunk or on something. "Where are my clothes?" He screamed at Jared. If words were spit it would have caught him right in the eyes. The wave of anger and energy hit him on a day he was not doing well. He yelled back at the patient. "You came in here without any!" Everyone stilled in the room well everyone but the patient. He just continued to be repetitive and redundant. The doc smiled at Jared not used to seeing him lose control. "He left his house naked today to attack someone walking down the sidewalk." "Why did you attack that man? What did you think he was a monster?" Jared was messing with this patient something that was usually not his way. They had to use a taser gun on him to get to him. So here he was in Jared's ER naked as a jaybird pleading innocence blaming all in the room on his moment of restraints and nakedness. Jared threw a sheet over him and walked out.

He looked for Jen but was pulled once more into a room to help with a patient. This time a female patient that the nurse needed help putting a catheter in the patients bladder. "Great," was all that escaped his mouth. The lady was very large so he had to pull one thigh away for the nurse to push the catheter into its proper place. The nurse struggled to find the proper hole. Jared pulled the large leg up more. The catheter began to be inserted and the lady screamed grabbing Jared's arm. As soon as she touched his arm she began to moan. He looked at the nurse wondering what the hell was she moaning about. The nurse pushed and pushed but the catheter wasn't in. The patient started to stroke Jared's arm as she moaned even more. The nurse started to laugh trying to subdue the sounds so the lady didn't hear her. Jared whispered, you need to go lower, she is enjoying this." The lady began to squeeze Jared's arm now while pushing her leg against his stomach. She arched some wanting more of the catheter to touch her. The nurse had to leave to get another catheter so as not to insert that dirty one. The lady moaned the whole time she was gone and stroked his arm. She added a few hip thrusts to the picture. The nurse finally back, found the spot and inserted the catheter. The moaning was replaced with a yell of pain. She let go of Jared's arm and tried to close her legs to this new feel. The nurse finished putting the catheter into her bladder. Jared let go of the ladies leg. But she suddenly grabbed his arm again. He looked back at her, "What do you need?" "I need you, I am single and looking are you interested?" The nurse laughed with a comment, "yes Jared is single do you want me to give you his phone number?" Jared stammered some. "Sorry I am not single but your offer is very generous." He walked out of the room pulled his gloves off and snapping them at the nurse. "Look ashamed!" He smiled and walked toward the back of the ER still looking for Jen. "This place is crazy." He was feeling better but still needed to find Jen. Two steps further and he was pulled into yet another room. "Jared quick we need you!" The patients heart had stopped beating. He began compressions, with each push he could

301

feel the ladies soul leave the body. Slowly but surely it squeezed out
of her flesh. The nurses rushed in with meds. His compressions would
push the medicines through the body since the heart had stopped its
beat. He saw the energy lingering, sweat formed on his forehead.
Pushing harder he felt it was not this ladies time to leave. She slowly
fell back into her body. In that instant she coughed. "Stop
compressions!" The nurse felt for a pulse. "She has a pulse." He
stepped away from the lady and out of the room. Worn out from
pushing but happy it had a good ending, for the moment anyway. He
saw Jen sitting three bays down. She made him smile his heart felt
gooey when he looked at her. "Gooey?" Vomit flew in front of him,
the good ole projectile kind. The patient was holding onto the rail of
the stretcher and vomiting everywhere. He stepped around the puke
determined to get to Jen. Another nurse called for him to do an EKG
quickly on the lady that he just did compressions on. She knows her
stuff but could bother the hell out of a tech. In the middle of chaos she
would want you to clean a patients mouth or prop a leg. Always the
patient's care but sometimes requesting some labor intensive duties
during hectic moments. He looked at Jen then sighed. The machine
was in front of him away he went. The tags went on the body to get
the tracing for the EKG. The skin was wet from sweat and bones were
brittle. He could see where he broke a couple of her ribs doing
compressions. Finishing it quickly he handed it to the doc. There was
a page overhead for another EKG and to transport one of his patients
to ultrasound. As soon as they hand him the EKG slip with the info on

it another doc came up wanting the blood results from an earlier enzyme test. A Nurse yelled at him "go get that patient in ultrasound Jared." "I need the results of the enzymes Jared where are they?" "We need this EKG now..Jared!" Jared knew what it was like to be in a tornado. He was in the middle of a swirl. He lowered his head pushed the EKG machine away, it rolled against the wall. Dropping the EKG order he walked away from everyone. "Enough!" Tossing his badge to the charge nurse he smiled. "I quit!" His locker never looked so good. Grabbing only his coat he slammed it shut.

Walking back into the ER he pulled Jen from the room, lifting her into his arms kissing her lightly teasingly then deeper, his kiss lingered while his mind traveled to places far away. But he was not with her in this image of time. Pulling quickly away from her, "No!" was the only thing that escaped. He wanted her with him beyond anything and into that place he knows called forever.

She saw his pain it was sudden and deep. A fog is a cloud, soft with moisture covering the grounds and the trees, a fog of love is soft with moisture. They were in this fog while he held her. Nothing existed but the two of them, soft of time caressed both of them. Whispers from the angels of love, of life, of reality, wrapped them both in an instant. A scream from one of the patients removed them from pure ecstasy. "Jen," he didn't finish the original thought. Not going to say to her he knew she would not be with him. No, he would not allow it to become words from his mouth into her ears, across her soul. Pushing with a fist of strength from his gut he stood away from her. Ignoring what he was just shown. Shown he had true love but not this place in this time of existence to have love. It was for the others, he was just to help open people to love. Show them what it was, show them the beauty of real touch of a kiss that comes not from lust but from original love. Jen couldn't breathe, her inhale had left. He kissed her once more then smiled. He looked at her with so much love, no one had ever looked her like he did. She saw the times with him. His laughter, the way he walked through her mansion mesmerized by it but not intimidated. His arms holding her while he immersed himself into her. Her breath found life once more. "I'm going to go shoot pool, I need your keys." "You can't leave you have to work?" "I just quit," Jen felt him reach into her scrub pocket on the side of her pants leg. Her car keys were there, he snapped them up and turned away. "I will pick you up at seven tonight." Waving to all he bid "farewell."

*

Jen let him go. Her patient was awake smiling after watching her get kissed. "My turn for a kiss?" He asked, she ignored him but smiled. Cory, the charge nurse was also one of his favorite ones in charge. She took the badge and smiled. "Good luck out there Jared." He winked at her and walked out of the back doors away from that place. The beast's mouth was opening and closing but he paid no attention. Spirits were hiding around the signs and bushes, he ignored them. This time of his life in a place of death blood guts and vomit was over. He would help people in a different way, he would open souls to love and help them find God. But not at that ER anymore. He Flipped open his cell and called John. He got Johns voice mail. "John where are you let's shoot pool." Jared climbed into the BMW smiling. This was a good day to live breathe and make love. He drove towards John's house. The air was stirring along the car, he tried to release old visuals of death and exhaled slowly pushing away any negative still residing in the walls of Jared. "Walls of Jared," he laughed at this analogy. Enjoying the way the beamer drove he accelerated. This is what Jen does now I know why. He was going 80 in a 35 zone. The radio needed to be on, so his mind said, but with that thought was a feel of push. A push from liquid that was not air and was not good, suddenly a shadow moved across the front of the car. Jared gripped the steering wheel and turned it sharply to the right to avoid hitting what he thought was a child crossing the street. The car rolled over tossing Jared. His head slammed against the side window. Pain was now in every part of him. The airbag smacked him in the face and caused his head to snap back. The dust from the airbag filled his lungs. His eyes burned from the powder from the airbag, mixed with the burning in his lungs and back. The car fell down a hill and finally stopped by a tree. The tree collapsed dropping what's left of the car to the street. Jared was aware of more shadows around him just before he passed out. He was bleeding, "Jen..I.." His words dripped against the dashboard along with the fuel leaking from the car to the pavement. Silence was the feel in this place of sleeping without sleep.

Chapter 39

Jen was near the nurses station preparing to get some morphine for one of her patients. She felt a sharp pain swirl through her body. Jared was standing beside her. He was trying to speak. She saw blood pouring from his head into his mouth. "Jared!" Jen reached to feel the vision of Jared in front of her but he slipped away. Fading away from her he no longer stood there, something horrible had happened. The feel of pain didn't leave her. Hurrying to find a phone she called his cell. It didn't ring, it went directly to voice mail. "Not like him to have his phone off." She didn't know what to do. Running over to Cory she told her she had to leave she knew something had happened to Jared she felt it. Cory was in the middle of handling a phone call plus guiding with a pointing finger the next patient back to a room. She looked at Jen with a puzzled look. "What? Jared is what?" Continuing with the conversation on the phone she turned away from Jen. She had no keys and no way to find him. "John I need to call John." But she didn't know his number. The trauma radio came to life with a report from EMS bringing in a patient. Jen was standing near the phone trying to figure out how to find Jared. She heard the report of an accident. Half listening half thinking of numbers and how to contact John she struggled to try to even remember his last name. Nothing was coming to her mind. Nothing but Jared bleeding and hurt. The voice of the EMT filtered into her reality of thoughts and fear. "I have a male in his mid-fifties involved in an MVA, he has multiple contusions. He is unresponsive. We have a line in him and have intubated him. His sats are 90, his heart rate is 45 his blood pressure is 80 over palp. We will be at your facility in five minutes. The doctor, announced overhead, trauma five minutes we will need respiratory." Jen felt Jared getting closer to her. "It's Jared, they are bringing in Jared!" "What?" Cory heard her and called for the trauma people to get into the trauma room and get ready to take care of Jared. He was well liked, Jen was a mess with worry. Kathy, the chaplain, was working on this day. She was anxious along with all in the ER. The doctor called for a chest tube set up. If he was intubated and still not getting oxygen one of his lungs was compromised. He got one of the techs to go to the blood bank to get blood. Everyone was ready to receive him.

The buzzer for the trauma room sounded as EMS moved quickly into the room. The EMT knew Jared and was upset. Subdued with a try to control emotions the trauma room had a silence unusual for the moment. Everyone knew this guy and they cared about him. Not that they don't care for those they don't know but this was Jared.

Jen was already in the room waiting for him to roll through the trauma doors. He looked horrible, covered in blood intubated, and limp. The tube to help him breathe was secured with a string that pushed against his eye. His left eye was swollen shut and purple. She saw a hint of blood beginning to come from his left ear. Not a good sign at all, damage to the brain. The EMT gave report once more about him to the docs. He was removed from the EMS stretcher with one easy pull. His body looked even more lifeless on the trauma stretcher. Jen wanted to help but she was pushed out of the room by Cory. "You cannot be in here you are personally involved you will be no help." Jen knew she was right and left. Looking back at him she saw his light energy hovering over his body. "No!" She pushed past Cory to lean to his ear. "Jared you do not give up I need you!" Cory let her move back to him.

Lightly touching him she was able to feel is injuries. Not only did he have a head bleed, he was bleeding internally. His walls of veins unable to hold the fluid of life. His left femur was broken, his C-spine was compromised, his clavicle was broken. Without the c-collar on he would have been paralyzed. The Doc pushed her gently away. "Let me get to him Jen." His energy was ebbing, weakening and rising more from his body. Jen moved to the bottom of the stretcher to watch his vitals on the machine. She knew she could help him but it will be slow and she had to do it without anyone knowing she was doing it. The hidden gifts of spiritual are more alive than people know. To keep the label of crazy or possessed away and to keep from being thrown into the looney bin. Always the quiet is the healer of flesh and bones. She touched his foot, it was cold. Acting as if she was feeling for a pulse she looked into him as a feel of pure energy moved through her from another place. It was like a line of silver moving through the top of her head down through to her hand into him. The mend had begun.

Light of God was mixing with the broken bones and leaking vessels. She stepped away, now it was up to Jared. If he wanted to leave to the place of forever, would he want to remain or come back to this place of pain and hurt. But Jen knew he felt her love. "He will come back to me." She whispered as the fight not to cry hit her hard. She tried to adjust to him possibly not wanting to come back. Walking slowly from the room she heard the orders given by the doctor, for pain meds, for the fast scan to look for blood in the belly, for x-ray to finish the view of bones. The ER was a fog through her eyes. Her only thought was of him. A residual of his injuries carried through her mind. Telling one of the other nurses to watch her patients, she walked to the lounge to take a break. Unable to be in the ER or to even think of anything but him.

Chapter 40

Within the walls of Jared…

The hospital was a virtual revolving door for the other side of life. With the constant passing of lives the door swings always open. Thus the fine line of reality and spirituality, filling with demons and angels. They travel easily through the building looking for those souls that are about to find out why they should have been a little bit nicer while they were alive. Those souls that will be thankful they gave a lean of help and gentle into other peoples day. Suffer the reward if you fling your spit into the hearts of life. It will not be a pleasant journey for a long time. They enjoy invading the rooms with a heavy feel of fear or sadness. Inundating the innocent visitors with that feel of doom and fear but there is also the ones of pure love that find and surround the ones who chose in life to give and show compassion. Jared was now in the place of both.

Time was fun right now for Jared. He was flexing within it's walls. Falling away then back into the way of his own flesh he was finding was a simple task. Yet there was a light near him that seemed to be available for his entrance. Nothing blocked the way and the pull to just relax into the feel of love and silence was tempting. He glanced at the tunnel, "not yet," his words of no words slipped into this place of time and no time. He was dead in all reality. But he was very much alive. He was energy as all were energy. And for the moment he was in stasis. Is this a test? Will he fail? Only the truth of time and it's walls know. Even in this way of fall he was comforted by a presence that was ever so near him. He heard Jen suddenly speak to his soul. She was sad and afraid, not wanting him to leave her. The flash was quick and time did its thing, becoming something of an ocean with lifts and those drops but with no movement of flesh. The current of energy is a flight when released from the body of flesh. He saw himself being thrown against the inside of the car. A silent laugh to himself, all of the years of preaching to others to wear their seatbelt and he didn't put one on for this glorious trip to freedom. What seemed like another flash of light he was lying on the ground while his blood fell onto the pavement. Blood had starting a journey from his brain through his ears. Kind of looks funny to Jared to see himself in patient mode. He had seen so many people bleeding, suffering, now he saw himself. But from where was he seeing this? Interestingly he felt no pain. He watched as the people appeared at the accident. One man yelled for 911 to be called. Another whispered to his wife, "this guy is dead look at the blood coming from his head." Someone threw their coat over Jared's face to cover what they felt was a dead body. Jared didn't like this at all. "Now that has to come off," his voice of no voice he heard but know no one else could hear him. Or so he thought.

The light got stronger from the tunnel with small sides and a narrow opening. Tad too narrow for someone with claustrophobia. He saw some of his long gone family members standing beside the tunnel. Just standing there not beckoning him or pulling him to the tunnel they were just standing there. He didn't really see them but was aware it was them? He questioned what he saw as he saw it. A flash once more, must be a passage of time? He had no idea just saw the flash felt the change and noticed the different surroundings. Life, what we experience, is just full of backdrops anyway, his random thoughts are solid in this random place of death or near death.

He saw Cory moving quickly around the trauma room that held his body. The vent pushed air into his lungs. But he felt nothing. He was not in his body he was near it watching all that was going on. He heard Jen, felt her pain. For a moment he seemed to just be at her side with just a thought. Kissing her neck lightly. She responded she knew he would be ok, she also told him to stop, oh he loved the feisty in her. Suddenly he heard a deep calm voice. "It is not your time Jared, return and guide others to me." He looked around the trauma room and felt a euphoria as a huge bright light surrounded him. "God?" He asked in a voice of no voice in this place of time with not time. Nodding his head with a smile he knew the answer. "I will do what you want, just let me know I will be able to return someday." Jared had a moment of fear that he might have messed up somewhere along the line of life with his anger, that he may miss out on this feel of heaven. "I am always with you..." The voice was strong and deep yet calm resounding with a feeling of love throughout his whole spirit.

The sounds of the trauma room returned. He could hear the docs, their tone was tense, they cared about me. He felt good in that thought but not that Jen was hurting. Looking around the room he saw entities of dark but there was a barrier of some kind. Is this the forever resting place, heaven? These thoughts made sense to Jared but what is a forever resting place? Is it full of recliners and the best pool tables with the best cue sticks?

He began to feel pain in his legs especially his right leg. He saw his soul was moving back into the broken body. He could hear Jen's heart pounding and feel her worry. Pain began to have its own life inside every muscle that was torn. Every inhale was one of intense pain. It seemed the pain meds were not finding their spot. And that spot was Jared wanting release. He became rigid, tightened muscles to try to stop the spasms that were finding his back and legs, spasms aren't natural. Your body hurt and then tossed a flex of muscle to push harder against that pain. Frustrated with the spasms that had found a temporary home in him he tried to relax to turn the pain into a different feeling. Voices from the outside of his mind traveled to his ears. "He is very diaphoretic; we better get an EKG check his heart." Why was he sweating so much? The EKG leads fall off of his chest unable to hold their place because of his sweat.. Still unable to speak because his vocal chords were being visited by the plastic tube that was sending air to his lungs, he tried to signal to get more pain meds. Cory saw his struggle. Leaning she whispered to him of more pain meds on the way and to relax. He held a thumb up showing he heard her.

Winds carry air to cool, winds carry leaves from the trees, a wind of spiritual was about to carry Jared to a place of silence and calm. The pain meds were delivered. Good for Jared, pain mode would ease some but not good for he would lose control of his thoughts and slip away into a place of vulnerable for the not good spiritual bad guys. Realizing this, he relaxed into it waiting. His muscles slowed their spasms being quieted by medicines to still their push. He saw a piece of light to this vessel, his body as he began to leave it's boundaries again. He rose away from his flesh as energy and saw his line of light that was a tether to his body.

Silence…

His body stilled on the stretcher. All pain was gone he was gone from his body away and walking into a place of silence. He could feel people of his past lives near that tunnel his mom was close but only smiled. He saw no darkness felt no pain. He was alive in a place of death. But this wasn't death it was a passage. A way of transition a way of peace. He looked down at his body on the stretcher. The silver tether was attached and strong. They were moving him to the CT to scan his broken bones and leaking blood vessels. He listened to the calm of this place he was in. He was drawn again to walk towards the tunnel he glanced to his right. A feel of something huge but very calm was near him. He was ready to do battle but the battle was not in this place of afterlife. The battle of evil and negative was in the place of earth and human life. He looked again at those walking around the trauma room caring for him. He saw the darkness mixed with light flowing around and inside those walking through their moments.

He heard their thoughts of distraction and insidious nature of the beast found their darkest secrets and fears. That is the battle ground, he realized that his battle had to be on earth in flesh, with a gift of vision to pull from those he was near to find their light. In this place he had moved into there was peace and a silence that was comforting. The battle of the demons did not take place here. It was over when one died. No battles to be fought, it was too late. He knew what he had to do and his path was to fall back into his body. "Yes, Jared help them find me." The strong deep voice circled him with peace.

He had to help those of life that slipped away into a place of sadness, of pain, of hatred. The silence within their soul that was the loneliest place in the universe. That place is one far away from the God, into the pit of darkness of negative, of hatred, of a level of vibrations that Jared saw on this side of reality. He tried to speak but of course had no voice. Yet he was heard by the large presence to his right. With no words he communicated with what he felt was God. A voice of calm with no voice found him once more. "Go back and help those of lost thoughts and scattered mind, help them find me." Jared began to fall, a feel of slipping quickly away from the tunnel and the air of peace. "Sin no more Jared…" He saw he and Jen making love and they were not married. He had to marry her before they could make love again. The tether to his body was tightening as he fell spiraling quickly back into the body given to him. Crashing inside his walls of flesh, intense burning pain was released into every cavity of his existence.

He jerked and raised to sit up on the stretcher. Cory ran over to him to push him back to lie down. "You will extubate yourself Jared lay down!" Jared wanted away from the restrictions of his body for a moment. He missed the freedom and lack of pain lack of worry. The feel of peace, the feel of love is what he wanted returned to his side. Not this pain. Screaming inside his mind he tightened his muscles once more then faded into a place of dreams as the meds took over. Dreams are reality with a swirl, he swirled through time, as images of his life flipped into his mind. He played pool and made love to Jen, crying with a feel of loss as he watched her walk away from him. His body was frozen by meds that caused him to be temporarily paralyzed. When light is given to heal another it doesn't stop its path unless blocked somehow by the one getting the gift. Jared was open to Jen's healing touch although it was unknown to him that she pushed that light into him. Time would slowly slip its pillow case over his pain. But with a slowness of healing, lessons are hard as he was the lesson. Slipping silently through his dream place he enjoyed the fall into a softness. Not the softness and calm of the place of forever, the softness and calm of the place of Jen.

Chapter 41

Reality Bites

There is a distinct odor to a person that had been lying in a bed soaked in blood. Small clumps of red, still vividly mixing with what was white clean cotton sheets. Jared could smell himself in this clump of blood place, It wasn't pleasant. He had painted the sheets with his fluids creating a canvas of surreal. The cold of it surprised him. Wondering why the tech for his room hadn't cleaned him up yet or put him on clean sheets. Reality, even he was ignored temporarily in the way of familiar and just another patient on a bloody sheet. Moving some he tried to shift his hips to the left and lie flat on his back. Pain was an interesting companion that seemed to yell on a constant into your brain. Voices with no voice, voices of ripping sheering heated pain. "Nurse!" He yelled as he strained to sit up to see who the docs were and if Jen was anywhere near. One of the night nurses walked up to him. She was new and didn't know Jared. "Calm down sir I will check with the doctor for pain meds." She walked away leaving him in agony. He could feel that he was not too badly broken. Felt like his right femur was broken and his clavicle didn't feel very comfy. He had that damned uncomfortable c-collar still on his neck. Most likely because the radiologist went to lunch or home and hadn't read his films yet. It has happened before it could happen again. But this time he was on the receiving end of incompetence. He didn't understand why Jen wasn't there. She must have assumed he would be taken care of. He fell back into a dizzying heat of pain and passed out. Dreams floated into him with screams of patients and laughter of Jen. A complete mix of life through a mist of some sort. He stood on the edge of an ocean, he was alone but for the total peace of God with him. The waters were calm and Jen was on an island far away in the waters. She was surrounded by people in white clothing of some sort. He moaned and jumped, which pulled himself from the dream. The nurse returned with some pain meds. "You are a mess young man." She called one of the techs to help clean him up. The aroma of old blood would soon be a memory and he was ready for that memory. They rolled him and changed the sheets then started to wash the blood from his hair. They used a cap that after heated had rinse free shampoo in it. He had always wondered if it really worked. All he knew was it sure felt good. He fell asleep after they were done but went deeply to sleep. No dreams, just sleep.

The night tech walked away from him and looked back when he heard a noise. Above Jared he saw a light that hovered over him. It faded and vanished suddenly but left a wonderful feel in the room. The tech smiled, he knew of this Jared tech, that he was special and helped many. He knew this because he was an angel. He walked slowly to the triage area and then walked into the parking lot. A light filled the night and he vanished as a human. He was one of his angels. He hovered over Jared while he slept, "help them find God Jared…" Jared jumped suddenly and then felt the horrendous pain that filled every part of his body. "Who woke me up?" He said slowly and fell back to sleep. His sheets were clean and all was wonderful. He was in love and he was doing the right thing.

*

Jen slept through the night somehow. She woke and got dressed quickly to go see Jared. She was off and needed to be near him. A black shadow followed her to the garage. She stopped and felt it push against her which caused her to be shoved against the rental she had. "Leave me you are not wanted here." It did not leave, it continued to press into her. She felt it feel her body and she yelled, "Leave me now! I love God!" The darkness shriveled away and she was released. "God how long do I…" she didn't finish her question. She knew she had to work the ER for many years to help others, her choice to bring more people to God. The sun was bright and she was late. Shadows of spirits followed her car all the way to the hospital. She missed him and wanted him in her life until and beyond death. "Is that possible?" She paused and slowed the car, "to have him at least until death?" She felt a horrible feeling of dread and pushed harder on the accelerator.

Chapter 42

John stood over Jared and looked at him and shook his head. He was wearing yet another weirdly striped shirt and tight black slacks. He had a piece of chalk used to chalk the cue in his hand and he tossed it and caught it repeatedly. "Jared you awake? You hear me?" He pushed on his arm but no response. He looked at his hands to see if they were ok to shoot pool, they were. "Jared!" He jumped at the sound of his voice which caused him to feel every bit of pain in his body. "What dammit!" His eyes opened to see his friend standing over him. "John no, I cannot shoot pool today and where the hell were you? I called you just before my wreck and you didn't answer?" John sat in a chair near the bed. "I was doing a young filly my friend." He smiled, "she wasn't half bad if I say so myself." Jared looked away disgusted, he tried to shift his hips some but the pain was horrible. "John you need to respect those women some more and romance them." He asked God to help him with the pain then moaned and pushed the call button. "I respect every bit of them my old friend, all the way down to their legs opening……" He stopped talking as a nurse walked into the room. "Jared are you needing anything?" The nurse was not bad looking as John examined her. "He is ok, but I am in need of some TLC." She ignored him, "Jared?" He looked at her and whispered, "any pain meds ready for me? I am suffering horribly." She nodded and walked away, "I will get you some." John watched her walk and smiled, "nice nurses here my friend." "They are too classy for you John so leave them alone." Jared fell asleep quickly and his monitor started alarming, it showed his oxygen saturation was 84% and his heart rate was 35, even John knew that wasn't good. He pushed the call button but no one answered. "Nurse!" The nurse that was just there walked slowly back in, "yes?" She then saw the monitor and called all to Jared's bedside. They rushed him into the trauma room away from his friend John.

John just tossed the chalk in the air and caught it and whispered, "get better my friend..." He sat down in the chair that was in the room and was concerned about his friend. Jared was his only true friend in life and he did not look good. He thought of all the times they had hustled and laughed, but Jared did always respect women. He felt bad suddenly on the casual way of his life with sex and alcohol. He lowered his head and prayed for the first time in his life. A peace filled him and a calmness followed. "He will be ok.." He walked out of the room and passed up Jen as she walked into the emergency room. "They took him back into that special room you guys do all the serious work in." Jen's eyes opened wide and she gasped. "Why, what is wrong!" He smiled, "I have no idea but he didn't look good." He walked away from her some then turned, "he will be ok don't worry about him, he is in good hands and God has him." He walked out into a new way of thinking. Maybe this God stuff had something to it, "we need to chat more often God." The day would be one of rest and contemplation and he would toss a few more prayers to his old friend.

Chapter 43

Jared saw himself once more above his body, he heard everything then saw Jen run into the room. He looked around and felt nothing near him, good or bad, he just hovered over his body. They were putting in another chest tube but he felt no pain. He saw light around Jen and smiled. She is a good person isn't she, yes came the word but was a voice once more with no voice. Why am I back here am I going to die? Suddenly a swirl of lights surrounded him. "You have a journey Jared, one of battles against evil and healing others." He felt himself moving slowly back toward his body. "You have to leave the hospital, it is time.." He slammed back into pain of his flesh. He could hear his blood pushing through his arteries. He opened his eyes and yelled in pain. "Somebody give me something for pain!" He tried to grab his side where the fresh chest tube went into his lung. "Do not touch that!" Jen yelled and cried then kissed him, "I love you Jared, get well and come home to me.." She stood back and walked away. She felt a shift and heard what she didn't want to hear. He saw the look in her eyes change but faded into sleep, they sedated him and gave him pain meds.

Jen cried as she walked away from him. "No, no no…" She walked back outside of the emergency room and leaned against the wall. "Why can't I have him with me?" Silence was an interesting thing on a cool evening with shining stars but this silence broke her heart. There was no peace in it, there was no happiness. She walked

324

out of the emergency room to her rental car. She had to get away, he was asleep anyway and it would give her time to pray and get back on her feet again. Back on her path and continue to do what she was meant to do until her job was done. She cried all the way back to her house. The day was beautiful with bright sunlight and that crispness of fresh air filtered around her. Her heart hurt, she loved him but she knew she couldn't be with him, she couldn't marry him, she couldn't live life with him. She pulled into her driveway and ran into her home. She walked past the torn painting and cried even harder. "You will be ok, he will be ok.." She calmed some when she heard the gentle voice of what she felt was God. It could be her angels either way it was from a place of love and light for it calmed her. She fell onto her bed and fell asleep quickly. She saw Jared walking away from her, he stopped and turned toward her then lowered his head and blew her a kiss. His eyes were brilliant with light but his walk was slow and his head was bowed. "Jared!" She sat up and yelled his name, it echoed throughout her house. "My love…" She lay back down and cried herself to sleep.

… The way of paths

Jared woke and was confused on where he was until he tried to sit up. Pain hit him in every direction from his broken pelvis to his chest tubes and the wonderful foley in his unit. He lay back down and began to cry, he pushed the call button and waited for a nurse. The air smelled of bleach and urine quite a combination but the usual mix to try to remove the wonderful odors in a hospital. "You need something Jared?" The nurse checked the amount of blood that had been drained from his pleural sac around his lungs. "Looks like the chest tubes are doing their work." She had light blue scrubs on and bright red hair. He didn't know her. "Where am I?" You are in the ICU don't you remember Jared?" She smiled and her eyes twinkled a little with a light. He strained a bit more and she changed to just light. A huge bright light that moved across him, "you will be ok just rest, you have much work to do." The image vanished and another nurse walked in, "whats up Jared you ok?" It was Danny an ICU nurse that he did know, "Danny I hurt like the dickens, any meds on the docket for me?" Danny smacked his leg lightly and Jared jumped in pain, "hey! pain here!" Danny laughed some, "sorry Jared I owed you that for the time you took three hundred from me at pool." Jared smiled and saw the angel move behind Danny and out through the ICU unit. He relaxed and waited for the meds. He looked for a phone but none available, he wanted to talk to Jen, he had to talk to her but he had time. He had to heal first and that would take time. Danny gave him the meds and he fell back to sleep.

His dreams were of traveling through time into another place, another lifetime. He saw Jen but she looked different he saw himself standing in front of a mirror and he was a young man with blonde hair and blue eyes. She walked up behind him and put her arms around him. He jerked awake, "Jen?" He woke in his bed at his apartment.

He could sit up and was in no pain. His sweat soaked the sheets and the silence was overwhelming. He remembered nothing about leaving the hospital or the chest tubes being removed and where was Jen? He looked frantically for his phone but could not find it. It was still dark and he needed answers. He got dressed quickly, he saw the scars of his accident and laughed at himself. "You had to drive like Jen didn't ya…"

His phone rang but was muffled, "hello! I can't find my phone!" Why he was yelling in the air he had no idea. He saw it lit up under his sheets and answered it quickly. "Hello!" Jen relaxed immediately to just the sound of his voice. "Oh Jared you are awake, did I wake you?" "Jen what happened, where are you? How can I be home already, when did they take…" "Jared calm down I will come over, get back in bed and rest some I am on the way, I love you Jared." She hung up too quickly he didn't have time to respond. He had no idea what time it was, he was confused. He sat down on the edge of the bed with just his jeans on. He saw his bag was packed and his P-coat lying over it. "What happened to time?" He saw a note from John on the table with a piece of billiard chalk on top of it. *Hey old friend, I guess you are going on your way into life without me. I want to thank you for being my friend through all the dark and stupid things I did. You are the only true friend I have ever had and I think that I will ever have. Thank you for letting me find the Lord. Sounds corny doesn't it, especially coming from me. I will miss you my friend, if possible please keep in touch. God bless you Jared, for He has blessed me having you as a friend.* He took the chalk and tossed it into the air. The note brought back all of the lost time. Jen helping him and John bathing him a few times. He laughed at the folly of that experience. He lowered his head, "thank you for your love.."

Chapter 44

.. It is finished..

Jen drove slowly to his apartment, she knew it would be goodbye. She had taken care of him while he healed but obviously he has amnesia to all of it. The many talks late into the night, the holding of each other and waking in his arms. It was all taken away from him. She loved him more than anyone ever in her life and he was leaving her. "Your will be done but I so wish…" "Everything will be ok Jen, this is not the time." She parked and sat still and prayed. She was a strong one and had battled many demons and suffered much pain, "this beats all I have ever had to do God."

Jared opened the door and pulled her into his arms. "I love you Jen so much." He kissed her gently then passionately. His hands began to search her body, to explore to remember where he had kissed where he had tasted. She pushed him away, "no Jared we cannot…" Her eyes had only love in them. He looked deeply into her eyes, "I know." "You think maybe we can get together in a few years and get married?" He laughed nervously and began to shake some. She started to cry a little, "well yes, please, if?" He sat on the edge of the bed and looked up at her. She was beautiful, more beautiful than anything he had seen in life. "I love you.." She sat next to him and whispered, "I know.."

"I have to stay here and you have to leave Jared, it is time for you to help others away from this ER and away from me." He remembered the voice with no voice, he knew she was right. He kissed her deeply and saw them again as different people. She saw his blonde hair and blue eyes and pulled away. "Jared? Was that you? Is that us?" He put on his black t-shirt then sat back down to put on his shoes, "yes we are lovers of forever Jen and into forever more." She whispered to him, "I will find you again." He chuckled, "you better I don't seem to do a good job of it." He put on his coat and picked up his suitcase. "I am heading east to see what I am to do and who I am to help." She had put more than enough money in his bank account for him to use for expenses. He refused it at first but he did need money and she had plenty of it. He would do odd jobs as he traveled and spread the love of God and heal as many as he could.

She walked with him out into the fresh morning air. The sun was just rising, he wanted to walk her to her car but didn't know which one it was. "What do you drive?" She pointed to a bright yellow jeep. He walked her to her car and smiled, "very nice and will be more fun than that beamer you had." His body ached and he felt some pain from his injuries but most of all his heart hurt down to his souls core. "I will always love you Jen." He kissed her slowly and softly, "don't forget me.." He walked toward his van, his head was bowed just as he got to his van he turned and looked at her. His eyes were brilliant with light, it was her vision, the one she dreamt of. He blew her a kiss and got in his van and drove away.

She crumbled into her jeep, collapsed into weeping agony. She tried to calm herself but she was lost inside the pain of losing him. She saw a river and on the other side of it was Jared. He waved to her, his hair was grey and he had a grey beard but it was him. She waved frantically back and yelled for him. She sat back in her jeep the tears slowed as she whispered, "I will find you soon…"

About the author

Mitch Bensel is a multi genre author in word and audio with spoken word cd's available. Mitch loves God and is a parent of three daughters and grandparent of two grandsons. Metal detecting and rock hound and enjoys a good game of three card poker. All books are available either on Amazon or lulu . com and other sites on the internet.

Available now~ CDbaby. com and Amazon and Lulu. com and other internet sites.

Whispers... spoken word CD

Walk With Me healing and guidance CD

The Pumpkins Revenge

The Butterfly Girl

Crooked

On The Edge of Evil

Circular Redundant Flip Flops, a collection of poetry

Available soon:

Sequel to Time of Death The Story of Jared

Just A Simple Rock~anthology of romance and mystery

She Said Hello~Murder mystery

Alexander~Murder mystery

Adventures of Danny and Jenny~ children's series

Rhythms of Life ~ poetry

Sequel to On The Edge of Evil

God bless all, everyday is special keep love in your heart and do no harm...

Write to the author Mitchbenselauthor@ gmail . com

on twitter @mitchbensel

FB Mitch Bensel

97423088R00186

Made in the USA
Middletown, DE
05 November 2018